MARI KAY

The Flower Grower's Daughter

Contents

III   Part Three

Prologue

My sisters and I clasped each other's hands, while the rest of the family stood in a line in front of us. The priest's voice droned through the liturgy. Shoes shuffled on the damp grass while stiff dress coats whispered against shirt sleeves.

I kept my eyes firmly fixed on my shoes. They weren't new, but they were my best. I'd spent time last night polishing them, checking the soles were clean as well. Now the buckles shone in the watery sunlight, the dew rising as steam around my feet as the morning heated up. The breeze wafted Yvonne's rose-scented perfume over me. As much as I tried to block out the words the priest was saying, I couldn't help but hear those dreaded final lines:

"We commend to Almighty God our sister and we commit her body to the ground, earth to earth, ashes to ashes, dust to dust. The Lord bless her and keep her, the Lord make His face to shine upon her and be gracious to her, the Lord lift up His countenance upon her and give her peace."

I

Part One

1

Spring 1942

"Come on Elise! Maman will wonder what has happened if you take such a long time."

I had dawdled behind my sister and brother, kicking up dust as I scuffed my feet. I looked up to see Yvonne stopped further up the hill, hand on her hip and a frown on her pretty face. "All right Yvie. I'm coming." I drew closer.

Yvonne extended a hand. "Do I need to hold on to you like I did when you were little?"

"Very funny, Yvie. How about you try keeping up with me?" I challenged her as I began to run. Her laugh chased me up the last part of the hill until I caught up to Leon.

At home, I threw my things onto my bed and went to find Maman and Grand-mère out by the flower beds at the far end of the garden. The late afternoon sun was hot through my hat and I saw the garden beds had dried to a pale brown. Perfumes wafted up from rows of lilies and roses, competing with each other for dominance in the heat.

Maman's flowers were always in high demand. We lived on the road to the local cimetière, on a hill above the town. It was a perfect spot to grow the flowers and sell them from a booth at the front of the house. Every Sunday local families would walk up to choose fresh blooms with which to show their respect at the cimetière.

Maman rose from where she had been crouching over one of the flower beds. She turned, smiling as I hurried over.

"Oof! Elise, gently my darling!" Maman stumbled back a step as I barrelled into her for a hug, laughing and wrapping her arms around me. Her skin warmed me where we touched. I buried my face in the worn folds of her apron. I loved how it smelled of flowers and sunshine. After a few moments, she carefully prised my arms from her, then lifted my chin to look into my eyes. "Does this mean you did well on your spelling test today?" One corner of her mouth lifted in her lopsided smile.

I nodded. "I came second in the class Maman."

"It just so happens that while I was busy in the garden, Grand-mère baked some treats for dessert before coming to help me. She must have known we'd have something to celebrate. Go wash up, I'll be in shortly."

2

Summer 1942/1943

"Elise, I am sure you can cope with this last one by yourself," said Maman, as she pushed herself up from the grass beside me. The three of us – Maman, Yvie and I – were working on the flower beds. "The box should be full but not overcrowded. Oh, I don't need to tell you this!" She reached over and gently stroked my face. "I shall see you inside. I think I have been working too hard in this heat!" She smiled again as she turned away, walking back to the house with slow, measured steps, a few last words of instruction drifting over her shoulder. "When you have finished, go and help Yvonne out by the calla lily bed. Don't take too long now."

"Yes, Maman." I watched her make her way along the path to the house. Something was wrong. I knew it was not the heat. Maman loved summer, she had always said so. As I watched, I saw her stumble and grasp the frame of the kitchen door. As soon as she was inside, I scooted over to my sister.

"Yvie," I hissed, gesturing towards the house. "Did you see? What's wrong with Maman?"

Yvonne shook her head. "Like she said, she's probably just

been working too hard. You know how she can get when the mood takes her."

I frowned. "But it's never made her almost fall over before. She loves being out in the sun. I think there is something else. Yvie," I tugged her sleeve as she started to dig again with her trowel. "I am really worried." I bit my lip to keep from crying.

Yvonne sat back on her heels and studied me. "You really are, aren't you? If it will make you feel better, I will talk to Papa. I'm sure it's nothing." She pulled me closer, hugging me. "Now, how about you get back to what Maman asked you to do, hmm? Unwell or not, she doesn't need the trouble of telling you off!"

As I hugged Papa goodnight later that evening, he whispered in my ear. "Yvonne tells me you are worried about your maman, little one."

I nodded, watching his face. "I saw her trip on the back steps."

"It is true that she has not been feeling the best lately, but she has seen the doctor. He thinks she has just strained herself with all the garden work lately." He smiled at me. "So no more worrying, all right? If there was anything to worry about, that would be my job. Now, off to bed with you." He ruffled my hair before opening the door and ushering me out.

3

Autumn 1943

"Elise, when you have finished eating, go and help Yvonne with the garden." Grand-mère's quick fingers flicked water as she signed her words before turning back to the dishes in the kitchen sink.

I licked the last crumbs from my fingers and placed my plate on the counter beside her. "Merci, all done." I signed back.

Skipping out the door, I picked my gloves up from the hall table, making my way through to the far end of the garden. I marvelled as always at the clever way Maman had laid out the flower beds. From certain spots you could see every colour of the rainbow in one sweeping view. Whites, palest yellows, all the way through to deep reds and purples so full they were almost black. The lawn was still damp with dew under my feet and at this time of day, before the sun warmed up the flowers, the raw aroma of the soil filled my nostrils.

I loved helping out here. As I walked towards Yvonne, my fingertips gently brushed the blossoms that edged the beds. I adored the tickling of the bottlebrush grevillea. The stamens of the lilies, proudly pushing past their petals, stained my skin with their golden pollen.

Maman smiled at me from the chair Papa had put outside for her. The sight brought me up short: though she refused to talk about it or let us 'fuss', it made it clear that something was very wrong with my dear maman. I forced a smile in return and made my way to the other side of the rosebed.

4

Winter 1943

"Elise." Maman called, as I shut the kitchen door behind me. As I drew near she smiled, though tiredness carved new lines into her face. "How was school today? Has Aimée's maman finished her dress yet?"

"Not quite, Maman. But she asked if I may come over this weekend? Her maman has said all of us can come and see how it is going." Aimée's older sister was getting married and my friend was to be a bridesmaid. We were all excited for her; the first of our group to see a brother or sister married.

"I am sure that will be fine. Now," –she waved a hand to the garden– "this bed is most in need, so if you'd like to start down at the other end and work towards Yvonne, you should get it tidied up quickly. Once that is done, I need a fair amount of whites and yellows, as they've been the most popular lately." A table had been set beside her, with her flower arranging tools and supplies close at hand.

I got to work. It was both tedious and rewarding – tedious in that the more I looked, the more weeds I saw, and rewarding when I could see the progress I was making.

While we worked, Maman picked up from where she'd left off a week before, sharing her knowledge of the flowers themselves, and what the market – our neighbours – demanded. Though I was just a child then, these times with my Maman would stay with me throughout my life; her peaceful patience at this time of suffering teaching me even more than her words.

5

September 1943

The new collège term had started. Our first day back was bittersweet.

"Where is Mme Allard?" Aimée said, as we put our bags in our desks.

I looked up. A stranger was sitting at the maîtresse's desk, apparently absorbed in the book in front of her. When the classroom door shut behind the last student, though, she shut her book and stood in one fluid movement. Her eyes swept over us, standing in silence behind our seats.

"Bonjour tout le monde!"

"Bonjour, madame."

"Asseyez-vous."

Chair legs scraped against the hard floor, filling the room with ear-splitting shrieks as we pulled our seats out and sat down. The noise settled quickly while the teacher waited in front of her desk.

"My name is Madame Gagnon." A giggle near the back of the room was quickly stifled. "I am sorry to say I must give you some sad news. Madame Allard has asked that you be told. She received a telegram last week and will be on compassionate leave for a little while. Her brother was a pilot in the Normandie squadron. Sadly Mme Allard's brother did not survive after his plane was shot down over the ocean." Though her face was stern, I heard her voice break slightly in her final sentence. "I am sure your thoughts and prayers will be appreciated by her at this time."

For the first time the war in Europe had touched very close to home. For several moments there was complete silence as we took in the dreadful news. A boy beside me raised his hand.

Mme Gagnon spoke again.

"If you have a question about Mme Allard, I am sorry, that is all I know at this point." He lowered his hand. The teacher nodded. "Now, let us turn to our books."

After my last class of the day, I walked home in silence, thinking of my maîtresse and her loss. I opened the front door, hung up my bag in my room and washed my hands before heading to the kitchen. Because my mind was still with Madam Allard, I didn't notice at first. It was while I poured myself a cup of water at the sink that the silence of the house encroached upon my thoughts. I frowned.

"Maman?" I called, walking back down the hall, looking into the rooms as I passed. Not finding her or my grandmother, I checked the back garden. "Maman?" My voice trembled. I reached the back of the garden with still no sign of my family. A bang sounded from somewhere near the house and I ran, automatically picking the quickest route. I got to the hall just as my papa came in the front door. He stopped when he saw me.

"Papa? What has happened? I cannot find Maman or Grand-mère anywhere!"

He strode forward and hugged me briefly. "I didn't know we would be gone so long. Please, go and turn down the blanket on Maman's bed. No questions yet, Elise, please. I need you to do as I say."

"Yes, Papa." Though every part of me wanted to cry out, obeying Papa was ingrained and I found my feet taking me to their bedroom, my hands reaching out and doing as he asked. I heard murmurs in the hallway and turned to see him supporting Maman as they came through the doorway. Maman's skin was white and her hair tumbled past her face instead of being smooth and pinned neatly in place.

Papa glanced up. "Would you help Grand-mère in the kitchen? I will just settle your maman and be with you shortly."

I had never seen my mother so helpless, nor my father so gentle. I backed out of the room.

Grand-mère looked up. It was uncanny how she could always tell when we entered a room, even when she wasn't looking. Now she beckoned to me. Her hands spoke quickly.

"You will have lots of questions. Your papa will explain. Set a cup on this tray for your maman." I did as she directed, taking it through and setting it on the cabinet beside their bed. As strange as it was to have him home on a weekday, it was also a comfort. He drew me to him and enveloped me in a hug. I breathed in his solidity.

"Little one, I will tell you more once your brothers and sisters are home, but you are not to worry. Maman was feeling unwell today so your grandmother got a message to me. That is why I am home. We must take care of your maman so she can rest and get well. Will you help Grand-mère to get dinner on the table?" He rubbed my back as tears threatened. "Keep

15

yourself busy for now. I will explain to you all at dinner. I will stay here with Maman for a while. Off you go."

It seemed as though Grand-mère had decided to use all the food we had available. I was kept busy peeling, chopping and washing the vegetables from the garden. She prepared pancakes and let me help whip some cream. We were to have dessert – a rare treat in the week. Part of me understood this was all a distraction, but I allowed myself to go along with it.

When our older brother and sisters were finally home, we gathered at the dinner table. Our plates filled with the main course before Papa began.

"You are all aware that your maman was taken ill today. We still don't know why, but your maman collapsed" –he held a hand up as a collective gasp of shock went up– "Grand-mère sent for me. Your oncle brought me home in his car so we were able to take Maman straight to the doctor. He has done some tests and now we have to wait for the results." He looked around the table, his own face reflecting our worry. "I know this is scary for you. As it is for Maman, Grand-mère and me. But all we can do now is take care of her, help her to rest, until we know more."

For the first time in my life, our bedtime routine was reversed: I went to Maman's room to say bonne nuit. I walked in slowly after knocking on her door. She pushed herself up to sit against her pillows, smiling at me.

"Elise, ma chèrie. Come, come."

I came close and felt her arms go around me.

"Thank you for helping your grand-mère with dinner tonight. It was delicious."

I nodded against her shoulder, not trusting myself to speak.

"Now, you mustn't worry, all right? I'm sure it is nothing,

I just need to learn to rest a little more, now I'm such an old woman, yes?" She laughed then, releasing me. I gulped and searched her face.

"You are not old, Maman!"

She laughed again. "That is sweet. Now, off to bed with you. You need to rest too, so you can grow strong. Bonne nuit my little one."

I was sure I would not be able to sleep for worrying, but my maman's voice replayed in my mind until sleep overtook me.

6

November 1943

Time stretched unfairly while we waited. Each day, as I went to collège and returned, I could see Maman was no better. Some days she was up and in the kitchen when I arrived back, but she moved slowly and her smile no longer reached her eyes. I was careful when I hugged her.

They sat us down, all of us. Then Papa stood near Maman, but did not touch her. He looked at her, and she lifted her eyes to meet his. Maman turned to us, and in halting words, explained what the doctors had found. It was cancer. I had not heard the word before, but the way Maman said it, I knew it was something — very bad. And apparently it was in her stomach.

"The only help I can get is in Australia."

Australia! Only Edmond, my oldest brother, had ever left Noumea, let alone the country.

"But I have told them that is out of the question. It is more money than we have in a whole year, to get me there and pay for the treatment. And there are no guarantees of success. So, we will keep going. We will pray and trust God. We will do our best." Her voice broke.

Papa placed a hand on her shoulder and squeezed gently. I could barely look at him. Even through his ravaged features, his agony for Maman was evident. That was almost harder to bear than Maman's words.

"I am so sorry, my little ones."

We sat for a moment, stunned into silence. Then Odette spoke up, doing her best to put our thoughts into words. One by one we went to Maman, both offering and needing comfort. Even the usually taciturn Edmond was moved to hug Maman, before turning to Papa and grasping his shoulder. It was in such moments that I recalled he was only twenty, barely out of childhood himself. When I finally reached Maman, she smiled, drew me in for the tightest hug I could remember, then began stroking my hair.

"Elise, my littlest one. My helper. I know this is scary for you. You must be brave, for me, yes?" Holding me firmly, she continued: "We must trust God's will, yes? His Word says we will share in the suffering of His Son. We will go to mass, and we will pray for strength." I nodded into her shoulder, not trusting myself to speak. Her hands on my shoulders now, she held me at arm's length. "Look at me, Elise." I raised my eyes from the floor between us, meeting hers. "I will need to rest more, so you and your sisters will need to share my work between you. While you are at collège, Grand-mère will do her best to help me, but she has her own work to do. So, I can rely on you, yes?"

Again, I nodded. She smiled, patted my shoulders and let go. As I left the room, I saw that my brothers and sisters had left before me. I made my way to the bedroom I shared with Yvonne, my hands brushing the wall, but as I approached the door I could hear sobbing. Yvonne. I spun around, running back down the empty hallway, my footsteps loud in my haste. I ran outside, around the back towards the flower garden. Once at the far end, I hid behind the tall frames of frangipani trees. My knees hit the soft earth, a sharp dead leaf digging into my skin as I collapsed, arms reaching out to hug the trunk of the nearest tree. I welcomed the scrape of its bark on my face. Hot tears burned down my cheeks, my stomach clenched and my mind fixated on Papa's expression, which had said more than Maman's words.

* * *

It was the end of summer. Somehow we'd got through another Christmas, though none of us had much heart for celebrating. I straightened up and brushed my hair out of my eyes. Though still early, the sun was hot and my face glistened with perspiration. Maman's garden had been neglected lately and weeds were starting to take advantage. I looked back along the section I'd been working on, checking I hadn't missed anything, when I caught sight of Maman's face looking out of her bedroom window, watching us. I smiled and waved. Yvonne was working across the flower bed, her back to Maman's window.

I turned back toward the garden, the smile fading. I sniffed as tears threatened. Yvonne looked up.

"What is it?"

"Maman is so thin, Yvie." My voice broke as I saw my own pain reflected in my sister's face. As one, we bent back to the soil, cleansing it of the unwanted growth.

7

May 1944

The house was quiet now, kept dimly lit day and night, to keep maman as comfortable as possible. I woke suddenly to see Grand-mère standing by my bed. "Grand-mère! What is it?" I signed, my hands moving quickly in the trickle of light coming in from the hallway.

"Ma chérie, you need to come now." Her eyes welled as her hands spoke.

I reached for my dressing gown and followed her quickly down to Maman's bedroom. I fell to my knees beside her bed and grasped her hand. It was so brittle, I thought I could break it if I held it too tightly.

Gradually sounds encroached on my consciousness: Maman's breath, rasping, slowing; quiet sobs of my sisters and Leon, the heavy breath of Edmond and Papa. I looked up from Maman's hand to her face. It seemed impossible that she could look so at peace; already far from us, slipping away from this life to the next. My eyes met Odette's, kneeling opposite me at Maman's other hand. Yvonne was sitting by Maman's head, stroking her hair from her forehead. Leon and Edmond perched at the foot of the bed, a hand each on her blanketed legs. Each of us touching her, none of us trusting our voices to let her know that she was loved, and would be missed. As much as we were loath to let her go for our own sake, we knew her suffering was coming to an end. Papa, I saw, stood behind my brothers. He alone did not touch her. They had walked together in this life for nearly 30 years. His grief eclipsed ours and it showed in every line of his face.

I turned back to see Maman. We had all heard it, that rattle in her lungs we had been warned of. Her chest rose as she took her last breath, her eyes fluttered briefly open as her head fell to the side, and she was gone.

8

July 1944

"Merci," I tried to summon a smile as I took the coins in exchange for the posy, but my eyes slid away from the sympathy in my neighbour's answering smile. He nodded and continued on his way. The afternoon sun was beating down on my head, my old sunhat barely offering any protection. When we had walked home from church earlier, the wind was brisk, fresh off the sea, competing with the sun climbing higher in the sky. Now there was no wind to move the heated air.

"Merci." I barely noticed my lips move – I'd said the word so many times already this morning.

Maman's flowers were still as popular as when she had been here to tend to them. Many of her customers had come to her funeral. I felt a hand on my arm.

"Merci to you. It must be very difficult to continue your maman's business. Je vous bénis ma chère. We do appreciate it."

I nodded mutely, tears threatening to breach my self control. She moved on, one of a steady stream on the way to pay their respects at the gravesites.

At last my stock was gone. I picked up the empty box, folded the deal table and carried it all back to the garden shed. Now it was our turn. Grand-mère was in among the flower beds, choosing just the right stems for Maman's grave. For a moment I thought I saw Maman by her side. I ran inside, desperate to be alone before facing the cimetière.

9

Christmas 1945

My errand today was at the fish market on the port side of town. The ocean glittered in the distance as sunlight glanced off its lightly rippled surface. Near the shore, homes of all shapes and sizes nestled between stands of palms and pines. I stopped to gaze out over the sea, imagining the islands we had learned about in school, far to the south and west of us. Nearer my path, flowers of every hue shone against the green foliage. I loved to notice the changes in gardens and along the roadside. The road itself was long and almost straight, its surface beaten down and flat from generations of feet and vehicles.

My basket swung on my arm in time with my footsteps.

"Ouch." Yvonne put a hand out to stop my basket, bringing me back to the present. I'd almost forgotten she was with me. This had been her job since Odette had begun working full time and now she was passing it on to me.

"Sorry, Yvie. My mind was far away."

Yvonne led the way to the fish market. The stall holders welcomed us, smiling and busy. At each one, she said the same thing: "Bonjour. You know my sister, Elise? She will be doing the shopping for us from now on."

And the response was fairly standard as well: "No! This can't be little Elise! Look how you've grown! You look so like your dear Maman, may she rest in peace."

I recoiled in shock at first but Yvonne squeezed my fingers in warning. I smiled tightly as we moved on, steeling myself for the next encounter.

At each stall my lesson continued, my sister showing me how to select just the right fish or fillet, and the way to negotiate the price firmly and respectably.

"Yvie, stop." I pulled on her arm as we came to the end of one row of sellers. "Can we sit for a moment, please?"

She shrugged her shoulders, sighed, and led me to the low brick wall at the edge of the market. "There. Now, what's the matter?"

"I just needed to stop for a little. You're used to this," –I waved a hand at the scene around us– "but I'm not. How do you stand it?"

Yvonne dropped her gaze as she answered. "I guess I have gotten used to it. But I should have warned you. I'm sorry. They mean well, I try to remember that. And I ask God for strength." She smiled gently and tapped my knee. "Shall we get this finished? Let's head over to the bakers. We might find a nice treat to have on the way home."

I brushed the sticky crumbs from my fingers on my skirt as we reached the top of the hill above the town centre, shifting my now full basket from my elbow to my hand.

"Yvonne?"

"Mm-hm?"

I looked over to see her pop the last of her pastry into her mouth. She nodded for me to continue. "I am worried about Papa. He's drinking again, like after the mine accident." I had planned out what I would say when the chance came up but instead I just blurted it out.

We walked in silence for a few minutes.

"I'm not sure what to say, Elise. We are all worried, even Edmond. Odette especially. She has even mentioned postponing her wedding."

"Oh no! That would be terrible. I know we will miss her, but it would be too hard on them both."

"Not to mention the cost of changing their travel plans to America. I told her that. I know it won't stop him drinking, but I said maybe it would help if she involved him more in the planning." She put her free arm around my shoulders. "Grand-mère says it will just take time, that we must be patient with him. It was Maman who helped him stop before, and she is not here to show us what to do."

Not long after this conversation, something else happened that would distract not just Papa, but us all. Yvonne met a young man. Being the dutiful daughter that she was, she had spoken with Papa as soon as she believed it was serious. Now here we were, preparing to meet Mr Carlisle as a family.

"Yvie, just sit down. Grand-mère has the dinner all in hand, I've set the table exactly as you asked." My hands on her shoulders, I pushed her backwards until the chair caught the back of her knees. Yvonne glared up at me but I just grinned in response.

"Aren't you Little Miss Bossy all of a sudden?" Yvonne said, shaking her head. Next minute we were laughing.

I sat heavily on the floor at her feet. "Someone had to be; it's pretty obvious you've gone all to pieces over Mr Carlisle."

I said his name in a teasing sing-song voice.

She tapped me on the top of my head. "I have not gone to pieces. I just –"

" – want everything to be right." I joined in on the phrase she'd been saying since last Sunday. She tapped my head once more.

Despite my best efforts, Yvonne jumped up and left the room again, muttering her 'to do' list under her breath. I sighed and followed. If this was what being in love did to a person, I was glad that I was too young to have to think about it.

During dinner it was entertaining to watch Yvonne try to elevate Papa's esteem for Mr Carlisle.

"So Mr Carlisle," Papa asked, his tongue struggling with the English name. "What is it that you do here in Noumea?"

Mr Carlisle looked up, a bemused look on his face.

Yvonne spoke up. "Papa, Mr Carlisle doesn't speak French. May I translate?"

Papa frowned but nodded assent.

Yvonne had learned English for her job. She passed on Papa's question. "Mr Carlisle is here with the New Zealand army to build the new hospital." She added her own words: "His commanding officer leaves much of the daily decision-making to him, Papa. He is very good at his work."

Papa stared at my sister, fork halfway between plate and his mouth. "Hmph" he grunted, then went back to his questioning. Yvonne reddened. I bumped elbows with her in mute sympathy.

It was almost like Papa was giving Mr Carlisle an exam with all the questions he asked through Yvonne. I stopped paying attention to the conversation, contenting myself with quietly watching my sister and this man who had captured her heart.

"You see?" I said as Yvonne and I washed and dried the dishes after dinner. "It was fine. I think Papa liked him."

She flicked soapy water at me, grinning. "It's not polite to gloat," Yvonne answered. Her face became pensive. "I hope you're right though. I couldn't bear it if Papa and Rex didn't get along."

Mr Carlisle – Rex – soon became a regular dinner guest. All too soon, Yvonne's left hand bore a simple jewel, and my worry for Papa returned. Now he faced losing two daughters.

10

1946

Odette married her GI fiancé. They left for America soon after. That left just Leon and I living with Papa and Grand-mère, and Yvonne, for now at least. Our oldest brother, Edmond, had left home within months of Maman's passing, when he joined the Bataillon du Pacifique.

Leon's eighteenth birthday had brought more change. All of a sudden, my playmate, my brother, whose chief delight was to tease me, was a grown man. He came to meet me at the end of school one day, not long before his birthday.

"Leon! What is it? Is something wrong?" He'd not walked me home in a long time. My friend Aimée grabbed the back of my blouse in a quick pinch; I saw her blush out of the corner of my eye and stifled a grin. Oblivious, Leon turned and fell in step on my other side.

"I just thought it'd be nice to walk you home today." He glanced around at my friends. "Just us, maybe. Is that ok?"

I stopped and looked at him. I could see something was weighing on his mind. Nodding, I turned back to the girls. "See you tomorrow."

"Don't mind us. We can manage without you, this once." Marine winked at me, grabbed Aimée's arm and turned towards town.

I smiled at my big brother and slipped my hand into the crook of his arm as we walked homewards. We continued in a companionable silence for a while. Dust from the beaten path found its way inside my sandals, irritating between my toes. I found myself pinching a fold of Leon's sleeve between my fingers, rubbing the rough cloth back and forth against itself. I realised he'd shortened his stride to match mine.

Finally I spoke. "I'm sure you didn't walk all the way to my school just to walk me home. So, what is it?"

He kicked at a pebble in his path. Shrugging his shoulders, he slowed down and looked at me. "I just…" He looked away. "I'm almost eighteen."

"Yes, I do know that. I have your present hidden somewhere safe."

He grinned and nudged his elbow into my side. "I haven't found it – yet. But that's not what I meant."

"You are starting to worry me, big brother. Just tell me." I nudged him right back. Just four years my senior, he'd always ignored my shyness, including me in his playtimes at home when I was small. He accepted me just as I was.

He stopped walking and stared at the ground. "I'm going to be working down in the mine." The words came out in a rush.

I felt the colour drain from my face. "What? No, Leon! But why? You already have a job up the top. Why change? What if you get hurt, like Papa did? Or worse?"

He raised his face, and I could see my own fears reflected in his eyes. "Apparently it's what happens. You work at the top until you're old enough, then they send you down below. But

31

I didn't know, I swear I didn't, Elise!" He grasped my hands. "The crew I work with, they're all younger than me. I never even asked Papa about what happened to the chaps who used to do our job. Well, you don't, do you? I was fifteen when I started. I just worried about doing my job right and not getting into trouble!"

I shook my head, my own words stuck in my throat. I knew this was terrifying him, but I couldn't think of anything to comfort him. Movement was at least doing something, so I tucked a hand back in the crook of his arm and continued our walk. We were almost home before I trusted myself to speak. "You just make sure you're always last in and first out. I can't lose you too!" He dropped a quick kiss on the top of my head in reply.

That night, I dreamt of Papa's accident. I used to have the same dream often, soon after it happened, but in the aftermath of losing Maman, it had been drowned out. In my dream, I heard the explosion. I was near the mine. The details were vague – I'd never been there in real life. I tried to run to Papa but the ground was littered with stones and tools, shaken by the force of the blast. I'd trip and fall, each time feeling more desperate that I was running out of time. I'd always wake up as I reached the top of the mine itself; the last thing I'd see was black dust filling the air, men stumbling out, coughing and frightened.

I woke up the next morning still tired and anxious. I took longer than usual to get ready, so I was surprised to see Yvonne still at the breakfast table when I got there.

"Finally! I'm going to be late for work, but I need to talk to you."

"Good morning to you too, Yvie." I surprised myself with my sharp tone.

She looked contrite. "Sorry, little sis."

I rubbed my eyes. "Sorry too, Yvie. I didn't sleep very well." Pulling a chair out from the table, I flopped into it, reaching for my baguette with one hand, a cup of chocolate with the other. The hot sweet drink was exactly what I needed, the first sip soothing me. I chased it down with a big bite of the bread.

Yvonne managed to sound concerned and impatient at the same time. "That's no good. But listen, can you come to see me when you get off for lunch?"

I nodded.

"Ok, I'll see you then. Have a nice morning at lycée."

She raced out of the room, patting my shoulder as she passed me.

"See you later, girls." I waved at my friends after the morning's lessons. Yvonne worked at a florist's in town. Working with Maman all those years had been great training. Plus Maman's reputation had been the perfect reference. Yvonne was standing in the doorway. As soon as she saw me, she called over her shoulder before joining me outside.

"We need to be quick before they close for lunch as well."

I hurried to keep up with her. Though we were roughly the same height, somehow she took a longer stride that I had trouble matching.

"Where are we going, exactly?" I managed to ask.

She grinned sideways at me. "You'll see."

"Yvie! You know I'm not great with surprises."

"Then you had better move, hadn't you?"

I scanned the stores in front of us, trying to work out which it could be. There was a clothes shop, a stationery store, and a photography store on this side of the street. Yvonne wasn't checking the road, so I assumed it was one of those. Sure enough, she stopped at the clothes store. Holding the handle, she looked back at me and grinned again. "Come on then. Suspense nearly over."

There was a lady behind the counter. She looked up as the bell over the door tinkled. The shop smelled of cloth and some light floral fragrance. The counter was wide and had a flap at one end, currently folded back, leaving a space between it and the wall.

"Mlle Bouchet," said the lady. "On time as usual. I appreciate that."

Yvonne smiled and put a hand on my shoulder. "Mme Dorey, this is my sister, Elise."

"Very pleased to meet you, Elise. You are a lucky girl to have such a kind sister!" They exchanged knowing looks. Mme Dorey must have seen my blank expression.

"Oh, it's like that. Right, well, Mlle Elise, if you'd like to step this way." She raised her arm to usher me towards a curtained alcove at the back. I raised my eyebrow at my sister. She giggled and nodded.

"Go on."

Once I was in the alcove, the storekeeper reached up and took a hanging clothes bag off the hook. She smiled at me and unzipped the bag. She manoeuvred the hanger down through its slot and then pulled it and the contents out through the opening. All with the bag between me and what was inside. She paused, clearly enjoying the drama of the moment.

"Are you ready?"

I bobbed my head. "Yes!"

She took the cover out of my way. "What do you think?" She was holding a white dress, covered in little dark blue spots.

My face split in a grin, and then I found myself laughing. "Yvie. This is what you wanted my 'help' with?"

"Well, if I'd told you it wouldn't have been a surprise, would it? Do you like it? Try it on. Come on, we're holding Mme Dorey back from her lunch."

The lady handed the dress to Yvonne and returned to the front of her store. I heard her click the lock and pull down the blind on her door. The dress felt so grown up once I had it on. The bodice fitted closely beneath a wide v neckline. The skirt was ankle length and gently flared. There was a narrow white belt that sat nicely above my hips. It was sleeveless.

"I love it, Yvie. But, why did you do this?"

She grinned once more. "Well, I thought it was about time you had something a bit more grown up. Since I'm getting married in New Zealand, you can't be my bridesmaid. So instead of a bridesmaid's dress, I got you this. Oh, Maman would love this on you."

I swallowed. Then grabbed her in a quick hug. "Thank you Yvie. It is beautiful."

"Excellent! Get changed and pass me the dress. I'll get Mme Dorey to wrap it up."

Yvonne's talk of her own departure and of Maman had threatened to undo me but I had gotten my emotions under control by the time I was dressed and back at the counter.

"Thank you, Mme Dorey. I'm sorry we've held you up. The dress is lovely." I spoke quickly, nervous as always when speaking to strangers.

"You are very welcome, and apologies are not necessary. I enjoy these little surprises!" She collected her own purse, unlocked the door then followed us out, pulling the door shut behind her.

Yvonne grinned. "Let's go home. Then you can show Grand-mère how lovely you look in that dress."

11

January 1947

Too soon, both Yvonne and Leon had gone away to their new lives. Leon had decided to move into a boarding house with some of the other workers.

"This way I save myself time to and from work. I can sleep that bit more, Elise. You know I'm going to need it!" Leon had explained, his tone apologising for his decision. I nodded. I did understand but would miss him dearly.

"Can you come back for dinner sometimes though? At least I'll be able to see for myself that you're still in one piece!"

He laughed. "Now you sound like Papa! He's already made me promise to come home for Sunday lunch every fortnight. So you won't have time to miss me, will you?"

Yvonne's last month flew by. Her fiancé had arranged it all from New Zealand. They were to be married almost as soon as she arrived there.

"I know it will be lovely that Papa can walk you down the aisle," I'd said to her. "But won't it be hard, not having us there?" I was sitting on her bed while she packed up the last of her things.

"Oh, did I not tell you?" Yvie said, trying to zip up her suitcase. "Odette's husband is sending her over to spend a week with me, up till the day after the wedding. Isn't that so nice of him?" She couldn't get the zip to close the last few centimetres. I sat on the suitcase, helping to flatten it just a bit more. Yvie managed to zip it closed. A horn sounded outside. The car had come to take her to the airport. She hugged me, her arms around me like a clamp.

"Goodbye Yvie, I'll miss you," I said through my tears.

Yvie wiped her eyes. "I'll miss you too."

Then she was gone. Suddenly I was the only child in the house.

Perhaps a month later, Papa invited Père Durand to lunch one Sunday. I had helped Grand-mère set the table and prepare as much as we could before we went to Mass.

"Let your papa know it's all ready once you put that down," Grand-mère signed as I carried the dish of hot vegetables to the table.

Papa looked up at my knock and nodded before I could say anything.

"Thank you Elise. Father, shall we?" Papa gestured for the priest to precede him to the table. Papa said grace over the food, then, as we began serving ourselves, I noticed a look pass between the two men.

"So, Elise, your papa tells me you have done very well in your first year at lycée. It is good to hear how well you have applied yourself to your studies."

I blushed. "Merci, Père."

Papa cleared his throat. "Tell the père about that last unit, Elise. I'm sure he will enjoy hearing what you learned."

Grand-mère watched our faces, content to observe rather

than contribute. I wished that she could speak for me! Instead she smiled and nodded encouragement.

Somehow I got through the meal, though I couldn't have said what anything tasted like afterwards. The scrutiny of our priest dominated my thoughts. The one positive I took was that I knew Père Durand was on the board that chose which students would get chosen for the higher classes for our second year. The classes that could lead to université. As Grand-mère and I washed the dishes, I allowed myself to think that I may have impressed him enough to be on that list. I dearly wanted to study ecology so I could continue where Maman's teaching had been cut short. There was so much more to know! Even though we were still looking after her flowers, I could see the difference since she was gone. She had never gone to université, she'd had a rare gift. I would need many teachers to continue her work to her standard.

12

Late March 1947

One day after school, as I came within sight of the house, I glanced up from the road and saw Papa standing at the window. He seemed to be looking out for me, raising a glass in his hand as we made eye contact. I swallowed the sigh that threatened, and knowing how observant he was, smiled instead and waved. He had been hard work since he'd come back from Yvonne's wedding. I never knew what mood he would be in. Especially with that glass in his hand. From this distance I couldn't really see the colour of its contents.

"Bonsoir Papa!" I dropped my book bag to the floor, shrugged off my coat and hung it on the peg in the hallway.

"Come in here please, Elise."

I could tell Papa was trying to sound casual as he turned from the window, raising his glass to his lips once more. Sensing his uneasiness, I came slowly into the living room. This was new. Was Papa nervous? He lowered himself into his armchair and motioned me to the other chair. Closer now, I could make out the distinct smell of the whisky. My stomach clenched as I sat back in the chair, pretending I hadn't noticed. I realised my fingers were picking away at a worn patch on the arm of my chair and I forced myself to stop, folding my hands together in my lap.

"Elise, I have made a decision."

"Yes, Papa, what is it?"

His ruined face gave nothing away; the scarring masked any emotion. Looking me squarely in the eye, he said, "You are almost sixteen. I am not convinced that lycée is the best place for you."

I sank lower into my chair. "Why, Papa? I made good grades this past year." I swallowed hard, trying to sound calm and mature.

He cleared his throat and continued: "That is all for the good. It is good to finish with a good review. But, I have been talking things over with Père Durand." He waved his free hand at me. "As I say, a decision has been made. Père Durand agrees that you should enter the convent over in Saint Louis. You will receive a more suitable education, and have a stable, safe home with the other women there. Your grandmother isn't getting any younger; frankly, neither am I. We will find somewhere smaller to live, somewhere easier to maintain."

"Papa, please! Why? You know I want to continue my studies to qualify to go to université! And what about Maman's garden? I have been taking good care of it, and I thought you were pleased that I have kept her stall going." My words began to trip over themselves. He rose from his chair.

"Elise, why do you think Père Durand came to lunch that day? He knew my concerns for you, now that your sisters have left home and married. It would be different had they stayed in New Caledonia, but now we must deal with the situation before us." He raised his glass and swallowed the remaining contents.

"I thought…" I remembered how excited I had been. I had got it completely wrong. My shoulders sagged as I realised Père Durand also oversaw the administration of the convent.

"I will give you some time to get used to the idea. I assumed you'd be excited. Talk to your grandmother. I'm sure you will find she agrees with me: it's the best thing for you." With that, he left the room.

My mind churned. I sat, I don't know how long, mentally arguing what I was unable to speak out. Finally as the sky darkened, I escaped my thoughts out in the garden. I brushed my fingertips over the flowers as I had always done until I got to the far end, turned and walked slowly back to the house. Grand-mère came through the kitchen door as I came near. She hugged me, then began to sign.

"I know you feel close to her here, my sweet girl. As do I."

I nodded, eyes stinging once more.

"But your papa only feels her absence wherever he looks. I'm sure I don't need to tell you how much he misses her."

I signed back, almost angry. "We all miss her, Grand-mère. Leaving will only make that worse!"

She patted my arm. "Sweetheart. You know we carry our grief in our own ways. My daughter is with me" —she laid a hand over her heart— "wherever I am. But your papa needs to leave here more than we need to stay. And he truly feels that the convent is better equipped to finish your education than lycée. We will still be able to see each other." She dropped her hands as I turned away, my hurt and anger like a brick wall between us. She tapped my shoulder, and I faced her again. "I'm still not clear why you are so against entering the convent, Elise. The life there is simple, and quiet. You would get to help in their gardens, just as you have done here. You enjoy so many of the things that you could continue to do with the sisters. The only difference would be that you aren't in this house. And you would be helping people. So what is it, my dear?"

I shook my head as tears threatened again. How to say it? It wouldn't look like anything special to anyone else. And until now, when I'd been forced to face it, I hadn't truly realised how much it meant to me. I looked out over Maman's flower garden. Though it was fully dark now, I imagined I could see the blooms, some closed for the night, some with their open petals facing the moon. At last I found the words I needed. "I want what you and Maman each had. One day. I want my own family. My own home, a garden to take care of. One day. And right now, I want to stay with you and Papa. Is that so wrong, Grand-mère? Am I being selfish?" When she didn't answer immediately, I worried I'd upset her by the mention of Maman. It struck me again, that as hard as her loss had been on me and my brothers and sisters, how much harder it must be for my grandmother to have her daughter go before her. She now looked past me towards the house. "Grand-mère? I'm sorry. I didn't mean to make you sad." I tapped her arm.

"No child, you didn't upset me. I'm touched, that is all. And you reminded me how it was for me when your maman was a babe in my arms. I'm old, and slow to not have considered this as your reason. Leave it with me, I will talk to your papa for you." She reached up, patting my face gently. "Come inside now, it's getting cold. I'll make us a nice hot chocolate, how does that sound?"

13

May 1947

I continued at lycée for several weeks. Papa had not raised the subject again since that night, and the lycée year was almost over. My last year there.

Any free time I had, I spent in the only place I was able to speak 'to' her, or cry when the grief was too big for words – among the flowers, out of earshot of the house. Maman had worked for so long to get the flowers to the standard she desired, coercing our land to work in harmony with her. And she had built a solid reputation in our community.

"Maman, I have tried to do what I can to look after your garden, as have Grand-mère and Yvie. But our best isn't quite the same as yours." She'd had a special way with flowers.

I arrived home one afternoon in the last week of lycée to find a letter waiting for me. It was from Yvie. The only other one I had from her had come about a month after she had left. She'd sent me some of the flowers from her wedding bouquet, dried between fine tissue paper. Now, I walked quickly out to the flower garden and sat on the grass to read her letter in private.

Dearest Elise,

I hope you have not been letting yourself get too worried about Papa's plans for you. I know how he is, and I know how you are – neither will have spoken to the other about it! Am I correct? You will be surprised to hear that he has telephoned me and explained the situation. A new decision has been made, which I hope you see as an improvement on going into the convent. Papa, Rex and I have agreed that you may come and live with us here. I will teach you English, and you can help me around the house until you are confident enough in that language to look for work. Now I have surprised you, haven't I? Your passage has been arranged. All you need to do is pack! I believe you have Grand-mère to thank for this alternative. Oh my dear, I do look forward to having you here! It'll be such fun!

Your loving sister,

Yvie

I read the letter through again. I was torn between gladness at seeing my sister again, as she had hoped, and grief that I would still be leaving the only home I had ever known. I stood up, tucked the letter into my pocket and wandered between the flower beds. My hands trailed over the petals, letting their scent and touch calm me as they always did. Gradually my thoughts settled and I accepted that there was no other alternative for me. I knew now that Yvie's departure had begun a countdown on my life here with my father, grandmother and my mother's garden. As I trailed back towards the house, my tears dried on my face and at last, I was able to go to my grandmother and thank her with a smile and a hug.

My possessions were few; I neither wanted nor needed lots of clothes, so I had only one suitcase. My bedroom looked sad, stripped of all that made it mine. I had packed my last few things, dressed tidily but comfortably for the journey ahead. I'd been extra careful with the dress Yvonne had given me last year. I'd not had many occasions to wear it yet. Maybe in New Zealand that would change.

Grand-mère wasn't coming with us to the port. In a way I was relieved as I knew it would be hard to say goodbye and neither of us liked drawing attention to ourselves in public. She came into my room. I stood and wrapped my arms tightly about her. I didn't want to let her go. I breathed in her beautiful smell, trying to hold it in my memory. Eventually we parted, each reaching for a handkerchief. She signed, "wait here" and left the room. When she came back in, she had a square package in her hand.

"What is this?" I asked, as she held it out to me. I took it, turning it over.

"Open it when you get to New Zealand," she signed, her hands almost dancing. "I know you will find it hard to be away from all of us. But you have a future in New Zealand that would not be possible with the sisters. This is a small part of home. Open it when you are alone in your new room. Keep it close to you, and remember how much you are loved. I will not be able to visit, so please write to me often, will you, my dear?"

Now I was crying again. I hugged her again, squeezing her. "Of course I will write, Grand-mère. And I will look forward to your letters."

"Take all you have learned here, helping me to take care of your maman. You are a good girl, Elise. I know you will learn the new language and ways easily. You will find your place. Your sisters and brothers have done it before you."

At my door, she gestured for me to pick up my case and follow her. She led the way to the lounge and looked out the window, waving me over to join her. She pointed. "Here is Papa coming now. It is time. Let us compose ourselves. Put on your hat. We have said our goodbyes. Believe it or not, this is hard for him too, ma chérie. Go now." She kissed my cheeks, turned me about and gave me a gentle push towards the door.

I sat silently, while all around me the commotion of the dock whirled. Shouts and engines and metallic clatters tangled together and jarred my ears but I paid scant attention. Cool wind gusted between the hulls of the various boats and ships in port, battling the heat of the sun on my skin and bringing with it a salty spray.

While I had gradually come to terms with the loss of Maman, I was now filled with a new pain. The agony was almost physical at the realisation I may never see home again.

When the horn sounded boarding time, I stood, shook myself and walked to the queue forming in front of the ramp. There was no one to see me off. Papa had said his goodbyes at the house. He accompanied me in the taxi, then walked me to the departure gate. As soon as he was satisfied I was where I needed to be, he turned and headed back to the taxi.

I showed my boarding pass to the purser, returned his welcoming smile and made my way up the ramp. I held tight to the slick damp of the steel railing, carefully placing each foot firmly before lifting the other. The boards beneath my feet were topped with some sort of rubberised tread. It felt hard and soft at the same time. The whole structure trembled with the footsteps of the other passengers boarding ahead of me.

I stood at the stern as the ship pulled out from the wharf, watching the only home I had ever known slip further and further away. The sea churned in our wake. Though I was calm without, inside my emotions felt like those waves, frantic white foam folding over the flat blue beneath.

How long I stood there, lost in my thoughts, I don't know. By the time I looked about me, we were fully at sea, no land in sight. I stretched and sighed. To my left, a family was gathered, the maman and papa pointing out parts of the ship to their three young children. I watched as the maman reached out to straighten her daughter's collar. My eyes stung. The maman straightened, and our eyes met before her family regained her attention, the children running off ahead of their parents along the deck.

I was alone with my thoughts again. Out here, with nothing to see in any direction but the ocean and sky, I pictured myself back at lycée with my friends. My throat tightened as the faces of my girlfriends flashed through my mind. Would I ever be able to see them again? I remembered when Odette was preparing for her wedding and her move to America. We'd hardly seen her for days on end in the whirlwind of lunch and supper dates with all her friends, making sure she'd forgotten no one. She'd come home with sets of notepaper and envelopes, regaling us with the promises that went with them.

"Margot and Françoise said they are going to save up to come visit me as soon as they can," she had said. "And Jacqueline challenged me to write every month. She said she'll always reply."

Yvonne and I had a lovely afternoon out with her before she left for America. It was a rare treat that included having our photograph taken outside a public house in town. I knew we were all thinking how much Maman would have loved to have been there with us.

The ship's bow lifted as we hit some larger waves. I pushed myself off the railing and stretched. It was time to learn my way around this ship. I moved off to my right, stumbling a little with the unfamiliar movement beneath my feet. I continued down the deck, until I saw a door into the stairwell that led to the passenger's quarters below the deck. The temperature rose by several degrees as soon as the door closed behind me. I hadn't realised until then how much noise the sea and wind had been making. Here, even though I could feel the low rumble of the engines, it was almost silent. I made my way to the stairs, and carefully descended. I checked my boarding pass for my cabin number – eleven.

I leaned against the door as it clicked shut, closing my eyes and turning the key on the inside before reaching up to remove my hat. Sighing, I opened my eyes to see what the room held for me. There was a bed, a round window, a small washstand, and a rail to hang my clothes. My little window showed me a clear view of the sky, darkening towards evening.

I saw that my suitcase had been brought to the room for me. I put my toiletries on the shelves. Once that task was out of the way, I sat on the bed, plumped up the pillow behind me, leaned back and closed my eyes. In my mind I walked the path from school one more time, past the gardens of the wealthier homes. If she was with us, Maman never missed a chance to teach my sisters and me about her favourite topic. I could almost hear her voice.

"You see how cleverly she has interspersed the wildflowers with the more delicate blooms? The wildflowers are strong and vigorous, protecting the others from wind and salt blown in off the sea."

As a child I remembered being curious about other lands that we read about in school. Lands so vast it would take days or weeks to get from one coast to the other. In Nouvelle-Calédonie, it took a couple of hours, at most, to travel east to west, and we could get from Noumea to the northernmost point of Grand Terre in about a day. Now here I was, out on that very ocean, sitting on a bed as if in a house. True, in a house the bed and room would not be one minute tilting as if on the side of a hill, the next falling back the other way. In an odd way I found it soothing, and I was soon rocked to sleep like an infant in its mother's arms.

A loud bell sounded. I wondered for a moment why I had fallen asleep at school. Then I remembered. Noumea, my home, was far behind me and the bell which woke me was likely to be the ship's dinner bell, going by the darkening sky outside my cabin window. Shaking myself mentally, I swung my legs off the side of the bed and straightened. There was a small mirror over the basin opposite me. "Ugh," I groaned at the state of my hair. Frizz.

Now I was properly conscious, I did notice the temperature had risen while I had been sleeping. I padded over to the basin and turned on the tap. There was an initial gurgling noise, then a thin stream of cold water squirted out. I quickly plugged the basin before too much water went down the pipe, then dipped my hands in. Shaking off the excess, I ran my now damp fingers through my curls, detangling as best I could. I wet my hands again, this time using the dampness to pat and shape the curls, trying to achieve a semblance of tidiness. Next was my face. When I looked in the glass again, I was satisfied with my efforts.

Passengers flowed down the corridor, and I allowed myself to be pulled along with them. All around I could hear what I took to be greetings in a variety of languages. Jacket sleeves briefly brushed against my arm as long legged men strode quickly past. At the bottom of the stairs, the pace slowed down a little, but soon we reached the dining room doors and were directed to fill the tables arranged neatly around the room. A tinkling of silverware against glass became more audible as the introductions died away. I turned in my chair to see the captain standing by his table.

"Je vous souhaite à tous la bienvenue à ce voyage. I would like to welcome you all to this sailing." He smiled, looking around the room. I smiled at the sound of my own language. He continued, switching between English and French, explaining safety and emergency procedures, introducing the members of the crew to whom we could go for any assistance while at sea. When he had finished, a smattering of applause broke out, and he bowed, still smiling, as he took his seat.

As our food was served, the ship's motion on the sea was tangible: the wait staff so well adjusted to it that their passage between the servery and the tables was almost a dance. No crockery rattled, and nothing spilled during the entire performance. I watched, impressed, seeing similar appreciation on the faces around me. When our table was fully served, we turned our attention to the food itself.

"Bon appetit," I was surprised to hear myself say. My fellow diners returned the wish, and we applied ourselves to the tasty fare.

Conversations among relative strangers sprang up throughout the meal. The clicking and clacking of cutlery on plates formed a percussion that accompanied the rise and fall of voices. In breaks in the chatter at my own table, I could hear not only French and English, but also a smattering of German, Melanesian and Asian tongues. Though I couldn't understand what was said, I had heard them over the years in Noumea. Every so often laughter would break out, and I would feel a smile stretch my lips in response. Much later, as I lay in bed waiting for sleep to come, I replayed the captain's words, mouthing the familiar words in French and trying to match the English ones in my mind. My basic schoolgirl English had left a lot out, I realised. It sounded like such a quick language!

I woke up with a start, for a moment forgetting again where I was. I rubbed the sleep from my eyes with my knuckles, the ship lurched and my elbow knocked painfully against the wall.

"Ow!" Wide awake now, I sat up, reaching for the drape over the window with my other hand. The view now was grey and leaden. The glass was splattered with sea spray. The ship lurched once more, as if to shake me out of bed to face the day. Taking the hint, I clambered out of bed, steadying myself against the wall.

Climbing the stairs to the dining room, I could hear the tinkle of cutlery and a gentle hubbub of chatter from the early risers. I collected a coffee and croissant from the buffet and walked carefully to a table close by. I put my cup and plate down just as the ship dipped into a trough between waves.

"Salut!" said a cheerful voice to my left. It was the young mother from yesterday.

"Oh, salut!," I smiled in return. "I am Elise."

"I am Lucette. My friends call me Lulu."

"Bonjour, Lucette. I am very pleased to meet you. You have a lovely family."

She smiled with maternal pride. "Thank you. We have been blessed. The children seem to be enjoying it so far, anyway. I noticed you are travelling alone, and thought you may like someone to talk with. Do you go to visit your family?"

"I am going to my sister. But to live, not to visit." She put her hand on mine and leaned towards me. "Alone? That must be hard at your age. Please allow me to be your friend, at least onboard. You may come sit with us at meals and we will walk together with my children. Let their antics distract you. Please say yes?" She smiled again, and I couldn't help smiling back.

"That is so kind, thank you. Yes, I would like that."

"Excellent! Well, no time like the present, as my husband always says. Come, let us find what my darlings have gotten up to and rescue the poor passengers!"

Contrary to her dire prediction, her children were sitting quietly as their father read to them out on the deck. He smiled as he caught sight of us, and put a marker in the book, closing it.

"Your maman has returned, children. Time to make our way to the chapel, yes?"

"Louis, I have invited Elise to join us and she has graciously accepted." She turned to me. "Oh, Elise. I didn't actually check with you. Do you attend church? Or rather, did you do so at home?"

"Yes, Maman felt very strongly about that. As a family we have always kept Mass."

Louis and Lulu glanced at each other.

"Excellent," said Louis. "Let us be on our way then." He

led the way to the nearest door, and on through the maze of corridors to the chapel. I had not noticed it when I had made my own tour of the ship. It was small, and there were a number of passengers already in the pews. One of the crew served as priest, leading us through the service so familiar to me. The only difference was that here, aside from the Latin parts, everything was said in both English and French. The few Melanesians appeared to understand the French parts. As I took the emblems, I gave thanks that I had found a friendly face, and through her, the opportunity to come to this service. I would do my best to hold on to the peace I felt here, and try not to borrow trouble by worrying about my immediate future.

In a quiet moment before dinner, I decided to make use of the blotter and inkwell in my cabin.

"Dearest Grand-mère,

I know I won't be able to send this letter until we reach Auckland, but I wanted to tell you how the sailing is, while it is all still fresh in my mind.

This morning I made a new friend. She is a little older than me, a mother already. Her name is Lucette, and it is so lovely to have someone to talk to from home. Lulu, she likes to be called. She made her children call me 'Aunt Elise'. Her husband, Louis, is a quiet man, clearly devoted to his wife and children. The boy, Paul, and his younger sisters, Michelle and Therese, range in age from three to seven. Lulu and Louis had been childhood sweethearts, she told me, and were married as soon as both families gave permission.

Lulu invited me to attend chapel with them. I hadn't thought of there being one on board, so it was a welcome surprise.

We had a lovely time learning our way around the ship together, and I sat with them at lunch. We played cards until it was time for

54

the crew to clear and prepare the room for dinner.

I am supposed to be resting, but I had to share my new friend with you. I know you would like her.

Oh, Grand-mère, I miss you already. More later."

I sat with Lulu and her family again at dinner. I laughed at the stories of their life back at the northern end of Grand Terre. Louis had completed his studies since being demobbed at the end of the war. This was the reason for their move to New Zealand. He had secured a position in a local authority which came with a house.

"If we move now, while there is work and the children are so young, there should be much better opportunities for them than we could ever hope for back home. You have to have the right connections to get the sort of work Louis wants there. And we don't."

I had learned that New Zealand was much larger than home. I couldn't get my head around living among so many people. Noumea, even counting the surrounding area, had a relatively small population. This young family had come to mean much to me in such a short space of time. It would be hard to say goodbye tomorrow when we docked at the port; they were staying in Auckland while I would be going on to Tauranga.

14

Winter 1947

If I had been more aware of the bustle and noise at the port back in Noumea, possibly the shock here in Auckland wouldn't have been as great. A cacophony of foreign sights, smells and sounds greeted me as I lined up to disembark. I reached the foot of the ramp, which felt no steadier coming down than it had going up in Noumea. Once more I clung to the rail and concentrated on each step. Setting foot for the first time in my new land, at first I thought the ground was moving beneath me, then I realised it was me: a leftover of the ship's motion in my muscles.

I heard the customs' official say something to the passenger just in front of me. After two days onboard the ship, I recognised English more easily, but still had no idea what he had said. The man smiled, and gestured at his clipboard, then towards my purse. He spoke again, and mimed opening a book. Oh, he wanted to see my papers.

"Elise! Elise!"

I turned to see Lulu, still on the ramp, leaning out over the rail and waving.

"Remember, we will write as soon as we are settled."

I waved in acknowledgement. We had exchanged addresses last night, and as I took out my papers, I made sure my address book was still there.

Once through customs, we were directed to the arrivals end of the port building. Through the door, I saw rows of seats filled with people waiting to depart. At their feet were bags, suitcases and a few kit bags belonging to recently demobbed soldiers and airmen. Beyond the rows I could see others milling about. It was a shock to see my brother-in-law in the crowd. I think I had expected Yvonne. Her husband and I barely knew each other. He hadn't seen me yet. I took advantage of the crowd, ducking behind some men, taking some time to compose my thoughts and prepare to deal with this man who was the head of my new home.

Mr Carlisle spotted me and waited for me to make my way over to him. He reached for my suitcase.

"Bonsoir, Monsieur Carlisle," I greeted him.

"Hello Elise," he nodded, pantomiming for me to follow him.

We wove our way through the throng. The crowd moved reluctantly away to either side of us as my brother-in-law pushed relentlessly forward. Once or twice a suitcase grazed against my leg as it swung wide at its owner's side.

The outer doors shut behind us, cutting off the clamour of voices. In the comparative silence, bus and car tyres whispered against the road, and the motors made a steady purr. Now we walked side by side. I was glad he did not appear to expect conversation. He set a brisk pace and soon I saw a large car parked about a hundred yards away. Mr Carlisle said something quickly but the words meant nothing to me. I hoped my smile would be enough to answer. As we drew closer, the front passenger door opened, and a slight figure emerged. I saw it was my sister and my smile expanded as I sped up to reach her.

"Yvie! Oh, Yvie, it's so good to see you!"

She waited beside the car, then held out her arms as I reached her, pulling me into a tight hug. "Little Elise! Let me look at you." She pulled back and smoothed back my hair from my face. She laughed. "Those curls! Still all over the place! " Holding on to my arm, she turned to her husband and they conversed briefly in English. Yvonne turned back to me as her husband went to the back of the car and put my case in the trunk. She switched back to French. "Rex does not speak French, and prefers I don't speak it in front of him. But he knows you have very little English, so I have an excuse for now." She winked at me. "I just asked him if we still have time to find somewhere to eat before we drive home. It's quite a long drive."

"Thanks, Yvie. I am quite hungry, so that would be nice." I lowered my voice. I realised he wouldn't know what I was saying but I felt impolite talking about him. "What am I to call him? I barely know him, so I feel a bit strange calling him by his Christian name."

Yvonne chuckled. Mr Carlisle looked over the roof of the car as he opened the driver's door, a frown creasing his brow. She rattled off something to him and he shut the door and came back around to the footpath. He stuck his right hand out to me, the frown deepening. I placed my right hand in his. He spoke slowly and carefully. Yvonne translated. "He says, you may call me Rex."

I stared at my sister then at Mr Carlisle, wondering how accurately she had translated. I reddened when I realised he'd caught me staring and bobbed my head. I hoped I'd recalled the correct English for bonjour from school. "Thank you … Rex."

Yvonne opened the rear door for me, and they each got in the front seats. As we pulled out onto the street, Yvonne became my guide, pointing out various landmarks. "We'll get out of the centre of the city first. Rex knows a few cafés that should be open. He grew up here in Auckland."

We pulled up on a street about ten minutes outside of the city. At mid afternoon, it wasn't much busier than Noumea would be during the week. Most businesses were still open, and there were plenty of people walking both sides of the street. We left the car and walked around the next corner. Large plate glass windows invited the gaze of passersby. Rex held the door open and stood back. I followed Yvonne inside as a waitress made her way towards us. The waitress smiled and led us further inside.

"Well, now is as good a time to start as any." Yvonne said, as we sat down at our allocated table. The waitress stood beside us, a pad and pencil in hand. Yvonne gestured for Rex to order. That done, he stood up and followed the waitress to the counter. She continued through to the kitchen as Rex flicked through a pile of newspapers before selecting one. Even after just meeting him again, I could see the tension in his posture. As for Yvie, I recognised the set of her jaw, though she was respectful towards her husband.

"Right, your *chaise* is in English, 'chair'. Go on, try it."

I had to laugh. She'd reverted to her teacher persona she used on me when I was little. Obediently, I repeated the word. "Share."

She nodded. Rex came back to the table with the newspaper.

"Very close. But the English say 'ch' much harder than we do. More like this:" She demonstrated again. It made her sound stern, almost annoyed. Keeping my jaw tight, I tried again.

"Chair."

Rex's lips were pressed tightly though he didn't lift his eyes from the paper. I tried to ignore him as I focused on my sister.

"And in front of us," she tapped the table top. "We say *table à manger*, but they just say 'table'. Your turn."

So began my slow slog into speaking English. Our refreshments arrived, and Yvonne gave Rex her attention for the remainder of our stop. I wondered how much say he'd had in my coming here. It was already obvious to me that he didn't enjoy sharing Yvonne's attention.

Soon enough we were on our way out of Auckland altogether. Yvonne kept up a running commentary, filling me in on the towns and regions we passed through. It was strange to hear the New Zealand place names punctuating her French. I found it to be an island of sharp contrasts: at times we drove through seemingly endless flat expanses, at others up and down through more hilly country. But all the time, the road twisted and turned. In no time at all I had no idea in which direction we faced. Barely a mile would go by without a bend in the road. Conversation naturally died off as Rex concentrated on the road.

For a couple of hours, we rarely saw much more than the countryside on either side of the road. Night had begun to fall; our vision narrowed to the beams of the car's headlamps. Finally I made out street lights in the distance, and hoped that meant we were close to the end of our journey.

Yvonne turned to peer over her shoulder. "Almost home, Elise. Tauranga is not as populated nor as large as Auckland, but it is still much bigger than Noumea. So we still have a way to go from the town border." With the ease of familiarity, Rex turned right and left as we headed through the township.

"Yvonne, it is beautiful!" I twisted in my seat and put both hands on the window. I gazed in wonder at the wide open streets. The streetlamps and the car lights revealed footpaths lined with store fronts of brick, stone and wood. Everything was closed of course, and there was no one out walking. "It is so clean!"

She laughed and translated for Rex. He laughed too, a rough bark of a sound, and replied to her. "He thinks you are easily impressed. And he says the dark hides many imperfections."

* * *

Thankfully my new home did have something in common with my old one: we were on the coast. Even better was that from the back of my sister's home, we had access to a tributary. We were able to get right to the water's edge. Rex had built a basic jetty. He pointed it out when they were showing me around the grounds early the next day. He'd spoken for several minutes before turning back to look at me. Yvonne was biting back a grin. He threw his arms in the air and said something more before walking back to the house.

"What was he saying?"

"Don't mind him. He is very proud of where he has got to and got a bit carried away. He was telling you how hard he had worked to get this land right on the water. Then he realised you didn't understand a word of it! And he didn't want to stand around and hear me speak French."

I realised why she'd started so quickly in teaching me. It

was going to be awkward until I knew enough English to take this thorn from Rex's side.

Yvonne was still talking. "One day soon we'll have our own boat, but until then, his little jetty is a reminder of his dream. For now, he goes for a swim every morning. That's his start and end point." My face gave me away – she laughed aloud. "Don't worry Elise. He doesn't expect company! I sit on the jetty and paddle my toes when it's a nice day. That's all." We looked at each other.

"Because girls don't swim," we chorused, laughing together as we remembered the childhood admonition.

Confirming my earlier thought, Yvonne continued: "Like I said at the port, he doesn't like me speaking French around him. So it's hard on him at the moment that I have to translate for you. But he will just have to put up with it for now."

"Why does he not like to hear you speak French?"

Yvonne shook her head. "He's never really said. When we met back home, of course he heard me speak English in the shops to the tourists. And all our conversations were in his language." She sighed. "But when Odette arrived for our wedding, I greeted her in French quite naturally. As soon as she left the room, he made it very clear that he did not want to hear anything but English in his home."

I looked over as she finished speaking, hearing the sadness in her voice.

She tucked a hand into my arm and turned us back towards the house. "I have missed speaking so easily. English is an awkward language, so imprecise!" She laughed again. "But I am starting your English lessons properly, right now! Starting with the names of everyday things. Just as I learned."

We made our way slowly through the garden to the back

door, Yvonne demanding me to repeat each word several times until she was happy with my pronunciation.

Once inside, Yvonne went off to find her husband, and I made my way back to my room. Though the house wasn't much bigger than what we'd had at home, the layout was a little confusing at first. There wasn't a central hall going from front to back for a start. I walked through the kitchen which led to the lounge. A second doorway off that room led to the small front hall. From there my room was one of three bedrooms off to one side.

"The one at the end is Rex's study." Yvonne had told me when showing me around.

I was thankful that my room looked out over the back. When I opened my drapes that morning it was to a view of flowers and the waterway. It almost felt like home. I felt the corners of my lips turn up, surprised at the lightness of my thoughts.

Whether we were cooking or doing other chores, Yvonne had me working hard at this new, tongue-twisting language. At the stores, she'd pick up a vegetable or bag of dry goods, and give me another lesson right in the middle of the shop. I'd redden, feeling the eyes of strangers on me. But she persisted and gradually the words started to make sense.

Because they lived quite a distance from the main shopping area, Yvie had got Rex to teach her to drive. On the days she had errands, she would drive him to work early in the morning, and collect him at the end of the day.

"Yvie, I don't know how you can be so brave." We allowed ourselves to speak French when we were alone. I held onto the car door, sitting in the front beside her. Up here, the road seemed to come up at me so fast. At first I worried we'd bump into someone in front of us.

Yvonne just laughed. She was no taller than me; she had the seat all the way forward, a cushion under her and one behind. She gripped the wheel with both hands, but somehow seemed perfectly in control.

"It's easy once you know how. I have had a lot of practice these past two years. Let's just find a parking spot." She turned left to pull in outside the grocery store. She manoeuvred expertly into a slot, moved the gear stick, took her left foot off the pedal and turned the car off.

"See? Nothing to it. Ok, now, inside, remember, English only. Yes?" She wagged a stern finger at me. The effect was diluted a little by her grin.

It had been several weeks already. My English was slowly improving, though I was always nervous using it in front of strangers.

"Come on, you will only get better at this by doing it. After this, we're taking lunch out to Rex. I thought you would like to come this time." She pushed the door and held it open for me, ushering me ahead of her. The counter stretched the length of the store to my left and a couple of women were already queuing up to pay for their orders. I juggled my basket from one hand to the other. Stepping to my right, I waited for her to pass me but she just nudged me forward. I gulped and tried rehearsing the unfamiliar words in my head as we walked around the store, collecting the fresh vegetables before lining up at the counter. When it was our turn, Yvonne moved up beside me. I looked down and saw she had her ration book in her hand.

"You order, like we practised. Go on."

I muddled through, reading laboriously from the list in my hand. My face grew hot as I stammered over the still strange sounds. At last it was time for Yvonne to hand over the ration book and pay for the order.

We loaded up the baskets and packets into the boot, making sure the precious eggs we'd been lucky enough to get were well protected and secure. Once we were sitting in the car, I sighed with relief.

Yvonne glanced over, eyebrows raised. Still using English, she said, "Remember I 'ad to do this too, Elise. Of course I learned some English back at the shop at 'ome, but when I got 'ere I found it was very different. I almost 'ad to start over! New Zealanders 'ave their own way of talking." She laughed. "So I know it's difficult. But I also know it will only get easier by actually trying." She started the car. "Ok, lecture over," she laughed again.

"Thank heaven for that. You were starting to sound like Monsieur Hubert." I answered in our own language. It was my turn to laugh as she gasped in mock horror. Monsieur Hubert was the headmaster at our old school, known amongst the students for his monotonous lectures.

We made our way south. There weren't many other cars in town, and by the time we were near Papamoa we were alone on the road. About half an hour after we'd left the grocery store, Yvonne turned onto the side road towards Rex's mill. We pulled off the road into the car park. A worker was making his way across from the office, and looked up as we drove in. He smiled, recognition on his face when he saw Yvonne. She paid him no attention so I waved. It seemed polite. He waved back hesitantly, looking back over his shoulder as he walked on.

Yvonne parked. I hopped out, clapping my hands to my ears in shock. Yvonne saw and shook her head.

"It does take some getting used to," she shouted over the din. Yvie reached in and collected the lunch basket. I turned to see if the man was still in sight, but he'd gone. I followed Yvonne as she led the way over to the office.

"Elise, open the door will you? My 'ands are a bit full."

I sped up and got to the door ahead of her. Rex was at his desk, papers strewn across its surface. He grinned at Yvie. "There's a sight for sore eyes."

I heard the sounds but they made no sense. It made me feel I still had further to go with English. His grin had not included me so I drifted over to the window, out of the way. The outside noise was drastically muted now the door was closed. The window faced a clearing, the ground beaten flat by constant foot and vehicle traffic. To one side was a large three sided building with a massive bench and saw in its centre. Logs lay piled beside the building, and I could just see the end of a tall metal structure. I realised it was the source of the clamour. The beaten earth narrowed to a track that ran alongside the log pile before it disappeared around a bend. Trees grew thickly on the opposite side of the track, while I could just see the tops of a thinner line of them behind the building. I could dimly hear the whining of motors and crashing of trees in the distance but there were no people in sight.

"Elise. Did you hear me?"

I turned reluctantly away from the window at my brother-in-law's voice. "I am sorry, Rex?"

"She understood that much anyway. Well done my dear." His smile didn't match his cool tone, which confused me. He turned back to me. "I asked how you are getting on with your lessons."

"Good, I think. Yvonne is a good teacher." I crossed my

fingers behind me, hoping I'd used the right word.

His interest already gone, he looked away from me again. "Thanks for lunch. I'll see you at seven." He stood up while he was talking and came around the desk to Yvonne. He gave her a quick peck on the cheek before turning back to his work. As I turned to follow her out the door, I saw him reach for a sandwich with one hand. The other was already holding his pencil again, eyes on a page filled with figures.

II

Part Two

15

August 1947

A couple of days later, we'd finished dinner but were still sitting at the table. Rex leaned back and looked down his nose at me, head tilted back. "So Elise. What do you think of New Zealand so far?"

I didn't answer immediately. "It is, pleasant?" I stared at my sister, hoping I'd got the right word.

"Pleasant, hmm? Ok, I'll take 'pleasant'. The housework must not take so long as when it was just Yvonne doing it all?"

I wasn't sure of the connection between my reply and the housework.

Yvonne pulled a face at him. "Stop teasing us, Rex. You know 'ow we fill our days." She turned to me. "He's testing your English, Elise, and trying to get a rise out of me. 'umour him, please, or 'e'll keep going all evening."

Nervously, I smiled at the pair of them. "Well, yes, I 'elp Yvie with the chores. And then we work in the garden and she tells me the English names of the flowers and plants." I saw Yvonne nod encouragingly and gesture for me to continue. "Yes. We sometimes go for a walk. She is introducing me to the –neighbours? Is that right?"

"Yes. So, you aren't rushed off your feet then?"

I glanced mutely at Yvonne; he'd lost me now.

"Rex. Be nice! You know 'ow long your Kiwi sayings took for me to learn." She turned sideways in her chair now, her back to him. "Rex means our days are not so full that I cannot spare you sometimes. 'E is building up to tell you something 'e 'as decided."

I looked back at him and saw him raise his eyebrows at his wife.

"Yvonne tells me that you are quite good at organising and tidying."

Yvonne stopped him. "That means putting things straight. You understand?" She nodded at him to carry on.

"You will come to my office tomorrow, and tidy up my papers and cupboards. Yvonne used to do it for me but now that she has the house to run as well as look after you, my office is suffering."

My eyes switched back and forth from him to her. Yvonne's expression was hard to read. "Yvonne, you will not mind?"

"Of course she won't!"

"Yes, it's fine, Elise. It is just one day. The files can't be too bad, it's not been that long since I did it for 'im."

"I would be glad to be of use."

So it was that I found myself being driven to the mill early the next morning. Yvonne and I had made the lunches the night before, and they were packed into a basket at my feet. Yvonne had said that Rex wasn't one for what she called 'small talk' in the morning. I gazed out of the window, happy in the silence, watching the shadows change as the sun rose. I knew the sea was just beyond the tree line. I felt that if I could only concentrate enough, I would hear the waves breaking as they reached the shore. I peered upwards, my face close to the glass, hoping to see a few early seagulls.

I felt him glance my direction now and then but I pretended not to notice.

Soon we were pulling into the car park. I followed him to the office. I saw his staff waiting for him by the wall. Conscious of their curious glances, I did my best to keep Rex between me and them. I realised I would get to know every inch of the path very well if I watched my feet like this each visit.

"Good morning chaps," he said in general greeting.

"Morning, Boss," they each said, not quite in chorus. I could pick out individual voices. I raised my eyes. The man who I'd waved at on my first visit was standing a little behind the others. I caught him grinning at me over his work mate's shoulder. I felt my face grow hot and I turned away, hoping no one would notice.

Rex was finding the office key on his keyring. He looked up as he walked up the steps. Over his shoulder, he said, "Everyone, this is Miss Bouchet, my sister-in-law. She's helping me today with the filing."

"Good morning, Miss." This time they did speak in unison. I blushed as I replied.

Rex held the door open and ushered me ahead of him. "I'll be back. Sit there," he pointed to a second chair by the far wall. "I'll just sort them out with their work for the morning." He grabbed a sheaf of paperwork off the desk and ducked back outside, pulling the door almost closed behind him.

The last time we were here, I'd not taken much notice of the room. Now though, knowing more was expected of me, I spent the next couple of minutes getting the layout straight in my head. Written English had come more easily to me than spoken, so the labels on the file drawers were helpful. I had figured out the system Yvonne had organised by the time Rex returned.

He rubbed his hands together. "All right. Hang your coat and purse over there," he said, nodding at the corner opposite the door. "So, first things first. Best you go through each drawer, one at a time, make sure what's in there is filed properly first. Anything you're not sure of, make a pile, then you can check with me all at once instead of asking lots of questions. Ok?"

"You understand?"

I nodded.

"Show me." He nodded towards the cabinets again. I swallowed. His manner was making me nervous.

"I start 'ere." I walked to the drawer marked 'Ab-Am'. "And make sure it is correct. If any are in the wrong place, I put them" –I looked around me– "'ere on this corner and then you will 'elp me. Yes?"

"Yes, exactly. We'll work till smoko – morning tea. We'll go across to the tearoom and sit with the lads for that." He moved around to his chair, sat down and was immersed in his own work within moments. He paid no more attention to me.

For the next while the only sounds in the office were papers rustling over each other, the scratch of his pencil as he worked, and the squeak of the filing cabinet drawer hangers as I moved them back and forth on their rails.

When I heard Rex finally push his chair back, I was surprised to see that it was morning tea time. My morning work had absorbed me. It made a nice change from housework and I felt like I had done something constructive. Rex looked briefly at the piles of files and folders I had out on the floor, but said nothing as I followed him over to the tearoom obediently. There was only one person there ahead of us. He'd put the kettle on and looked up as we walked in.

"Hey, Boss," he greeted Rex, reaching up into the cabinet for mugs for us.

"Ta James. I'm parched." Rex grabbed a box off the bench, and pulled out a tea bag for each of us, tossing them into mugs before handing me one. I sat down at the far end of the table from Rex. The rest of the workers trickled in, each greeting him with a quick word or a nod. The table filled before I realised who had sat on my right, and only then when I heard him speak. I kept my face steadfastly to the front, tongue-tied once more. I could just see Rex in my periphery. He was talking to the older chap beside him. At one point I saw his eyes flick to my left then back to me.

I tried to ignore the man beside me, which I think I managed as far as anyone would notice. But my arm felt warm. The chairs were fairly close to each other, so our arms sometimes brushed against each other. The couple of taller chaps made a bit more room for themselves by pulling their seats further out from the table, their legs stretched out in front of them. I forced myself to pick up my mug and drink. I tried to keep my elbows close to me, to make myself even smaller. Suddenly I wanted the break to be over. I'd felt more relaxed when I was working!

Back in the office I did my best to forget the atmosphere that had been building at tea time. When lunchtime arrived, I decided to say something if I was going to be able to eat.

"Excuse me, Rex?"

He looked at me, eyebrows up. "Yes?"

"Um, we 'ave been inside all morning. Is it ... ok ... if I take my lunch outside?"

"No skin off my nose."

I frowned in confusion.

"It means it doesn't matter to me where you sit." He waved a hand at the lunch basket.

Relieved, I grabbed my portion along with my coat and left the room. The noisy machinery was turned off, thankfully, I noticed first. At the bottom of the steps I glanced around, hoping a good spot would make itself plain. The majority of the work equipment and plant were off to my left, through the break in the trees. I turned instead to my right and walked towards another group of trees. The ground changed from gravel to scrubby grass, then as I entered the tree line the ground softened, sheltered from the sun by the boughs overhead.

I saw moss and small ground cover plants replace the grass. It didn't take me long to find the remains of a tree that had fallen at some time in the past. I spread my coat on it and sat down, my lunch clasped on my lap. I heaved a sigh at being alone at last and I smiled, closing my eyes and raising my face to the weak beams which had managed to penetrate the canopy. Though it was only sandwiches, it was the most pleasant meal I'd had in a while. Alone in a forest, no need to worry about talking to anyone, or using a language that was not my own. And no strange man giving me unsettling smiles.

Lunchtime was over. I had been back in Rex's office for almost another hour before he came back in. The door opened, and he hung on to the door handle while he stamped his feet on the rough mat outside. He looked up and saw me watching. I smiled but got no response. Apparently satisfied his shoes were clean enough, he came all the way inside, pulling the door shut behind him. I turned back to my task while he dropped into his chair like a paperweight.

He sighed. He slapped both hands on the desk, making me jump. "Back to the grindstone." He waved a hand at the files and papers on his desk. "Paperwork is the price I pay for getting to make the decisions. There are fortunes to be made and lost, young lady." He glanced up. "And I do not intend to miss my window of opportunity." With no clue what he was talking about, and no desire to continue the conversation, I set my mouth into a polite smile.

He cleared his throat and dropped his gaze, then the reassuring sounds of his pencil on the paper let me know my attention was no longer required.

The sun was lower, sending rays inside that bounced off the cabinets when Rex pushed his chair back, stood up and took the few steps needed to get to my corner of the office. I peered back over my shoulder.

"How far have you got?" His gaze swept over the piles still on the floor and chair before coming back to me.

"I've all the files for each customer together, and I've nearly finished putting them in letter order. You know?"

"Alphabetical."

I nodded and tried the word out. "Al-fa-betical. Yes."

"You think you can finish it tomorrow?"

I looked at the work I had already done and thought for a moment. "Yes, I think so."

"Right then, time to call it a night."

I frowned in confusion.

"Means stop. Tidy up what you can, grab your things and we'll head home."

"Yes, Rex. Thank you." I smiled up at him, hoping my efforts for the day may have improved his opinion of me. But he just nodded impassively and went back to his desk, picking up piles and stacking them to one side.

I waited at the foot of the steps outside while he locked up, the now empty lunch basket on my arm. He joined me and we walked over to the car. He'd gone around to the driver's door after opening the boot. I put my things in, closed the boot, stepping back in the process. I bumped into something. Someone.

"Oh, sorry. I did not know someone was be'ind me." My face burning, I turned to see it was the young man who'd grinned at me this morning. The same man who had sat next to me at morning tea.

"No worries. Miss Bouchet, isn't it? I'm Harold. Harold McRae."

I looked down to see his hand stuck out in front of him. Hesitantly, I placed my own hand in his. He clasped it and shook mine in one fluid movement. His palm felt warm and dry against mine. I wasn't sure when it was ok to let go. I glanced quickly over my shoulder to find Rex. I really wasn't sure what he would think of this. But he was sitting in the driver's seat, facing the front. His door was closed already.

"Um, Miss Bouchet? I wanted to ask you something."

I turned back. "Yes?"

"I was wondering if you were free on Saturday. After work, that is. Would you mind if I come to call for you? Maybe go to a café and have a cuppa together. What do you think?"

I had no idea what to think. I heard all the words, understood most of them. Enough to get what he meant. But I didn't have a clue what to do with them. I grasped the first excuse I could think of. "Well, um. Mr McRae?"

He nodded encouragingly.

"It is very kind of you to ask. But I do not think my brother-in-law would approve. 'e is my guardian, really. So thank you, but I don't think I can say yes."

He grinned. "Is that your only objection? Because I already checked with him. I mean, he's my boss. I wouldn't dare ask you otherwise!" His grin had a triumphant note to it now.

I glanced back at Rex again, just in time to see his eyes switch away from his rear view driving mirror. I pulled my hand back, and thankfully he released it willingly. Now I was torn between embarrassment and indignation. To have been the object of discussion without knowing it made me feel slightly ill. On the other hand, this Mr McRae was closer to my age than either my sister or her husband. It might be fun to spend time with him. And he had made sure to say it would be quite a public setting. I forced a smile. "Then yes, that sounds like a kind offer. I accept." I tried my best to sound more grown up than I felt at that moment. I was still uncomfortable as to how this had come about.

"I'll come and pick you up after work on Saturday then." He promised, the grin even wider as he hurried off.

I didn't accompany Rex to work on Saturday. I'd gotten the filing and sorting all finished as expected on my second day at his office, so I was free to fret at home all morning.

Yvonne had laughed off my concerns when we talked about Mr McRae. "Don't be silly, Elise. You're sixteen, far old enough to be asked out on a date. And, like you said, you will be in public the 'ole time. Now, the more important question: what will you wear?"

So here I was, in front of the mirror to check my hair was

behaving itself. As it wasn't cold, I was wearing a summer dress with a matching cardigan. I found Yvonne in the lounge.

"I've decided against the one you gave me, Yvie. What do you think? Is this all right for a café?"

She looked up from her magazine. "You're absolutely fine, Elise. Just right. If you're ready, why don't we go out into the garden while we wait? You know how flowers soothe you."

"Yes please! I didn't realise my nerves showed so much."

Rex arrived home, put his car away and found us out to the garden.

He gave me an assessing look as he spoke to Yvonne. "So you've made sure she knows what's what? And Elise, stick to English. I very much doubt he knows any of your lingo."

Yvonne shook her head, frowning at him. "She'll be fine. She's been a quick study. And I am sure 'e will be a complete gentleman." She patted my arm and smiled encouragingly as he walked away. "Don't you worry, ok? It's only a café, just afternoon tea and possibly a walk through the town." She checked her watch. "We'll go back in now, 'e's probably not far behind Rex."

In that she was correct. We had only been sitting in the lounge for about five minutes when a car pulled up on the street and a door slammed. My face burned and I looked at my sister. She smiled once more, waved at me to stay where I was before rising to go to the door. I heard them greet each other, then the door shut and Yvonne came back into the room, bringing Mr McRae with her. To my surprise I saw his hands grasping the brim of his hat, his knuckles straining white. He was nervous as well! I prayed Rex would stay wherever he was in the house until we'd left. I wasn't sure I could cope with him as well. I stood. Yvonne was glancing back and forth from me to Mr McRae. I saw him flick his eyes sideways at her before switching quickly back in my direction. He swallowed.

"Um, good afternoon, Miss Bouchet."

I stifled a giggle. This was not the time. I bobbed my head. "Good afternoon, Mr McRae."

Yvonne made a noise, halfway between a cough and a laugh.

"Well, now you 'ave greeted each other so formally, per'aps you should be on your way. Unless," she addressed him, "you wanted to say good afternoon to Mr Carlisle before you go?"

Now he went red, his eyebrows shot up as he twisted his poor hat between his hands. "N-no thank you Mrs Carlisle. There's no need to interrupt him. Shall we, Miss Bouchet?" He gestured toward the door.

I nodded goodbye to Yvonne on my way out of the room. I didn't dare catch her eye. He walked quickly to pass me, opened the front door and ushered me ahead of him once more. We walked silently but briskly to his car, climbed in and drove off. The silence lasted a few minutes longer before I felt his eyes on me.

"That could have gone better."

I looked over. He was grinning, his face back to its normal shade. "Yes, it could. At least it was only my sister."

He looked back at the road for a moment, then to me again. We burst out laughing. Partly at ourselves, partly in relief. He leaned forward and tucked his hands over the wheel, steering with his wrists.

"Have you been to many of the cafés here in town at all? Cos I thought I'd show you one of my favourites. It's over by the waterfront. Even on a windy day it's a great view from there."

"I've only been to one, with Yvie –Yvonne. It's just in town, near the grocery store we use. I would like to see the

81

waterfront. I enjoy looking at the ocean."

I sounded stilted even to myself. Mentally I gave myself a shake; told myself to relax. He smiled again. He was watching the road, for which I was thankful. I stared at his profile. I'd not really had a chance to properly study his face till now. He had reddish brown hair, cut quite short on the sides. His fringe flopped over his forehead, and I noticed he would push it back every so often. His complexion was paler than mine, but freckled like other red-haired people I'd met at school. I turned back to the road so he wouldn't catch me staring.

He took a few turns I'd not been down before, heading closer to the sea with each street.

"So, you haven't been here long. In New Zealand I mean. Have I got that right?"

I nodded. "Yes, I arrived only recently." Preferring not to talk about myself, I tried to think of a question for him. I had one hand resting in my lap, the other sitting along the edge where the window met the door. Which gave me an idea of what to say. "This is your own car? Sorry, I only wondered. Most people at 'ome do not 'ave their own cars. I wondered if this is maybe your father's car?" I blushed, hoping I'd not insulted him. But then he grinned over at me and answered cheerfully enough.

"Yep, it's all mine! I got it cheap, off a chap I used to work with. He was getting married, needed the money for a house. You're right though," He checked the road ahead, looked in his rear view mirror and made another turn. "If he'd not been desperate to sell, I couldn't have bought it. Most chaps don't have their own car by my age." He pulled into a car park on the left, finding a spot near the front entrance to the café. The engine stopped, Mr McRae got out his door, shut it and came around to my side. He opened my door, and with a flourish that made me blush again, escorted me from the car to the café door. "Ladies first," he said as he held the large glass door open.

"Thank you," I murmured, feeling the eyes of strangers on me as I stepped inside. Mr McRae led the way to a table by the window down to our left. He held a chair out for me, giving me the side facing away from the rest of the café. The gesture wasn't lost on me.

"They have cabinet food, and a small menu. But, as I've been here before, would you mind if I order for both of us? Unless there is something you especially fancy?"

Relieved, I agreed to his suggestion.

He looked over my head, and beckoned. A waitress appeared beside me.

"Afternoon folks. What can I get you?"

"We'll have a pot of tea, two cups please. And a jug of milk, ta. And could we get a plate of your savoury sandwiches? That'll do for starters."

She wrote it all down on a small notepad, smiled at me and winked before walking off. Mr McRae rubbed his hands together and grinned across the table. He seemed to be enjoying himself.

"So, there's the view I promised you. It's a smasher, isn't it?" He nodded out the front, as proud as if he'd designed the view himself.

"Yes, it is beautiful. Thank you for bringing me 'ere." His expression had given me the clue I needed to answer correctly. I filed that away for future reference. 'Smasher' appeared to mean very good.

"It's pretty calm just at the moment. If we get a storm coming in from the east, it can get a bit choppy. But look, the horizon's miles away. It's like the sky and the sea meet way out there." I watched him as he gazed out at the water. There was almost a longing in his face.

"Do you go out on the water very much? Sailing and such?"

"Me? No. I'd love to, one day. But that's a rich man's game, that is." He made a conscious effort to turn from the ocean. "Enough about all that. I want to know more about you, Miss Bouchet. What brought you here. From your accent, I'm guessing you came all the way from France?"

I laughed. "No, not so very far as that. I am from…" I almost gave the French name. I stopped myself and rehearsed the English in my head. "New Caledonia. Do you know of it?"

He shook his head. "Can't say I've heard of it. Where is it, compared to here then?"

"I think a little north and west of the top of this island. We are closer to Australia really. But, to answer the other part of your question, I am in New Zealand because this is where my sister is. You see," I stopped again. I'd not had to explain this to anyone since Lulu, back onboard the ship. Certainly not to a man I barely knew. I wasn't sure how much to tell him. How much was private to my family. "Our maman died three years ago. Then both my sisters married and moved overseas. My papa did not think it good for me to be at 'ome with just 'im and my grand-mère. I am sorry, I don't know the English word." I'd seen confusion on his face as I used my familiar words for my family. 'Sister' was the only family word I was sure of in English.

"So, let me try to work this out. 'Maman' – pretty sure you mean 'mother'. And 'papa' is easy, lots of rich Brits use that one. So, 'grand-mère'" –He closed his eyes for a moment, then opened them, grinning– "I'm guessing grandmother —as in, your 'maman's' maman? How'd I do?"

I laughed. "I'm not the one to ask, but it sounded right. So, in English I should say 'mu-ther'?"

"Pretty much." He fished around in a pocket with one hand, pulling a paper napkin towards him with the other. He found a pen in the pocket. "M-o-t-h-e-r," he said as he wrote the letters carefully on the napkin. "Does that help?"

I nodded, and accepted it as he handed it over. "Yes, thank you. Yvonne 'as been teaching me the different ways to say the letters in English. Writing is much easier to understand."

Our food and drink arrived just then, the waitress having appeared silently beside me once more.

"Enjoy." She smiled and moved on to the next table. Mr McRae reached for the tea pot.

"How do you have it?" He added the milk and sugar to the tea in my cup then passed it over. He waved at the platter of sandwiches. "Help yourself. Like I said, ladies first."

The sandwiches had been cut in quarters. The bread was fresh and soft, and the fillings were just enough. I thought they had done well, considering what I had learnt about rationing here.

We ate in companionable silence for a few minutes before Mr McRae resumed the conversation. Somehow he managed to get me talking about home and my friends. I found myself telling him things I'd not expected to share. Eventually I realised I had been doing all the talking.

"This is very unlike me. I apologise. Now it is your turn. Where did you grow up? Is it near this town?"

Mr McRae smiled. He looked around the café. "No apology needed, Miss Bouchet. But I'm afraid we'll have to leave that for another day. I think they are wanting to close soon. It seems we're the last ones still here." He laughed. I looked behind me. Startled, I looked back at him.

"Oh my! I am sorry, I have probably kept you 'ere far too long." I collected my plate and cup into a tidy pile, pushing my chair back and scrambling to my feet.

He laughed again. "Here, let me. And look, don't worry. I had no other plans so no harm, no foul." So saying, he stacked up my pile of dishes with his own and led the way back to the counter. The hostess behind it looked up and smiled. I sensed a bit of relief was mingled with her polite look. I blushed and looked away. I half-listened to them talk as he settled our bill. Then I felt him take my arm and we walked to the door, which he held open for me.

The car ride back passed in silence. I could feel him glancing my way every now and then. I felt completely talked out. We were perhaps a street or two before Yvonne's when Mr McRae spoke next.

"May I ask you a question?"

I looked over. "Yes, of course."

"Would you mind if I called you Elise? It feels very formal, and, well, rather fuddy-duddy to keep calling you Miss Bouchet."

I thought for a moment. "Ok, yes, that will be fine. But what is 'fuddy-duddy' please?"

His ever ready laugh burst out once more. "I guess it means like a boring old person. We're not old, are we?"

I grinned. "Of course not. So, would you prefer me to call you by your first name too?"

He checked his side mirror, then looked at the road ahead, slowing down as we approached an intersection. He made the turn before replying. "I'd like that, Elise. It's Harold, by the way."

It was my turn to laugh. "Yes, I know."

"I'd very much like to hear you say my name." He arched an eyebrow at me, glancing sideways.

"Pleased to meet you, 'arold,'" I said, somewhat nervously.

"Close enough. I have noticed that with other Frenchies I've met. Can't say an 'h' at all. Wonder why that is?"

"We don't 'ave the sound. Any word that starts with that letter is written but not spoken in our language."

"Cool. Good to know."

I saw him check his mirrors again, then he looked past me at the houses we were driving past. He slowed again, pulling in towards the curb. I glanced to my left. We stopped outside an empty plot between two homes. I looked over at Harold again. He moved the gear stick, pulled on the brake and turned his body towards me.

He started to redden. His expression grew serious.

"What is it?" I wasn't at all sure what was going on.

"I wondered," he started. He looked at the floor then back at me. "I didn't want to ask outside the boss's house. But, I've really enjoyed our afternoon together. I'd like to do it again — soon. Did you have a nice time? Would you see me again, like this?" His words came out haltingly, almost stammering.

Flattered, I nodded. I wanted to take away some of his nervousness. Somehow, seeing him this way made me a little bolder. I smiled. "Yes, 'arold, I enjoyed myself very much. I 'ave not talked so much ever! I do not know why I did. But if you are 'appy to see me again, I promise I will let you do all the talking!" I laughed.

He put his head back against his seat and closed his eyes as

I heard him sigh. He opened his eyes again and grinned over at me. "You've no idea how relieved I am to hear that." He reached over, grasped my hand in his. His hand was much bigger than mine, and his skin was rough and calloused from his work. "Look, I know you're only sixteen, and I'm twenty-two."

"Twenty-two? I thought you were a lot younger than that!"

He laughed. "I'll take that as a complement. But now that you know, is it a problem for you?"

I looked away for a moment, gathering my thoughts.

"'arold, if I 'ad known your age first, I might 'ave thought it strange. But," I squeezed his fingers. "I 'ad fun today. You being older than I thought doesn't change that. Although, you realise that makes you closer to my sister's age than mine?" It was my turn to laugh at his expression.

"Oh, so you like to tease me, do you? Now we've got that sorted" –he leaned closer– "would you let me" –my eyes were locked on his– "kiss you?"

As soon as he asked, I knew that was what I wanted too. I nodded mutely. I wasn't sure what I expected. I'd never been kissed this way before. His lips pressed gently on mine. I found myself leaning into the kiss. His hand let go of mine and curved around my head. My hand seemed to have a mind of its own as I realised suddenly that I was resting it on his shoulder. I had closed my eyes without knowing it as well. I opened them slightly and saw he'd closed his as well. I quickly shut mine again lest he open his and find me staring. I'm sure it was only a second or so, but it felt like time stood still. A thrill ran through me, from my lips all the way to my feet. His hand pressed a little tighter against my hair, and then it was over. We pulled away. His smile had a new note to it. A matching smile tugged my own mouth wide. I dropped my hand from his shoulder, my palm tingling from his warmth. I looked down, almost embarrassed. I felt like he'd seen more of me than I was ready to show. He reached over once more, picked my hand up and squeezed.

"I think that went quite well for a first effort."

I looked back and realised he was teasing. I felt as though a switch had been flicked and next thing I knew we were laughing again. Relief flooded me and the mood lightened.

"Right, I'd better get you home before they send out a search party."

The rest of the drive passed without remark. But once he had the car in gear, he drove one-handed and held my hand with the other. He pulled over again in front of the house, got out and came around to open my door for me.

"All right if I don't walk you to the door? It's not dark, after all."

"That's fine, 'arold." I grinned at the look on his face. I found I quite liked making him happy this way.

"I 'ad a lovely time. Thank you so much. And yes, I would like to see you again." I grabbed his hands briefly, squeezing as he had done to me earlier.

"I'll sort something out, promise. Do you like to go to the movie theatre? I could see if something is playing in town next week sometime."

"I've never been. I'd like that." I waved as he drove away, then let myself into the house.

16

Spring 1947

A few days later, Rex arrived home at the usual time, and as he walked in, he handed me an envelope without stopping on his way to the kitchen.

I waited until he was out of sight, then ran to my room and shut the door.

"Dear Elise.

I really hope Mr C didn't steam this open or anything! Crikey, that'd be a nightmare.

Here goes. Thank you for seeing me the other day. I really enjoyed myself, and I hope I'm not being presumptuous, thinking you did too? I know you said so, but girls sometimes say things like that, just to be polite.

In case that's a 'Yes, you did', then I'd like to know if you're free on Thursday evening next week. There's a Charlie Chaplin movie playing at the Regent. I'm not sure which one. If you do want to come, could you send a note back please? I think Mr C won't mind. Please say yes! I'll be there to collect you at about 6.30, if you do.

Yours sincerely,

Harold McRae"

I grinned to myself, clutching the little note to my chest. It was kind of sweet that he seemed to be as unsure of himself as I felt. I read it over again, savouring this first – a boy writing to me because he liked me. I quickly wrote a simple *'that would be nice, thank you'* note to send in return, and then it was time to go and help Yvonne in the kitchen.

Thursday evening I was waiting in the lounge, idle time on my hands from having eaten my dinner early. Yvonne and Rex were going out for dinner; she was still getting ready.

When the knock on the door finally came, I jumped almost out of my skin. I had to laugh at myself. Shaking my head, I stood, collecting my purse and coat on the way out of the lounge.

"Good evening, 'arold," I said. I stepped through and pulled the front door closed behind me.

"Evening, Elise." He chuckled. "That feels a bit weird, to tell you the truth. Calling a classy young lady like yourself by her Christian name!"

My face burned at the compliment. "If it 'elps, I've 'ardly ever been called 'Miss Bouchet' by boys. The only boys I've ever known to speak to 'ave been my brothers or schoolmates."

We stood awkwardly for a few moments. He was dressed in clean work trousers. His shirt was chequered dark blue and white. The collar was open, he wasn't wearing a tie. I looked down at myself. I felt a little overdressed in my smart skirt and jacket. He cleared his throat and I looked back up.

"You look nice. I like that colour on you." His cheeks turned red and I bit back a smile. It was good not to be the only one blushing. "Shall we?" he motioned towards his car.

"Of course. What time does the movie start?"

"About ten past seven. We've got plenty of time."

Sure enough, in what felt like a few minutes we were pulling up alongside a beautiful building with a wide entrance. I stared, mouth open.

"I 'ave never seen anything like it, 'arold!"

"Come on, it's even better on the inside." He took my hand and placed it in the crook of his elbow. "This is nice. I'm quite chuffed I get to be the one to take you to your first ever 'moving picture.'"

We joined a queue in front of a window off to our left. Couples and families with older children shuffled along in front of us. I looked around me, trying to take everything in. To our far right I could see a long counter, like in a store. There were shelves behind it with sweets and bottles of drinks. Paper bags, top corners twisted together, stood in stacks along the top of the counter. Eventually we reached the front of the line, and Harold bought tickets for us both. He grinned round at me.

"Want to hold yours? Here."

It was just a little thing but I was so excited to hold this piece of card. I thanked him.

"Are you hungry?" he said, pointing towards the counter. "We could grab a snack now and take it through, or wait until intermission. What's your preference?"

"I ate dinner already. I didn't know they 'ad food 'ere. What's in those paper bags?" I pointed.

"Popcorn." I looked at him, confused.

"What? You've never heard of it? Oh are you in for a treat! Come on." He grabbed my hand and half pulled me towards the counter. "This is called the concession stand." He grinned back at me over his shoulder as he forged ahead. There were quite a number of people in front of it already, but rather than forming a queue, they straggled out the length of the counter, in ragged lines two or three people deep. Harold checked the crowd, before adjusting his direction slightly and making for a gap I'd not seen. "You have to be firm in these lines. It's every man for himself." He straightened once more, looking over the heads of those between us and the counter. He checked his watch. "Come on, come on," he muttered, as he bounced on the balls of his feet. "The movie's gonna start soon." He raised himself up a bit more. He pushed forward as someone collected their purchases and moved off to the side. "I'll have two bags of popcorn and a packet of pastilles please." He passed over some coins, grabbed the bags, turned and nodded to me to make a path back out of the throng again.

I turned to make sure Harold was still behind me. I caught him glowering before he realised I was looking.

He grinned sheepishly. "Oops. I thought I'd add a bit of extra incentive to them to move out of your way." He winked and gestured with a nod. "This way."

I grabbed his elbow again. I didn't want to get separated. We made our way to the theatre door where we were greeted by a smiling attendant.

"Tickets please," she said. She lined the two cards up, and tore the ends off them before handing them back. "Your seats are over there." She pointed.

I looked over to see another attendant at the end of the seats to the right. I nodded my thanks. It was getting louder the further we got into the building. The lights were dimmer in here as well. I looked around and saw there were uniformed attendants scattered around the theatre, waiting to guide patrons to their seats. Looking down, I noticed we were on a sloping floor rather than steps. The seats led off in long rows to either side of the door. I followed Harold towards the next attendant, at times dodging around other people looking for their own seats. Harold's hand tugged mine and I followed him past those already seated. He checked our tickets and looked at the seat numbers.

"This is us. Here, let me take your coat."

The theatre gradually filled up as the lights dimmed. A low rustle of clothing against seat backs accompanied the murmur of patrons settling in their places. Harold handed me one of the paper bags.

"Go on, try it. You're in for a treat."

I unravelled the twisted bag top and peered inside. A buttery, salty smell wafted out. I smiled. Maman always said you taste first with your nose. I dipped my hand in, grabbed a couple of pieces and popped them in my mouth. Oh! The corn crunched between my teeth as my tongue welcomed the salty butter. I closed my eyes.

"I told you."

I opened my eyes and turned to him. I realised he'd been watching me and blushed, thankful for the lowered lights hiding my reddened cheeks. I swallowed and nodded. "You did. And you were right."

Suddenly music began, seeming to swell and fill the theatre. I tried to see where it was coming from but it seemed to come from all directions. Harold reached for my hand. As the music built up dramatically, the drapes at the front of the theatre swept apart, revealing a large blank screen. The room became fully darkened as the screen lit up. From the moment the first images came up I was captivated. I'd never experienced anything like it. I'm not sure I fully understood the story itself, but along with my fellow patrons, I laughed and cried and gasped as Mr Chaplin led the way through his strange world. I vaguely realised he was saying something about the years we'd just gone through but much of it was over my head.

At last the screen darkened as the theatre lights reversed their earlier dimming. I blinked and cast my gaze around the room. I could hear the odd whisper, but in the main the audience were subdued compared to when we sat down. No one seemed in a rush to leave, so it was a few minutes before we made our way back to the lobby and the street doors. Harold was still holding my hand, having relinquished it just long enough to help me on with my coat.

He sighed at last. "Shall we make a move?"

"Of course. Thank you for bringing me. It was … I'm not sure of the word."

"I know what you mean. I've been to the movies before. But I've never seen Chaplin, and if that was anything to go by, I can see why he's so famous."

At the car, Harold held my door open and soon we were on our way home. He pulled up to the curb side and reached for my hand yet again. He looked at our linked fingers before speaking. "Elise? I … I really like you. I know, we've only spent a few hours together. But, I haven't met anyone quite like you before. It feels like…" He looked up at me, grinning shyly. "Is it just me? Am I barking up the wrong tree here?"

I tightened my fingers around the palm of his hand. Part of my mind realised I had easily worked out the funny English saying. "I am only sixteen, 'arold, so I 'ave nothing to compare this with. But if you are asking if this feels like it's serious, then yes. I really like you too. And if you are going to ask if you can kiss me again, then yes to that too." I laughed at my own nerve in saying that. This time it didn't stop quite so soon and I found myself wrapped tightly in his arms as the kiss deepened.

When we finally broke apart I was breathless. Neither of us had anything left to say. He got out and came around the car again to let me out. This time he walked me to the front door. It was only on the doorstep that he spoke again.

"I don't think I want to wait a whole week before seeing you again. May I come by on Saturday after work? We could go to the café again, maybe a walk along the beach?"

"I'd like that, 'arold, I really would. Goodnight." I reached up and kissed him on the cheek.

For the rest of spring Harold and I saw each other almost twice a week. The café became a favourite spot, and more often than not I returned home with sand in my shoes. About once a month we would share popcorn at the movie theatre. As we got to know each other – our likes and dislikes – my shyness began to fall away, confidence replacing it. My spoken English improved as well now I had two tutors - Harold and Yvonne. Spring was in me just as much as in the world around me.

17

Summer 1947/1948

One Thursday, as the sun stayed longer in the sky extending the evening, Harold walked me to the front door after another movie. He put his hands on my waist.

"How about something a bit different this Saturday? I'd like to take you to dinner. A proper restaurant, not the café this time. What do you say?"

I reached up and kissed his cheek in reply. We shared a smile before I turned to the door and let myself in.

Saturday dawned cloudy and overcast. There was just a light breeze. Yvonne and I got some laundry out and on the washing line as early as we could, keeping watch on the clouds through the day. We worked in her garden, finding a contentment here as we had done in Maman's garden. The rich earthy aroma mixed with the heady scent of the roses and honeysuckle. That was a new name for me. When Yvonne had taught it to me, I tried it silently, the roll of soft and hard sounds satisfying to my mouth. Of course neither of us could quite get the English way of the 'h' sound, but that didn't lessen the beauty of the word.

Another new one was camellia. Though the garden had a plethora of flowers and plants, Yvonne and Rex had focused attention on this particular bush. They were attempting to create their own variety of the species. The flower itself reminded me of the simpler roses, with just one layer of petals. Working outside meant we were quick to notice the clouds as they changed.

"Come on, Elise. We've just got time to clean up before the rain arrives."

Rex got home as we got the laundry tidied away. As usual, he came straight to the point.

"So I hear you won't be joining us for dinner tonight." He looked me up and down with a frown. "You are going to change before he arrives?"

I reddened. "Of course, Rex. I was about to wash up. Excuse me." I bobbed my head and dodged past him. I heard Yvonne rebuking him quietly as I walked down the hall to my room. Though I had begun to respect him for his hard work at the mill, bringing it such success and providing work for his men, I struggled with his sharp tongue. I was never sure how to take him.

I took the cloth cover off my dotted dress, the one Yvonne had given me, and laid it out on my bed. I had been going to wear my better cardigan over it, but when I told her about the restaurant, Yvonne had insisted I borrow a short jacket of hers. I laid it beside the dress and took my shoes out of the closet. They needed a quick polish. I would see to that after my wash.

I stood in front of the mirror, checking my hair one more time. My grandmother's parting gift caught my eye. Picking it up, I spoke as if addressing her, whispering in French. "I really like him, Grand-mère. I think you would too. He is a little older, but I like that too. I will write soon." I hugged the box to my chest. She'd known exactly what to give me that would help me feel like I had a little piece of home with me. The dried bloom of frangipani inside the glass hadn't faded at all. I laid it back against the wall on my dresser top and picked up my purse, walking out of my room.

I heard his knock at the door as I was about to sit in the lounge to wait. Rex was there already. He waved a hand at me to stay where I was and walked out to answer the door.

"Come in, come in, she's just through there."

I heard a mumbled response and then he was at the lounge door, grinning shyly.

"Good evening, Mr McRae." Yvonne said. "Well, off you go then, Elise. Have a nice time."

As we left the room, Rex called after us. "Have her back at a reasonable hour, McRae."

Harold gripped my hand tighter. "Yes, Mr Carlisle, of course." He opened my door for me.

"Where are we going, by the way?" I asked once he was driving.

"You'll see. I know you live near the sea anyway, but some parts of the coast are spectacular. We'll be there soon." We continued down the coast a few minutes before Harold took a left turn. Gradually the view opened up and I saw the vast blueness of the ocean up ahead. Sun winked off the surface.

Soon enough there was more sea than land to be seen in front of us. To my left I could see a small inlet, beyond which was a finger of land pointing back up the coast. Directly ahead, past the green table top of a promontory, the blue stretched as far as I could see in all directions.

"Oh my word!" I gasped.

"Just wait. It gets better." I could hear the smile in his voice. I kept my focus on the view, impatient now to reach our destination.

We drove through a small township, more a village really. Children playing in front gardens, adults strolling leisurely down the footpaths. Here and there people sat on porches, drinks on the ground beside them, just watching the odd car such as ours go by. Harold seemed to know exactly where he was going. Soon we turned off the road proper onto a beaten track. He pulled off onto grass as the track came to an end.

"I hope you enjoy walking cross-country." He grinned.

I looked down at my shoes. "I guess I chose the right footwear at least."

"You can leave your purse under the seat if you like. You won't need it where we're going, and it'll be safe enough – I'll lock the car up." He looked around us. "Not that there's much chance of anyone touching it. No other visitors today."

The ground was firm beneath my feet. The grass was short, freshly cut. We chatted as we went, about nothing special, just passing the time. Harold led me further and further out onto the point of land jutting out into the sea. Where there had been a few hardy but short trees to our right, now there was nothing between us and the wind coming off the sea from three sides. My other hand was kept busy holding my hair back out of my face. Harold glanced over and laughed at my efforts.

"I reckon that's a lost cause at the moment, Elise. Don't worry, I won't let you get blown away!" I pulled a face at him. We stopped and he pointed. "This is what I wanted to show you."

I walked a couple more paces and stood still. I barely noticed the wind now, so arresting was the panorama laid out below us. Waves broke at the base of the cliff, lazily falling backwards off the rocks. Gulls called to each other as they rode the air currents off the cliffs. Having grown up on an island, the sea had been a daily sight. I felt like I was seeing an old friend after a long absence. It was as if we were surrounded by water.

After a while, Harold raised his arm to check his watch. "Sorry to pull you away from this, Elise, but we need to go now if we're going to keep our dinner booking." He was standing behind me, arms wrapped around me, a living cloak to keep the chill of the wind off me. I surprised myself at how natural it felt to be enclosed in his arms. I leaned my head back into his shoulder briefly, then stepped away and turned a slow circle, taking in a last look around us.

It didn't seem to take as long to get back into town as it had leaving. All too soon we were pulling into the car park of the restaurant. We walked close beside each other to the door which Harold opened for me. Inside, Harold gave his name to the gentleman behind the desk, who made a mark on his register, then stepped around and indicated that we should follow him. It was easily the most expensive-looking room I'd set foot in, and I tried hard not to gape at the opulence of the decor.

At our table, our host pulled a seat out for me first, then Harold. We shared a look and turned away. I bit my lip to keep my giggle inside. I felt more like a schoolgirl than ever.

"Can I get you anything to drink before you order?"

Harold raised a brow at me.

"Yes please. Do you 'ave lemonade please?"

"Of course, madam. And for sir?" Now my giggle did escape.

I coughed in an attempt to hide it. Our host pretended not to hear, and waited patiently for Harold's reply.

"Make that two lemonades, thanks. With ice, if that's possible?"

The gentleman nodded. "Your waiter will be with you shortly. Enjoy your evening."

Harold kept looking past me as the man walked away. When he looked back at me, I could see a gleam in his eye, and we burst out laughing. I flicked a look at our neighbouring tables, but no one was paying us any attention.

"Is madam happy with my choice of restaurant?" Harold quipped.

"Yes she is. And what does sir think?"

"I think it'll do so far. Mustn't be too hasty – we haven't tasted the food yet." He winked at me. "We'd better behave now. Let's have a look at the menu."

So saying, he made a show of turning serious and lifted his menu up between us.

I followed suit. I gasped as I realised what I was seeing. "It's in French, 'arold!" He peered around the side of his menu and grinned broadly. "Yep. Thought you'd like that. And since I can't read a word of it, you'll have to interpret for me. Or order for us both." He looked very pleased with himself.

I looked down again, blinking rapidly. It was suddenly very clear that it was this one point that had made him choose this particular place to bring me. A thought occurred and I checked the page again. "Oh, 'arold. Are you sure? I mean, I am touched that you brought me 'ere. It is stunning. But, it is very expensive!" The entré alone was more than we'd spent for the whole meal on our last outing.

"Don't you worry about that. I don't have much to spend

my hard-earned dosh on, just you." He grinned again. He saw my discomfort, put his menu down and reached over, picking up my hand from the table. "I just mean, I can manage it fine, and I reckon it's worth every penny, if I get to hear you speak your language and see you enjoy yourself. So, go ahead, read it all and give me your recommendations." He squeezed my fingers and released me.

I did as he asked and saw that though the dishes had clever sounding names, they were simple foods, prepared well, if the descriptions were anything to go by. As long as they knew what they were doing, and at these prices I certainly hoped so, I thought we would have a good substantial meal, whatever we decided upon.

"Much of it is similar to what my Maman and Grand-mère used to make on special occasions." I spoke as I continued to read. "The first course offers a seafood *bisque*," I glanced up. "You know this word?"

He nodded, gestured for me to continue.

"Or *Cepes a la savoyarde.* It is, um, vegetables. I am sorry I don't know the English word for *cep*." I looked up again.

He spread his hands wide. "I am in your hands, Elise. I will have whatever you choose. As long as it's not snails." He grinned. "I heard Frenchies like eating snails."

I laughed. "Maybe in France, but in my country we didn't 'ave many of those. So no, I would not consider them a food. They 'ave five main course options. Oh, look. One is also a seafood dish. So..." I carried on reading.

The waiter arrived just then with our drinks.

"Good evening, I am Marcel. I will be your waiter this evening."

We said good evening in return and he smiled.

"Are you ready to order, or should I give you a few more minutes?" Harold nodded at me encouragingly. I cleared my throat. I was very grateful that Yvonne had taken me to the café and taught me at least some of the general eating-out terms in English.

"We'll 'ave *une entrée - cèpes à la savoyarde*, then as our main course we will 'ave the *bouillabaisse*, thank you."

The waiter smiled. "Madam speaks French? It is refreshing to hear it." He leaned in, as if telling a secret, speaking in French:

"The New Zealanders we get here do not have the best French accents. You would be shocked at the way they murder our words! I've been here a long time, so I speak English like a native. But it's always exciting when I get to speak in my own tongue to the odd patron."

I glanced over at Harold, wondering how he felt about this unexpected turn.

But he smiled and nodded.

"Go on, I don't mind. I'm enjoying myself."

"I am from New Caledonia. I came to New Zealand only about six months ago. This gentleman," –I gestured across the table, heat in my face as I realised what I was going to say aloud for the first time– "is my beau. He was generous enough to choose this place on my behalf. At home I am restricted to English you see."

Marcel stood, a broad smile on his face, and bowed briefly to Harold. "Merci, monsieur. It is a wonderful thing you 'ave done for your young lady. Speaking our own language is a rare treat, even for me working 'ere." Turning back to me, he winked as he said in French, "I'd keep him on, if I were you. He seems very considerate of you." Straightening once more, he took our menus and left to deliver our order to the kitchen.

"So, what did he say?"

I coloured as I did my best to translate the conversation faithfully.

His ready grin was there before I finished, his hand reaching over to squeeze my fingers. "I hadn't expected us to get an actual Frenchman as our waiter. So I can't claim credit for that. But I'll take the compliment. Did you really tell him I am your – young man?"

I turned my hand over in his, squeezing his hand in return. "Yes. Do you mind?" I asked as I let go.

He picked up his napkin off the table, unfolding and refolding it. "What do you think?" He said this with his eyes down, so I couldn't read his face.

"About what?"

"Don't tease, Elise. That's my job." He looked up, that grin back once more. "About us. Are you happy to be – my young lady?" Now he was colouring.

I held his gaze and nodded.

He threw his head back as he sighed dramatically. "Whew, glad we got that out of the way. I don't know if I could have eaten otherwise."

I laughed once more. "Now you are doing your job! Teasing me."

The food, when it arrived, was delicious. Small portions, but I had anticipated that, given what I had been learning about rationing here. And the bouillabaisse was substantial. They obviously had a steady supply of shellfish. There was a jug of water on the table, and we helped ourselves liberally throughout the meal. Marcel approached us as we finished our main course.

"I trust you enjoyed that?" He smiled at us.

We nodded in unison.

"Thank you, it was wonderful."

"Would you care to look at the dessert menu?"

I checked Harold's expression. Though he was smiling, I could see a little tension in the smile. I looked back at Marcel and shook my head.

"Thank you, no. That was sufficient. In fact I think I'll 'ave to walk it off."

I waited near the door while Harold settled the bill. We walked slowly to the car.

"We have time for a walk, if you meant it before. We could drive over to the beach and walk on the sand."

"Oh, that would be a lovely way to end the evening, 'arold. The moon is bright enough, the views will be wonderful."

"Right you are, your carriage awaits, madam." With a flourish he opened my door, grinning at his own joke.

We didn't have far to go to find a park near the beach. Though it had turned out to be a mild night, I was glad of my coat. We headed for a path we'd seen in the headlights as we'd driven up. Harold led the way, walking briskly up over the path between the tussocky dunes. I caught up as he reached the top and we once again reached for each other's hand as we took in our first view of the ocean by moonlight. We shared a smile, then, with a gentle tug on my hand, he led the way down the other side onto the sand. Of course I had sand inside my shoes within moments but I wasn't the least bit bothered. We wandered slowly, the moon reflecting plenty of light for us to be able to take in the vista. At some point we stopped holding hands, and Harold's arm was draped over my shoulders. I wrapped my arm around his waist, clutching his jacket with my fingers. I have no recollection of how far we traipsed before Harold chose a large driftwood branch as a seat.

I took off my coat and laid it over the branch. It was just big enough for us to huddle close. He took off his short jacket, and laid it on my shoulders.

"There, that'll keep the chill off. There's nothing to you, is there?" he said as the jacket swamped me.

"All the girls in my family are small like me. Well, you've met Yvonne so you know. Maman wasn't much bigger than I am. The boys got all the 'ight and muscle." I laughed up at him. Next thing I knew we were kissing. His arms came around me hesitantly at first but as the kiss deepened, his embrace tightened. I felt as though my whole being was centred around that kiss. When it stopped, he leaned his forehead against mine. He pulled back just enough to look me in the eye. I moved my hands to his shoulders, gently pushing him further back.

"Maybe it is time to take me 'ome." Even as I said the words, I wasn't sure what answer I hoped for.

He covered my hands with his and smiled. "Is that what you really want?" Leaning in, he kissed me again. "Really?" I felt his lips make the word against my own.

"Maybe we could stay a little longer," I murmured between his kisses.

Clumsy as we were, it wasn't long until I was pulling my coat back on and vainly straightening my hair. Harold gently brushed the sand off the back of my coat then turned me around to face him. I was more shy now than before. Eventually I felt a hand under my chin as he tilted my face up and once more we stared at each other.

107

"Are you ok, Elise? Do you," he swallowed. "Regret this?" He waved a hand at the ground behind us. I shook my head numbly, taking a moment to find my words.

"No, 'arold, I do not regret. It was – wonderful. But I am a little ashamed, I think."

His face lowered as his shoulders hunched forward.

I quickly put a hand on his arm. "No, not like that. It's just that I've never even thought about doing this before. I'm worried that I was too ... willing, I guess."

He hugged me then, burrowing his face down into my neck. "Silly Elise! That's old school thinking, I reckon. Why shouldn't a girl like it as much as a boy?" His words were muffled against me, but even so I felt his relief. "I best get you home." He tilted his arm so the moon shone on his watch. "If we're quick, I reckon the boss'll still agree it's a reasonable hour." He winked.

We scrambled back up the dune path and ran to the car. He checked the back of my coat again.

"If they notice, at least you can honestly say we used it to sit on that branch."

I shook my head in response, a knot of worry building in my stomach. As Harold pulled up outside the house, I noticed a light in one of the front rooms was still on. He walked me to the door. Our footsteps sounded loud in the night air. We were almost to the door when the light inside switched off.

I glanced at Harold. "I guess that means I'm back at an acceptable time," I whispered.

"Goodnight Elise. Thank you for tonight – all of it. I don't really want to go, but I'll see you next week, ok?" He kissed me once more then trotted back up the driveway to his car. He turned and waved before climbing in and driving off.

After Mass the next day, I told Yvonne I was going for a walk into town. She looked surprised.

"Are you sure? That's quite a long way, Elise. Why would you want to?"

I had thought about this while I lay sleepless for hours the night before. I'd realised it would seem odd, and I couldn't tell her the real reason, so I'd decided on a completely different excuse.

"You know 'ow far we used to walk back 'ome, Yvie. This isn't really much different. It's maybe not as pretty a walk," I grinned. "But I realised 'ow little I'd been out and about on my own since I arrived. I'd like to get to know the area a bit more. This way I'll see more than when we drive. I'll be fine."

Yvonne arched an eyebrow. "Mmm. I dare say you can manage. Just remember it's as far back as it is to get there."

Laughing, I shook my head. "Oh Yvie, I'm not five anymore!"

Her eyes searched my face. I kept a small smile on my lips, and hoped my own eyes didn't give me away. She nodded at last.

"See you later then."

I took care to walk at my normal pace until I was well out of sight of the house. I sighed with relief to be on my way. My shoulders relaxed and I slowed down to a stroll. Thankful for the sunny but cool day, I put all other thoughts out of my mind as I enjoyed taking in the gardens I was passing.

The sun had risen further by the time I reached the start of the shopping district. Most of my walk had been empty of other people, except in the odd car which had driven by. I straightened slightly, rolling my shoulders with determination as I set my mind on my real destination. I had sat through the service that morning listening to the sermon and readings with a growing feeling of dread. By the time lunch was ready, my nerves were so tightly wound that I could barely eat.

I checked the street before crossing to the opposite footpath. I slowed again as I approached the steps leading up to the door.

"Come on, get it over with." I muttered. A quick look to my left and right satisfied me that there was no one I knew nearby – which was unlikely anyway, given how few people I knew here – and I climbed the steps to the church.

I was relieved to see one half of the door standing a little open. Inside I made my way first of all to the front, opening my purse as I did so. I bobbed a curtsy at the end of the front pew, then turned to the side where the votive candles stood ready. I dropped a coin in the slot and selected a candle. I lit it, closed my eyes and prayed briefly–for courage and guidance mainly. Once that was done I went back down the aisle and over to the wooden cupboards on the other side of the church. None were in use, so I opened the first I came to, shut the door quietly behind me and sat down to wait.

When the little shutter finally slid open and the priest's voice came, making the standard greeting, my nerves were at stretching point. I stammered out my confession, well aware that the expected anonymity was undone by my accent – there weren't many other new immigrants in this church, and no other French as far as I knew.

The priest was solemn but compassionate. I had been scared that he would be a lot harsher. Rather, he merely reiterated scripture that warned of this particular sin being 'against your own flesh'.

"However, with the upheaval of the war over so many years, sadly we have seen a rise in these situations. It's clear that things are not always as straightforward as we would hope — in your case I see that your tender age gave you little with which to stand against the temptation."

He led me through a prayer of repentance and forgiveness, gave me my penance and then he was gone.

"Go in God's blessing and sin no more."

His final words echoed in my ears as I slowly made my way outside once more. I'd waited a few minutes after he'd left, wiping my tears and composing myself. My face still felt hot. I decided to take a turn around a block, until I could regain a more natural colour.

* * *

Harold regularly came over once during the week and again on Saturdays after work. Weekday evenings we'd just take a walk around my neighbourhood, or go for a short drive, and on Saturdays we usually went back to the beach and his favourite café nearby.

A few weeks later I woke suddenly in the dark of early morning. Unsure at first why, I felt a surge within and ran to the bathroom. Back in bed, I wiped a sheen of perspiration from my forehead as I tried to work out what was wrong. When I woke next the sun was streaming through my drapes and I could hear my sister in the kitchen.

I went back to the bathroom, splashed my face with water and rinsed my mouth out. In my room, I got dressed quickly, tugged my brush through my hair, opened my drapes then left to face Yvonne. She looked up as I entered the kitchen.

"Good morning sleepy 'ead. It's not like you to sleep late. Are you all right?"

I nodded as I checked the kettle and turned it on. "Yes, I am fine. Just tired I expect." Something held me back from telling her about earlier.

The next morning was the same. I couldn't understand it; I had been fine most of the day before. When it happened a third morning, I knew I'd have to say something to Yvonne. She would be able to tell me if I needed a doctor or not. Maman's long years of illness loomed in my mind and a dread began to settle. Yvonne looked worried as I sat her down at the dining table with me.

"Yvie. I think I am not well. And I am beginning to worry."

She reached out and grasped my hand, lying on the table beside my cup. "Elise, ma chérie. What is it? You look frightened."

"I think I may 'ave what Maman 'ad," I sobbed out.

She pushed her chair back quickly and came around to me. I felt her arms come around me. "Oh my love. What makes you think that?"

I told her about the last three mornings, hiccuping through my tears. Her arms loosened and she straightened up.

"And you 'ave been fine through the rest of the day?"

I nodded. I had thought telling her would be a relief, that she would laugh off my worries and have a simple explanation. Instead, hearing the hollow tone in her voice, I felt worse. She went back to her seat.

"Well, Elise, we will need to see my doctor to be sure, but I don't think you need to worry about cancer."

I stared at her, stunned at her almost casual use of that word. "But, what then? Am I going to get better?"

She nodded. "In a sense, yes. But in other ways, no." She saw my confusion. "Elise, you are my dear sister and I am 'ere

112

for you. But I am also very shocked. 'ow could you?"

"I don't know what you are talking about. Yvie, you're scaring me."

She dropped her gaze. Hands gripped in front of her, she was clearly struggling to phrase her words. "Elise. You and 'arold. Did you allow 'im to," she paused. "Take liberties? Did you do more than kiss 'im?"

The heat in my face put all my former blushes to shame. I felt my stomach rebel and ran out of the room. I made it to the bathroom just in time. As I splashed my face with water again, Yvonne knocked on the door and entered.

"Do you see what I am saying? Do I need to say more?"

I numbly shook my head — carefully. "Yes, Yvie."

She stared at my reflection. "Elise. We will talk more. And we will get through this. But right now I am angry. So I think it best if you stay in your room today. I will tell Rex that you are unwell, but I don't think I can look at you just at the moment. I will put a plate of snacks outside your door in a while." Her expression was cold and I stood, stunned, for several minutes before I could bring myself to move.

Back in my bedroom, I curled up on the covers and gave way to my tears. Thoughts chased each other around my head. "She can't hate me more than I hate myself right now," I whispered into my pillow. I dreaded to think what my family back home would feel when they heard, as they were bound to. I knew I had let myself and everyone around me down. A bleak future paraded itself in my imagination: I would be cut off from my family and secluded from society by my shame. I couldn't foresee how I would ever find my right place now.

I woke with the stale taste of those recriminations in my mouth and my mind. I rolled over, seeing the irony of my situation. I had told my grandmother how much I wanted a family. But not like this, not like this. I wasn't much more than a child myself. But no one can sustain such self-pity for long, I realised as I started to climb back up out of my pit. At long last I began to think of someone other than myself. I wriggled around, propped my pillow behind me and sat back against it. My hands found their way to my stomach. A new life had begun within me. A new wave of shame came over me. I started to worry I had somehow rejected my child, even for a moment. They were not to blame. "I will love you and protect you, little one." I promised, though I had no idea how.

Yvonne arranged to have the car the next day and took me to her doctor. He confirmed her suspicion. The drive home was quiet. The car was put away, the kettle on and we were in the lounge before Yvonne broke her silence.

"We 'ave to face it 'ead on now." She caught my gaze and held it. "You know 'ow I feel. But, it 'as 'appened and we must make the best of it. Now it is definite, we will 'ave to tell Rex. That's first. I cannot guess 'ow 'e will react, so all I can do is prepare you. 'e will of course want to speak to 'arold."

I gulped and nodded. I had nothing worth saying.

"But, life is sacrosanct, so there is no question on that front."

I must have looked bewildered as she explained.

"Some, those who are not of our faith, would say a young girl like you should be encouraged to – end the pregnancy. Do you see?"

Horrified, I clasped my stomach. I had not heard of such a thing.

"So, go and rest now. This is all new to me as well, remember."

I got through the day in a haze, trying in vain to distract

myself from the worry of Rex's reaction. I replayed the night I'd changed everything in my mind. How thoughtless my past self seemed now. And as far as consequences went, I hadn't thought beyond having sinned against God. I hadn't considered this future as a possibility.

I had dinner made and was keeping it warm in the oven by the time Yvonne and Rex returned. I heard the car draw up, then muffled slams of each car door. I stayed in the kitchen, with no desire to see either sooner than necessary.

The lock on the front door snicked open, a few moments of whispered cloth as I pictured each of them removing their coats and hanging them up. I heard the door close, then footsteps coming down the hallway. The footfalls went silent as Rex or Yvonne, I wasn't sure who I'd see first, stepped from the hall to the carpeted lounge. I watched the kitchen entrance with trepidation, my stomach threatening to rebel.

Then they were both in the doorway, standing closely together. Yvonne's face was neutral. Rex just stared at me. I couldn't read him at all. He wasn't frowning. I waited. I didn't want to be the first to speak.

Finally he lifted his hands wide as he walked further into the room. "Well, this is a fine fix, isn't it? What am I supposed to say to your father? I hope you are aware of the shame you've caused your family."

All this was said at speed as his expression darkened. Every accusation hit home. Fighting back tears of shame and humiliation, all I could do was shake my head. Though it seemed inadequate, I said the only thing I could think of.

"I am sorry Rex. You are right and I am so sorry." I'm not sure what reaction he had been expecting from me, but this clearly wasn't it. I saw him visibly deflate. He looked around

115

at his wife. She nodded.

"I will have to speak to McRae of course. I expect him to do the right thing by you. He does know, doesn't he?"

I shook my head. "I 'ave only just found out myself. I didn't tell 'im about being ill at all. We were going to go out again tomorrow evening."

He rubbed his face, both hands briefly covering it. He glanced back at Yvonne again then me. "Much as I'd enjoy tearing a strip off him in front of his mates, that's not exactly going to help with production. So I'll talk to him when he comes to collect you. Needless to say, you won't be going anywhere!"

Yvonne pushed past him at that point. "Right, that's enough for now. Let's get this dinner on the table and try to find something else to talk about." She bustled around the kitchen, handing me things to take through to the dining room.

How I got through the rest of that evening and the following day, I really don't know. Before I knew it, Rex was home once more and it was almost time for Harold to arrive. I felt ill as I imagined the shock in store for him.

When he knocked at the door, Rex waved at me to stay where I was. Yvonne went to the door. I heard her greet him. The door shut. Yvonne led Harold through to the lounge. I saw him hesitate in the doorway, taking in the scene before him. Rex's face was deliberately blank. I could barely meet Harold's eyes, but when I did, I tried to telegraph some warning, but he merely looked even more bewildered.

"Evening all. What's all this? You look glum."

Yvonne pointed him to a seat and hurried back to her husband's side on the sofa.

Rex looked at me. "Shall I start? Or do you want to tell

him?"

Startled, I swept a look from him to Harold and back again. I shook my head quickly.

Harold stared at me. "Tell me what exactly?"

Rex waited until he had Harold's attention. "Do you remember the last time you were here? You, me, my wife and my sister-in-law? My sixteen-year-old sister-in-law?"

The colour drained from Harold's face. The mention of my age had been a telling shot.

Rex nodded. "Ah, I see the penny is dropping." He stared, his face filled with disapproval.

Harold's eyes flicked desperately around the three of us.

"Yes. You are going to be a father. What will your own parents say to this? Will they be proud?"

Harold's expression changed, and I saw for the first time, anger in him. He rose from his seat. "I guess you've a right to be angry, so say what you like about me. But do not" —he shook a finger at Rex— "do not mention my parents. You know nothing about me or my family." His voice shook. He walked over to me. "Before we say anymore, I think it only right that you give me some time to talk to Elise, alone, don't you? Don't worry," he held a hand up as Rex opened his mouth to speak. "I'm not stupid enough to think we're going out anywhere. We'll just go out into the garden. Elise," he reached a hand back for me, pulling me from my chair. "Go get your coat. We don't need you getting a cold." He turned to look me in the eye.

Lowering his voice, he said, "It'll be all right. Go on, we can talk better alone." He gave me a gentle push towards the hall.

When I returned, he was still standing, but no one was talking. Yvonne and Rex were pretending to read, he a newspaper, her a magazine. Harold was staring out the undraped window. He turned as he heard me come back. Rex looked up. I led Harold out through the kitchen to the back garden. We walked silently to Rex's little jetty. The stream burbled and glittered in the faint moonlight.

Unable to take the silence any longer, I turned to face Harold. I felt ill again, but now it was from fear of what he would say. Surely he wouldn't want to be saddled with a young wife and a child. We had barely begun to get to know each other. I would be nothing but a burden. Even though I was sure what was coming, that this would be goodbye, I wanted it over with. With every bit of strength I could muster I spoke with a steady voice. "Say something, anything, please."

His shoulders rose and fell. Then his arms came around me and he hugged me tightly, pressing his face down into my neck. "I'm sorry Elise. Sorry I brought this on you. Sorry I didn't think to, well, take precautions." His voice was muffled.

Weak with relief, I was glad of his embrace to hold me upright. My own arms wrapped themselves around him without conscious thought from me. We pulled apart. "I don't know what that means, but it's not like we planned it, is it? 'arold, I'm scared. What are we going to do?"

He laughed. "Do? There's only one thing we can do, if I value my own life, let alone yours!" He sank down to one knee."Elise, will you marry me?" He grinned at my gasp. Speechless, I could only bob my head. "It's not like we weren't thinking of getting to this sometime in the future, is it? Just a lot sooner than either of us planned. Come on, let's go tell him before he has a heart attack."

I pulled on his arm. "Wait, 'arold. Surely we need to talk more? It's not that simple, is it? My Papa must be told, and 'e will need to give permission, won't 'e? Because of my age? What if ' says no?"

Harold lifted my chin gently, forcing my gaze upwards. "Why would he say no? He wouldn't want you to raise this child alone, and cause a scandal, would he?"

"I guess not. But 'e will be so angry with me. I 'ave never made 'im angry before."

"Then it's just as well he lives hundreds of miles away! There's only so much you can put in a letter."

"There's something else, 'arold. Can I ask," I hesitated. "Why were you so angry when Rex spoke of your parents? You can tell me it's none of my business, but if it is something I will need to know anyway?"

He stared over my shoulder, his face now set in harder lines. "My parents have had a bit of a rough life. I wasn't an easy kid," he laughed, shaking his head. "To put it mildly. And my dad got injured early on in the war; he's never been quite right since. That was hard on Mum. I guess I'm just a bit over protective of them. If Mr C ..." His jaw tightened as he cut his own words off.

I nodded, my respect for him rising.

Back inside, Yvonne smiled with obvious relief at the news. Rex, on the other hand, had one more thing to say.

"It's only your duty, boy. Don't expect any gratitude from me. And you better get on with it, or Elise's shame will be public."

"Cup of tea time, I think. Elise, come 'elp me." Yvonne beckoned me to follow her.

With hot drinks in our hands, the remainder of the evening passed a little less heatedly. The fact that Harold had so quickly accepted responsibility had taken the wind out of

Rex's sails. Whenever Rex tried to lead the conversation to further decisions that needed making, Yvonne steered us back to safe ground by asking Harold another question about his life outside work.

I fell asleep quickly, exhausted by the emotional day. When I awoke, it was again for a hurried dash to the bathroom. Afterwards, I made myself somewhat presentable by donning my dressing gown and running my brush through my hair before making my way to the kitchen.

Yvonne was coming back in from the garden. "Morning Elise."

"Good morning Yvie." Putting the kettle on, I raised a cup towards her.

She nodded and managed a small smile.

We moved around each other as I made our tea and she laid out the flowers she'd brought inside, trimming their stems and arranging them in the vases set out on the counter. The silence spoke clearly of the tension still between us, and I knew it was going to take time before I was fully forgiven.

I'd never had a real falling out with any of my siblings before and I didn't quite know how to deal with it. Several times I started to say something but stopped before a sound emerged. Yvonne accepted her cup with a nod of thanks, then left the room without a word. I stared after her, tears stinging.

After a few minutes I helped myself to a couple of plain biscuits from the pantry and took them with my drink back to my room. I opened my drapes, climbed back into bed and plumped my pillow behind me. The day promised to be long, with nothing to distract me from my thoughts.

Later on, I found Yvonne sitting in the lounge, magazine on the arm of her chair as she stared out the window. She stirred as she registered my return.We held each other's gaze for a moment, then at last she smiled.

"Come, Elise, sit down. We 'ave much to talk about, yes? I'll make us a drink first."

I sat down, curling my legs up beneath me, making myself small in the corner of the sofa.

She brought a tray through, a pot of tea, cups and a plate of sandwiches filling it. Silenced by surprise at the change in her, I nodded my thanks as she put a side table near me, laying my filled cup and a side plate on it before offering me the sandwiches. I selected a couple, setting them down for a moment. She settled herself with her own portion, then sat again.

"First I want to apologise for 'ow I treated you this morning. Of course I am shocked and disappointed, but I ''ave already said all that. While you were gone, I realised that you must be just as shocked, and scared. The last thing you need from me is more guilt or shame. We're Catholic, we 'ave plenty of practice at both of those!" She laughed.

I'd been taking a sip of my drink as she spoke and choked at her quip. But it broke the tension and I was able to laugh at myself as I found my hanky and cleaned myself up. "Yvie, I am sorry too. Rex was right, I 'ave let everyone down. You don't know what a relief it was last night, when 'arold said he wanted to marry me." I looked down into my cup as emotion threatened again.

"Look at me, Elise. A lot was said last night, some that needed to be, some that went a little too far. That side of things is done now. I will write to Papa and the family, and I will tell them only that you are to be married. The details will stay between us 'ere. No good can come of worrying

121

our father and grandmother. If we get organised, no one will know that events occurred in the wrong order."

She was as good as her word, and in what seemed a very short time, we had the church booked and a private dining area at a central hotel.

"Yvie, are you sure you can afford that?" I asked when she told me about the hotel.

"Yes, I am sure. Now, stop worrying. Papa is sending a little to 'elp with it as well, and Rex was 'appy to do this rather than 'ave people traipsing through 'ere. This way we don't 'ave to bother cooking or planning a wedding breakfast. We just choose from their regular menu. It's not like we'll have lots of guests, after all."

I stared at her, wondering how she could say Rex was happy about any of this.

* * *

Yvonne had a list to which she referred daily once Rex had left for work. She had organised it so that each time we had the car for groceries, we would also check something off her list that couldn't be sorted over the telephone. Today we were going to look for a dress for me. I had suggested I wear my favourite, the one she'd given me. She'd shaken her head firmly.

"Elise, this is already rather" –I saw her searching her mind for the right word– "unconventional, so no, you are not walking down the aisle in a spotted white and blue dress!"

We had parked by the grocery store and were now walking to the department store further along. Yvie pushed open the big glass door and led the way through to womenswear.

"Take a look around, Elise. You start that side, I'll go this way. We're looking for white or cream, all right? I'll come and find you."

I went on through, making my way through to the dresses at the back. There wasn't a huge selection. Shortages still affected what was available. Looking at the labels on a few that caught my eye, most items were made in Australia or America. At least with my height, the mid-length frocks would be almost ankle-length on me, making them more appropriate for our purpose. I had one possibility over my arm when Yvonne came over. She had found two for me to try on.

"Come on, the fitting rooms are this way." She led the way. The fitting room assistant showed me to an empty cubicle, holding the drape aside as Yvonne followed me in to hang up the garments. "Let's start with your choice," she said, holding the skirt away from the wall, studying the dress from shoulder to hem. "It's at least the right sort of colour, and not too fussy. We short girls can't carry off fussy clothes." She grinned. "I'll be just outside. Let me know when you're ready."

It looked better on the hanger than on me, so I moved quickly to Yvonne's choices; another dress and a skirt and jacket suit. "What do you think?" I asked, twitching the curtain open again once I'd fastened the dress.

"Mmm, turn around please?" Yvonne stood back and surveyed me as I turned slowly. "I'm just not completely sure. Try the other outfit; we can always come back to this one."

I did as she asked, enjoying the way the skirt flared slightly, accentuating my narrow – for now – waist. The jacket buttoned up to a high collar and finished with a wide peplum. I looked in the mirror as I buttoned it up. I smiled at my reflection and called Yvie back in.

She pulled the drape aside, took one look at my smile and

nodded. "I agree. This is very you. It's definitely smart enough to get married in. Now, a blouse and a nice pair of shoes I think."

"Yvie! I can't let you keep spending so much money. I'll never be able to pay you back." I bit my lip. I loved how the suit fitted me and how it looked, but I suddenly felt that it was wrong to accept such generosity after my disgrace.

Yvonne came into the cubicle and pulled the drape shut. She put her hands on my shoulders, making me look her straight in the eye. She whispered, speaking French. "Now listen, because I don't want to have this conversation each time we have to spend money to get this wedding sorted out. Yes, you are getting married far sooner than you thought you would, and not under the best circumstances. But you are still getting married, Elise! If we don't do this properly, we will invite gossip and none of us need that. Let me do this. You only get married once, all right? Rex and I have talked this over and we are in complete agreement."

I stared for a moment. I found it hard to believe that my brother-in-law would be so understanding or compassionate. Yvie must have worked hard to convince him. "Thank you, Yvie. I am truly grateful."

She smiled, switching back to English. "Let's finish getting you turned into a bride. Come on, we'll leave the rejects 'ere; the assistant will put them back in the right places. You get changed back into your own things, and we'll turn back into Kiwi girls, yes?" She stepped back through the drape.

I quickly changed, doing my best not to let my thoughts spiral as her assurances raised a whole new set of problems to my mind.

Back on the shop floor, I meekly followed Yvonne as she

selected blouses of different shades and styles, holding them up to the suit I carried by its hanger. Finally she nodded with satisfaction.

"This is it. It works with the suit, but is simple enough you can wear it again after," she looked quickly around us. Seeing no one close by, she continued quietly.

"After you have the baby."

My face burned. She laid a hand on my arm but said no more. I followed her to the shoes section.

By the time we got to the sales counter, we were laden with our selections. At the last moment, Yvonne had decided I needed a necklace as well as some new handkerchiefs and a purse. The sales assistant rang up the purchases as I did my best to ignore the total climbing on the register. She put the items neatly in bags and handed them over with a smile.

Yvonne thanked her, I merely smiled my thanks, taking both bags from her.

We got into the car. Holding the bags of my bridal outfit on my lap, I blurted out my fear.

"I know you said you forgive me, but I am so ashamed. I feel as though I will be acting out a lie, when I dress up as a bride. Yvie," the tears came then. "What will 'appen to me? What will 'appen to my child because of my sin, my shame?"

Wordlessly she pulled me into her arms and held me, letting me cry on her shoulder. Even through my fears, I was angry with myself for putting my burdens on her again. She rubbed my back, just as our Maman used to do when we were children.

"You sit there and gather your thoughts while I get our groceries. We'll talk more at 'ome."

The drive home was quiet. I was lost in my self-loathing and grief. Though I could forgive myself for being fearful, reminding myself how young a mother I was going to be, I couldn't do the same about my behaviour today. I felt like I had been ungrateful for the grace that my sister had shown me, in treating me like any other girl about to be married.

We unloaded our purchases into the house, still not speaking. Yvonne made us tea as I hung my new clothing in my closet, put the shoe box on the shelf and the other accessories on my dresser. I went to the bathroom and splashed my face with cold water. I didn't look in the mirror. I felt drained and numb now. Thanking her for the cup she handed me when I reached the lounge, I sat on the sofa, tucking my legs up under me. I could feel Yvonne staring. At last I met her gaze.

"Let's get back to what you said, yes?"

I nodded.

"Firstly, yes, of course we know it is a sin. But we also know about confession. And God's forgiveness. So I think that should be your first step in coming to terms with this."

"I did go to confession after that night. So why do I still feel this way?"

"Maybe because now it's about another life, not just yourself? Anyway, when we go to mass on Sunday, you can stay behind and go to confession again. I'll take Rex away for a walk so you don't feel watched or rushed. My next question may seem odd to you. But, do you know anything of Grand-mère's past?"

Confused, I shook my head. What had Grand-mère to do with this?

"It was her Maman who left France to live in New Caledonia. Did you know that much?"

I nodded.

"Well, what you probably don't know is that she didn't 'ave

126

a choice. I won't go into detail, but Grand-mère has never known 'er father. L'arrière-Grand-mère was not married. She was sent to New Caledonia as an exile, in shame. She conceived Grand-mère out of wedlock. Oh, she eventually did marry, more than once. But my point is this: 'ave you ever thought of Grand-mère as anything less than other people's Grand-mères?"

"No! Of course not. She is wonderful. I always felt like I was spoiled to 'ave 'er and Maman living with us." This news shocked me. Grand-mère had never said anything bad about her childhood. "But she used to talk about 'er maman and papa, about them as a family."

Yvonne nodded. "The truth is that 'er maman married the man Grand-mère called papa when she was three years old. But they told 'er and 'er sisters at a young age, so they grew up knowing 'e was not their birth papa. Instead they were taught that 'e chose them as 'is own. Do you see what I am saying?"

I sat for a moment, staring into my cup. New thoughts now chased the old accusatory ones around, vying for dominance. At last I looked up. "I think so? You mean that I 'ave not condemned my child because of my mistake?"

She laughed. "That's a start at least. Plus you are marrying the child's father. You won't be doing this alone. And we are doing everything we can to make sure you won't be subject to public shame either. So, can we put the self condemnation be'ind us?"

"Yes, Yvonne. I will do my best. Grand-mère will be my reminder if I begin to feel sorry for myself again. And thank you again for the clothes. I am grateful. I am sorry that I didn't seem to appreciate all you are doing."

She flapped her hand dismissively. "Right, go and try the

whole lot on for me. I'll see if we need to make any adjustments. Then it can go away until your wedding day!"

I blanched at the phrase, making her laugh again.

Saturday came around again, and brought Harold back to me. Rex had muttered something about horses and barn doors after agreeing we could go to our café, as I now thought of it. In the car, we breathed a sigh of relief in unison, laughing at ourselves.

"It's hard enough just visiting there, I hate to think what it's like for you living with him." Harold shook his head ruefully, eyes on the road.

"It was bad at first, but Yvonne and I cleared the air, and I think she 'as spoken to 'im. I don't get so much trouble from 'im anymore. Maybe with you, it's because 'e can't say anything at work, 'e must save it up." I grinned.

He gasped in pretended shock. "Elise, are you cracking a joke? Well I never! What's next?"

When we stopped laughing, I stretched my arms out in front of me, feeling a tightness I hadn't noticed being released.

He noticed, grinning sideways at me. "It's good to see you, Elise. I have been worried. Are you all right? You know." He gestured towards my stomach.

I nodded. "Yes. I still get ill most mornings, but Yvonne read up about it for me. I 'ave ginger biscuits beside my bed and a glass of water. That makes it settle quicker. And I am learning to just take it slow getting up in the morning for now." I saw he'd gone red, though he tried to sound as though he always had this sort of conversation. I patted his shoulder. "It is kind of you to ask. I will not tell you more unless you ask. Neither of us is used to this. Ok?"

His hands relaxed on the steering wheel and he sat back in

his seat. "Deal. I hope our table isn't taken. I feel like watching the sea from the comfort of the café is just what we need today."

We were in luck. Going by the busyness of the staff when we arrived, clearing and wiping down tables, they'd had a good day so far, but only a few tables still had patrons seated at them. Harold pulled me along after him to the table in the corner by the front window. He dragged a seat out for me, then went to the counter to place our order.

"Just what the doctor ordered," he said as he walked by me to the seat on the other side of the table. He sat down heavily, sighing with exaggerated relief. Our food and drinks arrived. I stared at the lavish spread that Harold had ordered.

"Did you not 'ave lunch today, 'arold?" I said in surprise.

He chuckled. "It's not that much, cheeky girl. No, I saw that they had some special cakes in and I felt like spoiling my fiancée."

My face went hot at the word, making his grin widen.

He pushed the platter towards me. "Ladies first."

I pretended to make a serious study of the whole selection, then reached for a little cake with pink frosting. Its top had been cut and re-positioned, then decorated to look like butterfly wings. I lifted it onto my plate. I heard his sharp intake of breath and looked up. As I did so my eye caught a glint on the platter where my cake had sat. "Oh!" I shot a look from the plate to Harold.

"Surprise!" He reached over and picked the ring up with one hand, while reaching for my left hand with the other.

"I figured I should make it official. It's not flash, but I thought you'd like it."

The metal was warm as he slid it onto my third finger.

"There. What do you think?"

I was stunned. I sat with my hand up in front of me, frozen. I caught my reflection in the window, seeing the ring adorning my own hand twice over. I turned back to Harold. I smiled. "I love it." Behind me, a silence I hadn't noticed was broken by a round of applause. I jumped and twisted around in my seat. The staff and patrons behind me had clearly been let in on Harold's surprise. I couldn't help but smile broadly, their joy in a stranger's happiness contagious. I bowed my head in thanks and turned again to my Harold. I laughed inwardly at that thought. Harold was thoroughly enjoying being a spectacle, I could see that. Glad to have the attention all behind me once more, I took a bite of the cake, which proved to be as tasty as it was pretty. He chose a cake for himself and for a while we just sat, drinking our tea and taking a second cupcake each. The sea's gentle movement beyond the window was soothing and held my gaze.

Finally he brushed his hands together over his plate, balled up his napkin and pushed back his seat. "Shall we?"

I nodded and stood, picking my purse up from the spare seat.

Hand in hand, we made our way to the beach and walked slowly along. He lifted our linked hands, twisting them around so he could see my ring. He grinned.

"It suits you."

I sighed happily. "Yvie took me shopping this week. She and Rex paid for my whole wedding outfit! I've never bought so many things to wear at the same time. Do you 'ave a suit to wear for the ceremony?"

"Mm-hmm. That's not a problem. It's not the latest fashion or anything; I had to have one for my older brother's wedding a few years ago. It's just been hanging in my wardrobe ever since. Shoes, on the other hand, do need sorting. I'm not great at shopping."

"Would you like me to come with you? 'elp you choose?"

"No, that's ok. I just have to make the time, is all. They'll be black, so other than that, I guess it's just trying some on. Don't worry, I'll be ship shape and Bristol fashion on the day?" He chuckled at my confusion. "It's another silly old English saying. Means I'll be tidy and fit to be seen."

"If you're sure. Yvonne said to ask you if you'd like to come to mass with us. Something called the reading of the banns? Do you know about that?"

He looked over, brows raised. "I'm not much of a church-goer, but I have graced them with my presence on special occasions." He winked.

I shook my head in mock reproof.

"Seriously though, I remember something about that when my brother was getting married. Yes, I'll come. But tell her it'll have to be next weekend. I'm seeing my parents this one, to give them our news."

"Yvonne will understand. I hope it won't be too difficult for you."

He shrugged. "They'll be a bit shocked, but happy I'm settling down, I guess. That's what I'm banking on anyway."

We walked on, then retraced our steps back to his car. Once we were driving, he raised the subject of our future.

"I guess we should seriously start looking for somewhere to live, hey?"

"But I thought I would just come live with you?" I was startled.

He shook his head. "I only board where I am. As a single

bloke, there was no point in me having a whole house or flat. But now, we're going to need a bit more room, and pretty quickly too."

"Oh, of course. I 'ad not realised. Where do we start?"

"Leave it with me for now, I'll ask around, see if anyone knows of something going. I'll take you with me if I find anything, how's that sound?" He reached over and squeezed my hand.

"Ok, yes."

After mass the following morning, Yvonne did as she'd said, leaving me sitting in a back pew to wait for the priest to be free. As a girl, I'd not had much practice at going to the confessional, and here I was, back a second time in not many weeks. The priest was kind.

"I am sorry, my child, for this outcome, at your tender age. I can't say it's unexpected. However, you aren't the first and you won't be the last. God's word tells us in the Psalms that children are a heritage from Him, a reward even. All children. We can't always understand His ways, in situations such as yours, but if we did, He wouldn't really be God, now would He? Our blessed Mother Mary was even younger than you when she was blessed to carry our Lord, do you remember? I forgive you, in the name of the Father, the Son and the Holy Ghost."

I made the sign of the cross as he spoke, my heart lightened by his words.

"Go in peace. I will see you and your young man next week for the reading of the banns, yes?"

"Yes, Father."

"I look forward to meeting him. It's not everyone in his shoes who stands up to his responsibilities in our modern world, sadly." We left the boxes at the same time. He smiled down at me as we met outside. "I am sure your sister is looking after you. That is a good woman you have there. Let her guide you and you won't go far wrong. Goodbye, Elise." I left quickly and went to catch up with Yvie and Rex.

18

Autumn 1948

The weeks before my wedding flew past and very soon I had only a few days left.

By now my morning sickness had all but gone and I found I had more energy again.

I woke from a deep, dreamless sleep on the day I was to be married. The weak Autumn sun peeped through beneath my curtains. I stretched, turned over and sat up just as there was a knock on my door.

"Come in, Yvie." I swung my feet to the floor, reaching for my dressing gown.

"I brought you a cup of tea; thought you could do with a slow start to the day."

"Thanks, Yvie. You look after me so well." She sat on the bed beside me. We sat in silence for a few moments, just enjoying each other's company. She patted my leg before standing again.

"I'd best get on, Elise. Come and 'ave some breakfast when you're ready."

Now the day was actually here, all my worry about it seemed

to have gone at last. Going to my closet, I lifted out my wedding suit and lay it on the bed. I smiled as I remembered what it looked like on the day we bought it.

Breakfast over, I bathed and washed my hair. As I dried myself, my hand lingered over my stomach. For the first time I noticed a distinct change: the soft roundness I was used to had been replaced by a firm bump. I ran my fingers from one side to the other, marking out the extent of the change and surprised at the suddenness of it.

"My skirt!" I muttered. It had been a perfect fit. What if I couldn't get into it now? I hurriedly finished up and got back to my room. I took the skirt off the hangar and held it against me. There was only one way to know and I couldn't put it off. I stepped into it, easing it up over my hips. I got the waist button fastened, breathed and slowly pulled the zip up. The relief! Yes, it was tighter, but it closed all the way to the top. I took it off again, instead dressing in my normal clothes for the morning.

* * *

"Shall we go over the ceremony once more, Elise?" Yvonne placed her butter knife across her plate as we finished our light lunch.

"I think I 'ave it clear now, thank you Yvie. I 'ad better get changed." I collected our dishes, ready to take through to the kitchen.

Yvonne waved a hand. "Don't worry about that, I'll see to it. Off you go."

Rex drove Yvonne and I to the church. She sat in the back with me for a change, holding my hand one minute, the next reaching up to fix a stray curl for me.

Rex stopped the car in our assigned space outside the church. He came around the car and opened the back door, assisting first Yvonne, then me, out to the footpath. I looked up to see the priest and his servers waiting at the door.

"This is it, my dear little sister. Come on, let's not keep them – or 'arold – waiting any longer." Yvonne gave me a quick hug as she spoke.

Harold came forward as we stepped over the threshold. He reached for my hand.

"Welcome. Let us begin." The priest smiled kindly down at me. He led the way as one of his servers opened the interior doors. I had asked Yvonne to choose the music. The verger of the parish had given us a list of choices. Now "Jesu, Joy of Man's Desiring" filled the church. I was glad to have Harold's arm to hold on to as we followed the priest down to the sanctuary.

He turned to face us at the altar and made the sign of the cross, and my wedding officially began. I was thankful for the formality of tradition that meant I just had to follow along, responding along with the whole assembly to the prayers and readings.

Under cover of the first psalm being sung, Harold leaned in close and whispered. "How bad's my singing?"

I stifled a laugh and shook my head. Glancing down at the paper in my hand, I joined in with the assembly. "The Lord is kind and merciful."

Finally we reached the homily and were able to sit down. My feet were pinching in the new shoes from standing for so long.

"Please stand for the statements of intent. Witnesses, please join us."

"Elise, are you here to enter into Holy Matrimony of your own will, not under any coercion?"

"I am."

"Harold, are you here to enter into Holy Matrimony of your own will, not under any coercion?"

"I am."

Questions over, it was time for our vows.

"Please turn and face each other."

"Do you, Harold, take Elise to be your lawful wedded wife? To have and to hold, in sickness and in health, for richer, for poorer, as long as you both shall live?"

Harold smiled. "I do." He slipped the ring onto my finger.

"Do you, Elise, take Harold as your lawful wedded husband? To honour him and love him, in sickness and in health, for richer, for poorer, as long as you both shall live?"

"I do." I realised my hand was shaking as I tried to put Harold's ring on his finger, but I managed not to drop it.

"Having made your vows before God and man, I pronounce you man and wife. May God bless you and keep you, strengthening you as you walk together from this day forward as one."

We faced the altar again, hands now joined, while the final prayer was read. Now it was my turn to lead Harold as we took the gifts of communion together: his first experience of this holy ceremony.

"Blimey!" Harold muttered as the last words of the blessing died away and we preceded the priest and his servers back up the aisle. "I didn't realise we'd be on our feet so long. I could do with a beer and a sit down about now."

I tightened my grip on his arm. "It is nearly over, 'arold."

My face started to ache from holding my smile in place for so long. At last, those who were to join us at the wedding breakfast left first, while the rest stayed to give us their congratulations. Those who had come for my side, were friends or colleagues of Rex, who had brought their wives. I felt humbled by the efforts Yvonne had gone to, trying to make my wedding day look as ordinary as she could.

"Well, Mrs McRae, shall we?" Harold gestured towards his own car.

Yvonne walked over. "We'll see you there soon." She patted my arm and grinned. "Being the centre of attention wasn't so bad, was it?" With that she walked quickly back to Rex.

In our car – I surprised myself at how quickly I'd come to think of it as ours rather than his – Harold leaned over and kissed me.

"That's better, without the audience!" he said as he straightened and started the engine.

We walked into the private room in the hotel restaurant and our guests broke into applause. I felt my face grow red once more. Having only ever been to Odette's wedding, my own wedding breakfast was a new experience in every way. We were all seated at one large table so I wasn't the focus of attention here. Now the attention was directed to those giving speeches.

Harold stood as his brother, the best man, sat down with a sigh of relief, duty done.

Harold cleared his throat. "Thanks for that, Len. Thank you all for coming and celebrating with us. Mr and Mrs Carlisle, I just wanted to say thank you for organising everything." He swept his hand to indicate the room, then grabbed my hand. "I – we really appreciate it. Mrs Carlisle, please pass on my gratitude to your dad for sending Elise here" –he grinned down at me "and for giving us his blessing on our marriage. I hope he'll be able to visit soon so I can thank him in person. And most of all, thank you to my beautiful bride, Elise. Will you raise a glass with me." He grinned at me, his own glass held high as he finished. "To Elise!"

I blushed as they followed suit, my name proclaimed loudly.

The food was served and I finally had a chance to properly study Harold's family. There was a strong resemblance between him and his father, both sturdy and average height, with similar colouring. His mother was completely different, and if she'd not been sitting with his father, I would never have realised who she was. Small like me, she had blonde, almost white hair worn in a wartime style knot at the base of her neck. Her skin was pale, and her eyes an almost watery-blue. Both of them were dressed very formally. I never heard her utter a word the whole day.

Our families were the last to leave. Yvonne hugged us both, Rex shook Harold's hand then gave me a quick kiss on the cheek before hurrying off ahead of Yvonne. Going by her expression, I think we were equally shocked. Harold's father shook his hand, nodded at me, while his wife stood behind him.

"Thanks for coming, Mum and Dad," Harold said, reaching for his mother and giving her a hug. They hurried off.

* * *

Harold drove to the bed and breakfast establishment a little way out of town where we were to stay that night.

And so started my married life. As I fell asleep, my mind

replayed the day. It had been almost perfect. I stroked my stomach, at last at peace with the secret we'd hidden from everyone except Yvonne and Rex. This child would know happiness in his life, I promised as I drifted off at last.

"This is the way to start our life together, now isn't it?" Harold said.

I looked up from scraping the last of my egg from its boiled shell, and followed Harold's gaze. The sea was still, its surface reflecting the morning sun like a polished mirror. "Yes, my love. It's perfect." We had been served breakfast at a little iron table on the back porch. The back garden had been planted with short bushes rather than trees, taking nothing away from the magnificent views. Mount Maunganui was visible to the left, and a small island out in the bay was almost directly in front of us.

I sighed in delightful appreciation. "So, what is your plan for the rest of today? You never did tell me."

He winked, grinning broadly. "Yesterday was supposed to be the main event! I didn't want today's plans lost in the noise. I thought we'd have a nice long drive before we head to our new digs. I know it's nothing flash, but I didn't feel like unpacking and getting all domestic straight away."

I had to agree, a drive did sound like more fun. Though I was looking forward to making our new 'digs' as he called our flat, how I wanted it. I hoped he'd get us there before it got dark. I was even looking forward to cooking for him.

Driving beside the sea was both energising and relaxing. I reached for Harold's hand, the first time I'd beaten him to it. He looked over and smiled.

"So, I figured we'd see how far we could get by lunchtime, find somewhere that does fish and chips, and grab a spot on the sand. Nothing beats fish and chips with the smell of the sea in your face. What do you reckon, Mrs M?"

I laughed. "Mrs M indeed. I thought we were past the last name thing. Yes, that does sound like a great plan." I wriggled down in my seat and stretched my legs.

We reached our new home late that afternoon. As I stepped through the front door, seeing it for only the second time, I was glad I'd not pushed to get here earlier. I knew now that the day spent by the sea, in the sun, would buoy me through the amount of work needed to make this dismal little place into a home.

I felt Harold watching me so I pasted a smile on my face before turning to him. I reached for his hand. "Thank you."

"What for?"

"You did all the 'ard work, finding somewhere for us in such a short time. Now it's my turn. I'll make us drinks if you bring our things in. Then you can put your feet up if you like while I 'get all domestic' as you put it."

He whistled. "Look at you, calling the shots and all. Being a married woman has changed you already."

Suddenly worried I'd done something wrong, I began to apologise.

He chuckled and grabbed me in a hug. "I'm teasing you, silly girl. Of course you're in charge of how this" –he waved around the room– "how it all looks and works. I bring in the folding stuff, you make us a home. That's how it should be, right?"

I studied his face, searching for any hint of unease.

He held my gaze, a small grin starting to show. "Satisfied?" he said.

I breathed out, relaxing. "Yes." I stepped away. "I'll get the kettle on then."

As I moved about the flat, I sent up a quick prayer of thanks for Yvonne's foresight. While we were shopping for clothing, and making all the wedding bookings, she had set Harold the task of buying whatever he didn't already have for the kitchen and living room. This past week he'd had friends help him move his few pieces of furniture from his room to here.

I got the kitchen sorted then prepared an easy dinner, putting the pots on the stove until I'd need them. Then I turned my attention to the bedroom. I called over my shoulder for Harold to come join me.

"What is it?" His voice trailed off as he looked over my head.

"Oh." I stood aside to let him through. His friends had at least put the bed in the right room, but it was standing on its side, the legs in a bag on the floor, and his pillows, linen and blankets were piled haphazardly just inside the door.

Harold kicked the pile out of his way and grabbed a bed leg from the bag. "They just screw in, so you want to grab one as well?"

I stood back once all the legs were screwed in tight, watching as he carefully lowered the bed onto them.

"So, what do you think? Against this wall, in the middle or would you prefer it over there?"

I was pleased to find how well we worked together. I enjoyed the way he invited me into each decision, no matter how small. We stood on each side of the bed as he helped me get the bed made.

He threw a pillow at me. "I'll leave the rest to you. I know my stuff isn't pretty, so when I get paid this week, how about you go find some new sheets and stuff to make it more to your taste?"

"That would be nice. I can see 'ow a bit more colour would brighten the room." A twinge caught at my back and I winced. Harold noticed and looked concerned. One hand on the painful spot, I held the other out. "It's ok, I think I just bent wrong. I'll sit for a minute." I sank down on the edge of the bed.

Frowning, he came round and squatted in front of me. "You sure? Anything I can do?"

I shook my head.

"If you're sure? Maybe we should leave the rest of the big jobs till tomorrow."

When I finally served our dinner, his appreciation of the meal made me forget all about the twinge in my back.

I was thankful for the years of learning from Maman, Grand-mère and my older sisters. The only hiccup had been battling the old stove, which appeared to have a mind of its own.

Our first week as a married couple fairly flew by; each day filled with shopping for the flat, finding the grocery shop in the area and learning to live together. And of course, all the time our baby was growing inside me. I realised as my clothes were becoming a closer fit that very soon my condition would show. I mentioned it one night to Harold at dinner.

He finished the mouthful he was eating then put his cutlery down for a moment. "Do you need money for new clothes then? Can it wait another week or so? We've bitten into my savings a fair bit getting this place to rights. I could do with us slowing down on spending, for a couple of weeks anyway. Our brother-in-law isn't the most generous boss, where pay is concerned."

I was worried now. "I am sorry, I didn't realise. I expect I can ask Yvonne for some of 'er old things that I can make over.

She likes to keep up with changing fashion, now that she can afford it. She 'as offered before. I'll 'ave another look at the 'ousekeeping to see if I can cut back a little."

He went back to his meal, nodding and speaking around the next mouthful. "Great, that'd really help. Listen, do you mind if I pop out for a bit after this? I told my mates I'd take them out for a drink to say thanks for their help moving my gear in. I won't be out too late."

"No, of course I don't mind. Please give them my thanks as well. I'll just clear up and 'ave an early night I think."

I fell asleep before he got back, but woke as he tried, unsuccessfully, to get into bed quietly. I kept my eyes closed. As he turned over I could smell the unmistakable sourness of beer waft over me. I suppressed a shudder at the memories which came with the smell. In minutes he was snoring but I took longer to get back to sleep.

We had arranged to have lunch with Yvonne and Rex after mass on Sunday, so I took the opportunity to ask Yvonne about the clothes while we were in the kitchen by ourselves.

She nodded over the pot of gravy she was stirring. "Of course, Elise. We'll 'ave a look through after lunch. The boys can entertain themselves, I'm sure. Though it must be a bit strange for 'arold, having lunch at the boss's 'ouse."

I laughed. "That was mentioned on the way over. But 'e will get used to it. Oh, but next week, 'is parents 'ave asked us to come to them. You don't mind?"

Yvonne turned with the pot in hand. She poured the contents carefully into the gravy boat before answering. "Don't be silly. Of course you must get to know them as well. Now, carry that platter through for me, will you?"

We carried our loads through, returning to collect the rest

of the dishes.

"Gentlemen, lunch is served," Yvonne called through to the lounge.

We went home with a small suitcase of Yvonne's old dresses and skirts. She'd made up a small sewing kit from hers for me to make some simple alterations.

"Don't throw the off-cuts away though, Elise. You can use them to make a couple of simple dresses for your baby. The colours will work for a boy or a girl, especially in the first few months. Can you remember your sewing lessons from Maman, and from school?"

I assured her I did, mentally noting to do a bit of practise before I tried to actually make anything.

"If you like, we can go look at patterns at the 'aberdashery in town one day. That'll 'elp."

As I told Harold about it all, I realised I was becoming excited at the idea of a project. I'd not really had a lot to do, outside of setting up the flat. At Yvonne's I'd just helped around the house, other than that fateful few days working with Rex.

Harold smiled, eyes on the road. "I'm liking this. Hearing you all enthusiastic and inspired. I'm looking forward to seeing what you make!"

Back at the flat, I laid out the garments on our bed, looking them over as I tried to imagine what I'd do with each one.

"Is there a library nearby, 'arold?" I asked as I went back to the living room.

He looked up from his newspaper. "I think there's just the one in the centre of town. There's probably a bus you can catch to get there. Maybe you should have a look tomorrow. You don't want to spend every day cooped up here when I'm at work, do you?"

I nodded but he'd already disappeared behind the spread pages. It reminded me of Papa. Back home, the newspaper was only once a week, arriving late on a Friday. Papa would spend Saturday afternoon in the same occupation as my husband did now.

The next morning, once Harold left for work, I set out for the library. After a short bus ride, I soon reached the street I was looking for and saw the council building on the other side of the road. Inside, I took the stairs to the library level. The heavy glass-paned door creaked as I pushed it open. I was hit with the dusty aroma of hundreds of books, mixed with the old-world smell of wood polish. It wasn't a huge library, but even so my shoulders dropped as I surveyed the lines of bookshelves stretching ahead of me. The timetable of the returning bus on my mind, I walked to the help desk to look for a librarian in the hopes of speeding up my search. Just as I reached it, an older lady came in from a door set behind the counter. She smiled as she saw me.

"Good morning, how can I help you?"

"I'm looking for some books on sewing please."

She explained that I would need to join as a member before I could borrow anything, and gave me a small form to fill out. Once the membership process was complete, she handed me a small card with my name on the back, alongside a membership number she allocated to me.

"Let's go find those sewing books you wanted," she said, leading me away from the front desk.

Though not a big reader by habit, the colourful spines and covers intrigued me. So once she had led me to the section I needed, I spent a happy ten minutes browsing, flicking through beautiful coloured pages of dresses, skirts and children's clothes before making my selection for my current project.

My friendly librarian produced a book-bag to make my return journey easier. "Now, remember to bring these back in two weeks. We can issue an extension at that time if you need them a little longer. Enjoy your reading."

I waved my free hand on my way out.

Over the next couple of weeks while Harold was out at work, I'd spend the morning on housework, then get out my books and the clothing I'd got from Yvonne. At first daunted by the thought of revising my old sewing lessons, I found the books gradually eased my concerns. They'd been produced during the war, explicitly to advise women on how to make over what was available so as to save fabric for the war effort over in Europe and England.

I took the books with me to Yvonne's on our next visit.

"It seems the austerity measures in the northern 'emisphere didn't reach us 'ere in the South Pacific, thank 'eaven!" she said as she perused the pages. She looked over at me. "The pieces I gave you 'ave much more fabric in them than those women 'ad to work with. You'll 'ave no trouble finding a pattern that suits you."

I agreed. "You'd never know this was made from a flour sack, would you?" I lifted the book to show her.

During the week I took a chair outside to sew in the sunlight. Now I had got two of her offerings made over. "Thank the Lord, I'm finished," I said aloud, as I cut the thread. I held up the skirt I'd shortened, critically assessing the hemline. The dress I'd let out before that was hanging on the washing line to air.

That day at the library, I'd also found a section on motherhood. While the first few I'd picked up offered advice on raising children, the next appeared to be just what I needed: the index showed chapters that dealt with what I could expect up to and including the birth. The book had been a goldmine of information that I'd never have dared ask anyone about. Suddenly I missed my maman so very much.

"Maman, I need you," I whispered, head against the shelf of books. "What would you tell me? Oh, Maman." I sniffed loudly as I fumbled for my handkerchief. Pulling myself together, I added the book to my pile, determined to learn all I could before my child was born.

As my figure expanded, I kept myself at home more and more. I wrote more frequently to my family and to Lulu, and the highlight of a day was to receive their replies. My grandmother and my Auckland friend were my only other sources of advice about my pregnancy, adding a layer of personal experience to the more objective information I had gleaned from the library book.

One Sunday, when we had been married about three months, we were having lunch with Yvonne and Rex as was now our habit. Rex was unusually attentive to my sister.

"Let me get that for you." Rex reached over with the jug of water and filled Yvonne's glass as soon as she set it down. Minutes later he stood quickly and left the room, returning shortly with a cushion from the living room. "Here you are," he said as he placed the cushion behind Yvonne's back, patting her on the shoulder before sitting once more.

Remembering the early days of my maman's illness, I tried to spot anything similar in my sister. Did she always take sips of water so frequently? Was her appetite the same as usual? I felt a jolt in my own stomach that had nothing to do with my growing child. Yvonne seemed cheerful enough, laughing at Harold's light conversation. I switched my attention to Rex but I couldn't work it out.

At last we finished the meal and moved through to the lounge. Yvonne poured the tea into each cup, handing them around, then sat close to Rex on the sofa. He stretched an arm along the back, pulling her closer still.

He cleared his throat dramatically. "Harold, Elise. We have something to tell you."

I clutched my cup tightly and glanced at Harold. He seemed unconcerned, wearing instead a look of polite enquiry.

"Elise, it's good news. Relax before you break my china!" Yvonne was laughing.

I recalled our parents gathering us to tell us of her diagnosis when I was just a child. I felt hands around mine, bringing me back to the present.

"Elise, I promise. It's not like that," Yvonne said, holding my eyes with hers. "I'm expecting, Elise. Do you 'ear me? We will 'ave little ones to grow up together." She prised my fingers from the cup one by one.

Like thick honey running from a spoon, her words flowed over my anxious thoughts. I searched her face.

She nodded.

I threw my arms around her, pulling her on top of me. Laughing, I hugged her as tightly as I'd gripped the cup, I banished the memories that had promised to undo me just a few minutes before. She patted my back.

"Ok Elise, it's ok." She gently pulled away.

"Congrats, folks," I heard Harold say.

Yvonne returned to Rex's side, tucking her feet up beside her like we'd done as girls and snuggling into him. His arm tightened once more.

"Elise's old room is now the nursery. In fact, we've already made a start on redecorating. Yvonne, take your sister through while Harold helps me clear the table."

Yvonne led the way down the hall. She stood in the hall, letting me go ahead of her into my old room. The smell of paint and wallpaper paste assailed me. I held a hand to my face to muffle it as I gazed about the room.

"Yes, it's rather potent, isn't it? We 'ave the window open in 'ere as much as possible. But what do you think?"

Three of the walls were now a soft shade of buttery yellow, while the wall containing the window was papered in stripes of cream and yellow. In the centre of the room was a wooden trestle table, with a roll of narrow paper still in its wrapping.

Yvonne moved around me and picked up the roll, tearing a section of the wrapping open.

"This will go around the top edge of the walls. See? It's an English alphabet with cute little animals. We decided yellow and cream would be fine for a boy or a girl."

I nodded. "I love it, Yvonne! You've done so much. Wait, 'ow long 'ave you known?"

She grinned mischievously, reminding me of a much younger version of herself. "We suspected for a while, but we wanted to be very sure before we told anyone. And, Rex wanted to 'ave this at least started. 'e's been in 'ere every evening working on it for about two weeks. I can't tell you the lengths 'e's gone to, to make sure you'd not notice anything until we were ready to share the news!"

A slow whistle came from behind me. Harold walked in. "He has been a busy fellow, hasn't he?" He stood in the centre of the room and turned slowly on the spot. He walked over to the wallpapered wall, reaching out a hand to run it down a join. "I'm impressed."

"So you should be," said a voice behind him. " It's not as easy as it might look. When you buy your own place, you might be glad to have an experienced hand to teach you." Rex stood in the doorway, a superior look on his face.

Harold grinned. "I think I'd rather pay someone than try this myself. I'm not cut out for decorating; give me a saw or an axe and trees to attack any day of the week."

Yvonne and I spent more time together from then on. Shopping became a fun day out as we searched stores for nursery furniture: brand new for her, second hand for me of course. I slowly learned to make more informed decisions as the months went by, Yvonne's example building my confidence.

"It's just like the fish market back 'ome, Elise, you decide a price and stick to it."

Though we couldn't decorate the second bedroom as Yvonne and Rex could theirs, week by week I was slowly making it more suitable for our baby.

"'arold, I 'ave something to show you." I took him through to the baby's room and pointed to the neat pile of not-so-new but brightly patterned drapes. "Aren't they so much nicer? Would you mind 'anging them for me, please? I can't quite reach."

"Where did you get them? They look new." He looked worried.

"They were at a second'and store. The lady said some people just give them away when they want a change."

He shook his head in wonder. "Their loss then. Right, let's get these boring ones down." He fetched a chair from

151

the dining room, climbed up and began unhooking the old curtains from the track. Soon the grey ones were gone, and the bright, cheerful ones up in their place.

In another store we'd found a small crib that I convinced Harold to paint for me. I'd had to show him how much a brand new one was, compared to what I'd paid for the crib, before he gave in. Rex and Yvonne gave us some paint they had left over from their nursery.

A second set of drapes was sacrificed to make cushion covers and a coverlet for the crib. Thankfully, Yvonne and I were able to find brand new crib sheets at a very reasonable price. My sewing was improving, but I was slow and soon running out of time. As my stomach swelled, I found my energy level dropped and I needed to take naps every day.

One evening when Harold arrived home from work, he went through to the baby's room. At first I thought he was checking on my progress, but when I followed him, a heavy sigh escaped him.

"What is it, 'arold?" I followed his gaze, but couldn't see anything amiss.

He turned and brushed past me as he left the room, his expression dark and closed off.

We ate in silence. When I could no longer stand it, I asked "Was the meat all right, 'arold?"

He shrugged, cleared his plate and left the table.

Because I now needed to sleep during the day, there were some days when I didn't have dinner ready to serve him when he walked in.

"I'm sorry, 'arold, it's only cold cuts tonight. I was so very tired today."

He surveyed the table with a frown. "I suppose I should

be grateful there's anything ready to eat." He grumbled as he served himself.

After that first week when he'd gone out with his friends to thank them for their help, there would been a month or so when he'd stayed in every night. One morning, he kissed me quickly goodbye.

"Oh, I nearly forgot. Don't worry about dinner for me tonight. I'm meeting up with the boys."

My face fell.

He sighed and shook his head. "Don't be like that. I haven't seen them for ages. This way you don't have to bother with cooking."

I smiled, waving goodbye, but once the door was shut I found myself in tears. The day loomed long before me. I was growing stout as the day of our child's delivery drew closer. Was that why he barely spoke to me or looked at me when he was home? Was that why he didn't want to even have dinner with me? With no way to answer those questions, I washed my face and got on with my housework.

When I woke the next morning, the room was still dark. I lay there a moment, wondering what had roused me. Harold snorted, rolling over in his sleep. I had no idea what time he'd got home. But as he turned in bed, a wave of sour, stale beer washed over me. Memories flooded in. I sat up, reaching for my dressing gown and slippers and left the room as quickly and quietly as I had woken. After a quick cup of tea and a piece of dry toast – all I could manage to force down at this hour – I busied myself getting his breakfast and lunch made.

"Right, I'm off," Harold called through the bedroom door while I dressed.

" 'ave a nice day." No kiss this morning then. I tried to

153

tell myself I didn't care but this was the first day since we'd married that he hadn't kissed me goodbye.

I was glad that Saturday's were already washing days, as I awkwardly bent to strip the bedding, holding my breath against the foul odour.

When I'd done all the chores I could find to do, I sat down and opened up the pregnancy book.

"Oh!" I had turned to a new section. It explained about lesser known changes – like the sense of smell. Now I realised why I'd had such a strong reaction to the smell of alcohol that morning. Apparently I was fortunate to still enjoy cooking meat: for some women in my state, that went off the menu until their child was born.

Friday nights alone became a routine. So far as I could tell, he had never come home actually drunk, but that awful smell woke me every Saturday. I learned to read the weather early on, getting the sheets on the line to catch any breath of wind and every warm ray from the sun. Those weekends I successfully banished those memories that threatened me. But if it rained, the laundry would dry more slowly inside, spread over the backs of the dining room chairs while I rested from my efforts. Then I'd see Edmond, my older brother, and Papa in my mind's eye. Back in those dark days after Papa's accident, I had been very young and most things that happened in the world of adults around me went right over my head. Papa's accident changed that forever. Impressions, disjointed pictures played out, seen still from my childhood perspective. Maman dropping a bowl as I sat having lunch in the kitchen. Even my deaf grandmother had jumped at the crash as the ceramic bowl shattered over the stone floor. Edmond running into the kitchen, face grey, covered in dust or dirt, words tumbling on top of each other. Screams waking me and my sister in the night, sending me scurrying into her bed for comfort; eating dinner with just Maman, Grand-mère and my younger brothers and sisters; Papa and Edmond coming home late, navigating the path up our hill with great care only to oftentimes bump into the side of the house. As if they'd forgotten where the door was. I remember giggling the first time it happened.

"Hush Elise!" my mother had snapped, her tone sharper than I'd ever heard. I'd risked a glance around the table but no one would meet my eyes.

I don't know how long that season lasted for Papa and Edmond, but it was as if we were in our own private winter; the sun didn't seem capable of penetrating the gloom that had settled. Once the bandages were off, Papa wore a hat, pulled down low over his face, even at the dinner table. Edmond wore a frown that seemed etched into him, never changing. Each memory would hit with an almost physical force as week by week, I saw my husband's face take on that same frown.

My only escape from the miasma of worry over my marriage was my weekly visits to Yvonne. Now that we could share this time as first mothers, our relationship grew ever closer. And, being just that little bit ahead of her in this one thing, there were now times where I could advise her or help ease a worry over a twinge or change.

Our Sunday lunches at Yvonne's got awkward. Each week after we'd eaten, Harold would clear off his plate, push it away, knife and fork lined up neatly in the centre, saying. "Right, I'm off." Then he'd stand up, thank Yvonne for the meal and disappear. It had become a habit. The first time it happened, Rex and Yvonne carried on as if nothing had happened. When it happened a second time, Rex got up from the table and began clearing the dishes, giving Yvonne a quick nod.

"Elise, let's go out to the garden. I don't know about you, but I need to walk after a meal now." Yvonne stood at the door, beckoning me to follow.

Maybe the walk would rid me of the queasy feeling in my stomach. I pushed my chair back and stood.

Outside, we walked in silence at first. I trailed fingers over the flower heads lining the path, letting their soft edges soothe me. The myriad of perfumes invited me to breathe deeply, letting them calm me further. Some were so familiar, like the frangipani, evincing the tropical fruit aromas of home. Others I'd grown to love since moving here, like the manuka with its sweet, heady smell that drew in bees when it flowered.

"Elise, I need to ask you something. Please do not be offended."

I rubbed the pollen between my fingers, focusing on the soft grittiness against my skin.

Yvonne touched my sleeve. "Elise, look at me." Satisfied she had my attention, she continued. "'ow long has that been going on?" She waved vaguely towards the street, where we'd all heard Harold drive off. "Is 'e all right? Are you both all right?" Sighing, I looked over her shoulder, dimly taking in the harbour waters glittering in the sunlight. "I really do not know, Yvie. 'e doesn't talk to me very much, and when 'e does, I 'ave usually done something to displease 'im." I kept my face turned, determined not to give in to the self pity that gnawed at me.

We walked further from the house, Yvie leading the way. When we reached the edge of the water, she lowered herself carefully to the ground, gesturing for me to do the same. We took off our shoes and put our feet in the cool water.

As the current gently lapped at my ankles, I felt myself relax and let go of the anxiousness that gripped me daily, feeling my lips pull in a smile for the first time in weeks. I leaned back on my hands and turned my face to the sun. Once more silence enveloped us. Though nothing had changed, the silence was less charged now. "What is it about being near water that makes everything seem fine?" I mused.

Yvie chuckled lazily by my side. "I don't know, and I don't care. That it does is all I need to know. Now" –I felt her turn her gaze back to me– "Elise, do you think," she stopped.

I met her eyes at last. I knew what she was trying so delicately to ask. I nodded. "Yes. Oh, 'e never comes in the way Papa and Edmond used to, barely able to walk. I will say that. But 'e smells of beer and smoke. Every Friday, Yvie. And 'e comes in later than 'e used to." Unable to stop myself at last, tears sprang and I clutched my face in my hands. "Yvie, I don't know what I did wrong or what to do to fix it. I'm scared."

Her arm came around my shoulder as she pulled me to her, letting me have my moment of weakness. "Why did you not come to me sooner?"

I sat up again, fumbling in my cardigan pocket for a handkerchief. I shook my head as I blew my nose and wiped my eyes. "I took a vow, remember? To put 'im first, for better or worse? I do not want to speak ill of my 'usband and I wouldn't 'ave said anything if you 'ad not pushed me."

"That's what big sisters are for, little sister. If you can't tell me, then 'oo? Now " –she patted my back quickly, then drew her feet out of the water, shaking them– "we need to decide what, if anything, we can do to make this time easier on you. Would you like me to say anything to Rex?"

Startled, I shook my head. "No! Please no. If 'arold found I'd said anything, especially to 'is boss – that's still 'ow 'e sees Rex – I don't know what 'e would do. And I do not want our private life to affect 'is work. With 'ow 'e is about money, that would be a disaster!" I paused, gathering my thoughts. "Even telling you, feels almost like I am betraying 'im. Maybe I should not 'ave said anything." I shook my head again, pulled my feet from the water and dried them on the grass. "Please forget what I said, Yvie. It will sort itself out. Please?" I helped her stand, holding both her hands a little longer, hoping the strength of my grip would convince her.

She considered me silently, then nodded. "If that is what you really want, then yes. Of course I will keep your confidence. But Elise, please do not put yourself or your little one in danger. If anything were to 'appen to you, I could not forgive myself."

"It's for the best, Yvie, you'll see. I was just feeling sorry for myself. I 'ave a lot to learn about being a wife. Maman—" My voice caught in my throat. I took a breath and tried again. "Maman set us a good example. Now I must follow that." I squeezed her fingers then released her. This time I led the way along the path. "You know what I would like, Yvie?" I said, changing the subject completely.

"What's that?"

"Would you 'elp me get some flowers going in my garden? The smell out here is so delicious! I'm sure it would brighten my 'ouse up to 'ave some there."

It seemed she'd been waiting for me to ask, as she overtook me and guided me to her garden shed. We collected some small pots, a trowel and secateurs. We spent a happy hour gathering cuttings and digging up a small plant here or there to transplant, nestling each gently into a pot of soil. Yvie reminded me of the names of each in English and what each needed in terms of light and care.

By the time Harold returned, we were pleasantly tired from our exertions and I was ready to go home and get started in my garden. If he was surprised at my lack of concern over his absence today, he didn't show it. He merely took in my selection of pots and carried them to the boot of the car.

* * *

I was even more careful with my spending now, saving on groceries in any way I could while still putting a good dinner on the table for Harold. The only money I spent on baby needs or the garden was what I managed to save from the housekeeping allowance he gave me once a week.

We'd been living in an unacknowledged strain for several months when he surprised me one Saturday at breakfast. He'd been reading his newspaper, when suddenly he snapped it back into its folds and slapped it on the table.

"Have you made any plans for dinner tonight, Elise?"

I stared for a moment, stunned that he even addressed me. "I 'ave a joint in the pantry that I was going to roast."

He waved a hand dismissively. "That can wait another day or so, can't it? It won't spoil? I realised we haven't been out together since" –he waved a hand again, in the direction of my figure– "you know? So, I thought, how about a walk by the sea and a light dinner out tonight? What do you say?"

I felt my face lighten, relieved that he seemed to be his old self. "That would be lovely, 'arold. Yes, I can put the meat back in the cooler for Monday." I grinned like a schoolgirl.

He reddened slightly, clearing his throat. "I'll just need time to clean up when I get home from work, then we can go early enough to get our table." He pushed back his chair and continued on in the way he'd done for months now. But as he was about to go through the front door, I heard him walk back down the hall to the kitchen, where I was already at the sink, rinsing the dishes. I felt him kiss the top of my head. "I'll see you later," he said gruffly, then walked quickly out of the house.

I stood stock-still for several minutes after he left, my hands locked around the edge of the plate I had been rinsing. The baby wriggled inside me, a foot prodding my ribs, breaking me out of my stunned stillness. Rubbing my stomach in gentle circles, I spoke to my unborn child. "Good morning, little one. Maman and Papa love you."

When we arrived at the café, Harold held the door open for me. The waitress looked up as I entered, smiling in recognition.

"Hey there, Mrs M! Long time no see." She bustled over and grabbed my hand in a quick squeeze.

"'ello, Sandra." I smiled in reply.

"Give me a minute, and I'll free up your table," she said quietly, winking, then hurried away, pulling out her cloth.

Harold came alongside me, one hand on my back to nudge me away from the doorway. "Maybe we should do this more often, for special service like that."

We watched as the couple at the table listened to Sandra. It looked at first as though they were not going to move, but something she said appeared to convince them, and they stood together, collecting their plates and moving to a table away from the window. Sandra wiped the table down and turned to wave us over.

"I worked my magic, they'll be fine." She leaned in closer. "Just maybe don't look their way for a minute." She went behind the counter and filled a plate with a few cupcakes which she then took to the displaced couple.

Harold picked up the menu, scanning it quickly. "It looks like they've not made any major changes since we were here last. What do you say to the shepherd's pie?"

"Perfect, thank you, 'arold."

I enjoyed the evening off from cooking, and Harold seemed to be more relaxed than I'd seen him for a long time. I couldn't think what had changed, but I refused to spoil it by asking him. Having my husband back to the way he used to be, even if it was just for this evening, was a relief. We talked without reservation for the first time in what felt like years.

After we'd eaten, as promised, he led me down to the sand and we walked slowly, enjoying the sea breeze. He helped me remove my shoes then took his own off, rolling up his trouser cuffs for good measure. I relished feeling his hand wrapped around my own. It seemed he felt the same when he swung our clasped hands forward and back.

"Listen, Elise. I know I've been a bit of a bore lately. Tonight was, well" –he stood still, turning me to face him– "my way of saying sorry. I guess I got a bit scared."

I shook my head in wonder. "Scared? What about?"

He waved his free hand at my stomach. "This! It was one thing to know we were going to be parents, but then, seeing you change so much; and all the things you kept talking about that we'd need. I couldn't see how my pay was going to cover it all, or how I was supposed to know what to do as a dad. And I guess you've figured that when I panic, I'm not much fun to be around." He pulled me in for a hug. "I started blaming you in my head. Can you forgive me?"

I nodded into his shoulder. "Of course, 'arold." I pulled back and looked up. "But what's changed? Why now?"

He had the grace to look a little sheepish. "You can probably thank your sister for that. Indirectly at least. Did you say something to her?"

I felt my face grow hot. "Sort of. But I told 'er to forget about it. I was just feeling a bit sorry for myself one Sunday. I'm sorry, 'arold! I never meant to say anything. It's our business, no one else's."

He laughed then. "Trust you! I act like a total numbskull and you try to blame yourself. You don't need to apologise. I didn't really give you much choice did I? Waking up every day like a bear with a sore head, and coming home not much better."

I hadn't realised how worried I'd been about him finding out until I noticed then a release in my muscles.

He rubbed a hand down my back. "Anyway, she didn't forget, clearly. That boss of mine stood me on the carpet at work a few days ago. He laid down the law about, how did he put it?" He frowned for a moment. His brow cleared. "Oh yeah, being a man about it. That I had no one to blame but myself for the situation we're in so early in our marriage. I think one of the boys must have dobbed me in as well, because he mentioned a certain establishment I've been seen at. Mr C said he knows the owners, and has told them not to serve me if I'm there again before the baby's born. And, if I am seen there, my job will be toast."

I stumbled, grabbing his arm. "Oh, 'arold!"

"No, love, it's ok. I get it. Here I was harping on at you for anything you spent money on, and I was drinking away more of my wages than you asked for. I'm sorry."

From then on, it seemed he had indeed turned over a new leaf. He came home straight from work, and if he sometimes seemed a little restless at dinner, at least now I knew why and found subjects to distract him. Now and then I'd encourage him to take a walk after dinner. I was growing too tired by the end of the day to accompany him.

19

Winter 1948

We'd gone to bed at the same time one Friday night, but while Harold fell quickly asleep, I found it difficult to get comfortable. I tossed the covers on and off, one moment too warm, only to grow cold soon after. Eventually I got up and waddled – it really was the only word for the way I walked now – to the kitchen, one hand supporting my belly. I set about making myself a cup of tea, but as I sat down to wait for the kettle to boil, a cramp gripped me suddenly, forcing a cry from my throat. I grabbed the edge of the kitchen table. Just as suddenly as it had arrived, it was gone. My tired mind failed to make sense of what had happened. I got up, poured the hot water into the tea pot and carried the pot and a cup through to the lounge. A second cramp hit as I bent to put the pot on a side table. My cup fell from my hand, bouncing onto the table then the sofa. I stayed bent, breathing fast, my mind focused on the cramp. It was only as this one also passed that I noticed the tightness was across my distended stomach. I slowly straightened, stood for a moment, thinking, before nodding to myself. I made my way delicately back to the bedroom. Touching his shoulder, I gently shook my husband.

"Wake up please, 'arold."

He grunted but remained asleep.

I shook him again, a little harder. "'arold, I need you to wake up. Please."

He rolled over, eyes still closed. "What is it?" His voice was muffled under his arm.

Just then a third cramp hit me, and once more I cried out, the hand I had still on his shoulder clenching involuntarily.

"Elise?!"

"Oh!" I clamped my eyes shut as I fought the wave of pain.

He threw the covers back and fumbled to stand in front of me. He took my hand from his shoulder, turning me around slowly. As the pain subsided, my face relaxed and he lowered me onto the bed. He crouched down beside me. "What do you need me to do?"

I breathed with my mouth open and held a hand out – wait. "I think you need to get dressed and find a telephone. Call my doctor. 'is telephone number is in my purse." I closed my eyes again, curled up on my side.

The next few hours blurred as my mind turned inward and the world around me seemed to be out of reach.

* * *

I woke to the sun streaming onto my face, confused for a second. I opened my eyes to orient myself. Oh, yes. I patted behind me to find the edge of the bed much closer than I was used to. Looking down, I saw crisp white sheets in place of my own soft cream ones. I rolled onto my back, realising as I did so that I was propped on several pillows. The sunshine which had woken me was pouring in from the window to my right. At home, the window was on the other side of the room, and the sun didn't reach there until later in the day. A noise on my right made me turn my head. The door opened and a capped head peered around the door jam.

"Oh good. You're awake then. Good morning, Mrs McRae." The nurse swung the door fully open then swept into the room. She came over to the bed. "How are we feeling this morning? You certainly worked hard last night!" She smiled kindly.

I pushed myself more upright. As I did so, she reached behind me, fluffing the pillows and standing them up against the bedhead. I smiled and thanked her breathlessly. I leaned back against them, worn out from the simple exercise. She stood expectantly. I realised I hadn't answered her question.

"Sorry. A little sore – tender really – but I am all right, thank you."

She patted my shoulder. "Tender and sore is to be expected. You just produced a whole new person! You'll start to feel better over the next few days." She lifted my arm and pressed two fingers to the inside of my wrist. Her other hand lifted her fob watch from the front of her uniform. She stared at it for a minute before laying my arm back down and tucking the sheet around me. "That's all good, your pulse is pretty normal for the circumstances. We'll be bringing breakfast through shortly, but would you like to see your son?"

My eyes were suddenly hot as shame ripped through. I'd not even thought to ask for him! A great mother I was starting out to be. My nurse, observant as I guessed she'd have to be in her work, patted me again.

"Now, now, don't take on so. You've been awake mere minutes, from a well deserved sleep. He's fine, we took him into the nursery with the other babies. He's also had a great sleep. Wait there, and I'll bring him through. Then, if you're up to it, I'll show you how to get him feeding. How does that sound?"

I nodded, not trusting my voice.

She bustled away, and I took the few minutes alone to regain some self control. She was right, I had barely woken.

"Young man, come meet your mummy." Her voice came through the open door before I saw her. A cot on wheels came first, her hands visible on the frame as she came through behind it. "Let's get you two acquainted. Do we have a name for him yet?"

I shook my head. "We talked about a few choices, but we didn't make a final decision yet. He arrived a bit before we were expecting." I managed a thin smile.

She shook her head. "It happens often. Not usually with a first child, but you are young and he was impatient to meet you! Is your husband coming to see you today?"

I used my hands to try to sit up straighter. "I think so, later on. 'e will 'ave to go to work, and 'e will want to tell our families."

"Excellent! That means we girls get this young man to ourselves for a few hours, and it gives you time to learn how to assuage his hunger. May I ask, are you French? I couldn't help but notice you have a bit of an accent." As we'd been talking, she'd checked the baby's diaper, wrapped him firmly in a light blanket, and lifted him into her arms. Now she nudged the cot out of the way with one hip, then brought him to the edge of my bed. "Mrs McRae, meet the new Master McRae." So saying, she leaned in and laid him gently in my arms.

I stared at the little screwed up face before me. I don't think

I'd ever seen such a small person. His skin was a bright pink, as though he'd just been scrubbed in the bath. He had a little dark hair, standing up on its ends from the crown of his head. Both arms had been bound against him by the blanket, tiny fists scrunched at either side of his face. As I watched, he blinked both eyes a couple of times before his brow lifted and his eyes went wide. He appeared to be looking all about him but without turning his head.

"He'll figure it out in a minute. He's learning to focus."

I nodded, hearing her but unable to take my eyes off my son. He jumped as a tear landed on his cheek. I lifted him to my face, unwilling to support him on just one arm, and wiped his little face against mine. My own eyes closed as I breathed him in for the first time. I searched my memory for words to describe the smell. Fresh air and sun on dried laundry, mixed with something like vanilla. That was the closest I could come up with. I buried my nose into his neck. Along with the heavenly aroma, his skin was soft and warm against mine. I felt him answer my embrace as he rubbed his face into me, those tiny fists working to free themselves from his blanket cocoon.

I whispered. "'ello my son. It is good to meet you at last." At the sound of my voice I felt him relax completely into me and his breathing lightened. I opened my eyes and turned to my nurse.

She nodded, smiling. "It's ok. He's fallen asleep again. Remember, he's heard your voice from the inside for nine months. He knows he is safe now." She laughed quietly. "So much for feeding him. We'll try after you've eaten." She leaned over me again, showing me how to hold him safely in my left arm. "Now you can keep a hold of him while you eat your own breakfast. We have to feed you up so you make plenty of his food!"

My baby stayed fast asleep as I ate. I revelled in the twin joys of holding my son and being waited on.

In between the various nurses stopping by throughout the day, I napped. I was surprised at how tired I remained. I woke to feed my son and myself then slept some more. A nurse came and took my baby back to the nursery once they were satisfied he had fed. I lost track of time as I drifted in and out of consciousness. So it was somewhat of a shock when I awoke to see Harold standing in the doorway. He smiled.

"Hey there sleepyhead." He came all the way in, one hand behind his back. "I brought you something." With a flourish he brought his hand in front. He held out a colourfully wrapped bouquet. "Ta da!" He laid it on my bed, leaning down to give me a kiss.

"Oh, 'arold, they're lovely!" I hugged him tightly, then picked the flowers up, holding them up to breathe them in. "They smell almost as good as our son." His face dropped. I laughed loudly, glad to have caught him off guard. "Thank you." I waved him back to me and kissed him once more. "I mean it, they look and smell beautiful. 'ave you seen the baby yet?"

He searched my face, then smiled. "So, now you've had a baby you've learned to tease me? I can see I'll have to watch you. And yes, I saw him last night before they chased me out. They have a waiting room for us chaps. Once they made sure which one I was, they brought the little guy out to meet me. He was very red!"

I swiped a hand at him halfheartedly. "Well, 'e 'ad worked 'ard for hours!"

Harold's face grew serious again. "Yeah, you had me worried

for a while there. I couldn't believe how long it was taking. I guess you were pretty knackered by the end?" He grabbed my hand, squeezing it. He looked down at our hands then raised them, turning them over so mine was on top. He kissed the back of my hand.

I reached over, finding myself comforting him. I realised, being out in that room, not knowing what was happening to me, had been almost as hard on him as my exertions had been on me. I was learning that he wasn't great at relinquishing control. He found a chair, placed it next to my bed and flopped down into it.

"I asked a nurse if we can see our son together. She's checking with that matron in charge. Figured I may as well make myself comfortable while we wait."

At last the nurse came in, our son cradled efficiently in her arms. "Here we are then, young fella. Time to get properly acquainted with your dad. Mr McRae?" Her look made Harold hasten to stand. She passed the baby over, and in a matter of fact manner showed how to hold him safely.

Harold smiled his thanks.

"I'll leave the three of you alone for," she checked her watch. "Let's say half an hour. Then I'm afraid the new dad here will have to make tracks, as it'll be time for baby's next feed and lunch for mum here."

I thanked her as I watched Harold, just as I had that morning, fall completely under the spell of our young son. His face softened in a way I'd never seen. As if he'd always known what to do, he extricated one hand and gently stroked the baby's cheek.

"We need to decide on 'is name. I can't keep referring to 'im as 'our son' or 'the baby'."

Without taking his eyes away, Harold answered readily. "He's Stephen. After my granddad. Stephen James. You happy with that?"

I tried it out in my mind. Stephen James McRae. "Yes, I think so. When did you choose that?" Stephen now had a fist wrapped tightly around Harold's fingertip. Harold finally looked up at me. "It was one we'd already talked about so after I'd seen him last night, I thought about it until I fell asleep. I was still tossing up between either of those as a first name, until just now. I can see he's got my granddad's eyes. You are sure you're all good with that?"

I nodded firmly. "Completely. To be honest, I'd not thought about 'is name until this morning when the nurse asked about it." We grinned as he perched on the edge of my bed beside me, moving Stephen around so he was facing us both.

"Welcome to the family, Stephen James McRae." Harold kissed me and handed our son to me.

"I'll go fill in the family, shall I? Of course, I told Mr C at work as soon as I arrived, but I've not had time to tell my folks yet. I'll check with the venerable Matron how long until she lets you come home. You two get some rest ok? And don't worry about me, fending for myself like a bachelor for a few days!"

Cuddling Stephen to me, I smiled in satisfaction that my husband seemed to be back to his old self, taking charge and caring for me. Us.

By the time I was due to go home, I had grown confident in feeding, changing and bathing the baby. The nurses were patient but expectant about my progress. They didn't let me back away from doing any of it myself after that first day, and gradually withdrew their help. My natural tendency to stay out of the limelight vied with the understanding that this was for my good: I would have no help at home in these maternal duties.

Harold arrived in the afternoon of my last day at the home, surprising me with a new carrycot. It was the one thing left on our list when I went into labour.

"It's perfect, thank you, 'arold." I was up and dressed, so we put the carrycot on the bed and I folded a little blanket, lining it. Stephen's nursery crib was now in my room, so I lifted him out and laid him gently in his new bed, removing the home's swaddling and replacing it with our own which Harold had also brought in.

"You'd think you'd been doing that for years," he said, as he watched me wrap Stephen in the sheet the way the nurses had taught me.

I tied the cover over the baby's legs and tummy. Being appreciated was a brand new sensation.

I sat in the back of the car, Stephen's carry cot on the seat beside me. I kept one hand resting on the cover over his tummy. Suddenly I was aware of every bump and stop, worried that the cot would slip and my child would get hurt.

Despite my trepidation, we made it safely home and Harold carried Stephen while I hefted my luggage through to the wash house. I walked back through to find the two of them together on the sofa.

Harold grinned. "I could get used to this. Sitting and looking at this wee chap."

I took the baby from him, settling Stephen on my shoulder. I found myself talking to him as I walked around my house for the first time in several days. I showed him his room, opening his drawer to see the tiny clothes nestled there waiting to be put to use. I took him through to the back garden, telling him about the flowers and trees as if he could understand me. The door to the house opened so I turned.

"Yvie! I didn't know you were coming!"

She hurried over, smiling. "Never mind that." She gave me a peck on the cheek before firmly taking Stephen from me. "Let me see you, mon chéri!" She laughed at my expression. "Just because you are 'is maman, you think you get to 'ave all the cuddles? Thanks to you, I am an aunty before I am a maman myself, so 'e will be my practice, yes?" She laughed again so loudly that Stephen started and began to grizzle.

"You're off to a great start there, Aunty Yvonne, making 'im cry the moment you set eyes on 'im." I took him back just as firmly, rocking side to side while letting him nuzzle into my neck.

My sister looked momentarily taken aback but recovered quickly. She flapped a hand at me. "No matter. 'e will get used to me. 'ow was it? Are you all right?"

I realised what she was really asking. Her nervousness for her own time showed through. "I am fine. Yes, it is difficult, and painful, I won't lie." She blanched. I laid a hand on her arm. "But even then, you know why it 'urts, and you know it will be over and you will see your child. At least, that was 'ow I felt. All my mind shut out what was 'appening around me, and I just 'ad to concentrate. I slept very well after, I can tell you!"

Her face relaxed. "Thank you, Elise. That does set my mind at rest."

I led the way back inside, to find Rex and Harold already settled in the lounge, tea made on the side table.

Life settled into a new routine, my days now revolving

around Stephen's needs. My energy gradually returned to normal. I spent most of my time in the kitchen, as I could have Stephen in his carrycot on the table while I worked. Harold came home straight from work now and I always had the evening meal ready for him.

One night, I woke to hear Stephen crying. Not like his normal whimpery cries that told me he was hungry. Somehow I knew he was in pain. I raced to his cot.

"There there, my child, maman is 'ere. What is it?" I jiggled him up and down, clasped to my shoulder. He rubbed his face frantically against me, his cries continuing. Reluctant to turn on a light, I instead opened the drapes to let a little moonlight fall on his face. His cheeks were red and his little legs were drawn up against his tummy. As I watched, he screwed his face up even tighter and let out a wail. I dimly remembered one of the mother's help books I'd read and I realised what was going on. "Oh dear, you 'ave a sore tummy my love? Come on, I think I remember what the book said to do." I turned him around and laid him along my forearm, tummy down and snug against me. Walking up and down our short hall, I rubbed his little back. His crying gradually slowed and his legs relaxed until I heard a loud belch. There was a sudden wet warmth on my wrist. "Oh!" I was louder than I realised, startling my son. Back in his room I managed to find a clean cloth diaper in the dark, using it to clean us both up.

So began the broken nights of near constant colic. After that first night, I had to try something different almost every night. My own tiredness often meant that I didn't always wake as quickly as I would like. At the start, Harold slept through the disturbances, but as I became more tired, Stephen's cries grew more strident, waking even his deep-sleeping father. Harold would wake me before pulling his pillow over his head to try to go back to sleep.

One morning, after a particularly rough night, I hadn't long got back to bed before it was time to get up again. Harold sat at the table across from me, staring at the toast on his plate. "Hardly what I'd call a decent breakfast for a working man." His tone was sharp and I flinched as though I'd been slapped.

"I'm sorry, 'arold, I 'aven't 'ad time to cook. Stephen…"

His chair scraped harshly as he pushed away from the table. "Yeah, I know. He was crying enough to wake the whole street! You need to sort it out, I've had just about enough. I need my sleep, for crying out loud."

"I am trying, 'arold. I've tried so 'ard. Maybe I should take 'im to the doctor?"

"Yeah, and where am I supposed to find the money for that?"

I stood, speechless at his coldhearted words.

"I'm off. I'll find myself something for lunch. And don't bother about dinner. You just get that kid sorted, hear me?"

I jumped as he slammed the front door behind him. A wail came from Stephen's room.

Once more I tiptoed around Harold in the mornings, determined to do nothing to further aggravate his mood. There were nights when I woke up alone, his side of the bed cold, unused.

20

Spring 1948

Stephen's cries hardly registered. I sat in the living room of the little house, lost in the fog of my thoughts. Harold had not come home from work. Again. Each time it happened, I worried that it was my fault, but without any idea as to what I could have done. He got so angry at times.

My son's need for me went unanswered until a pounding on the front door jarred me back to the present.

I pressed on the arms of the chair and stood up. "There, there, my son, Maman is back now my love." I lifted him from the carrycot, arranging him on my shoulder to soothe him as I walked out of the room towards the front door. "Yes, yes, I am coming. 'oo is there please?" I asked, opening the front door. Two uniformed men stood at the foot of the porch, frowning up at me.

"Sorry to bother you, ma'am, but we are looking for a" –the older one checked his notebook– "a Mr Harold McRae. Is he home?"

I gripped my son more tightly. My stomach twisted. "I, I'm sorry. No, 'e isn't back from work yet." I looked from one to the other. "Why? 'as something 'appened?"

"You could say that. However, we can't discuss that with you at this time. When do you expect him home?"

My tension was unsettling Stephen further and he grizzled against my neck. I jiggled him gently up and down, trying to comfort us both. "I don't really know. 'e comes in late some days, straight from work on others."

The one with the notebook jotted something down. He looked up, touched his hat peak and bobbed his head. "Sorry again for disturbing you, ma'am. We'll pop back a little later, see if he's turned up. In the meantime, if he does come home, might be best not to mention our visit. All right?"

I nodded, not really understanding, but wanting them gone.

Inside, the door shut once more, I changed Stephen's diaper and put him to bed, snuggling his comfort toy beside him. I retreated to the living room, having made myself a cup of tea. Now I was more worried than ever. I had no experience with the law, hadn't a clue as to what Harold could have done to come to their attention. As well, I did not know what, if anything, I would say if he did come home. Yes, as my husband, he deserved my loyalty. But could I disobey an officer of the police?

My drink was cold by the time I remembered I'd poured it. Still Harold wasn't home. I went to bed, my mind in turmoil but unable to stay awake.

I woke the following morning to see the other side of the bed still empty. I rolled onto my back again, staring unseeingly at the ceiling. Throwing back the covers, I picked up my dressing gown, donning it as I made my way to Stephen's bed.

"Good morning, little one. What a good boy to be so quiet." I smiled as I lifted him up, snuggling him into my shoulder, breathing in that wonderful baby smell. "Papa will be 'ome soon I expect. Let's make ourselves presentable for 'im, shall we?"

Anxiousness gnawed at me but I had to keep on with my day, for my son's sake. I did my best to keep things as normal as possible, part of me listening for another knock at the door. It came at last as I was putting Stephen down for a nap around the middle of the morning. I tucked him in and went to the door, shoulders tense. The same men stood impassively on my doorstep.

"Ma'am. Sorry to disturb you again. May we come in?"

I felt cold as I stood back, holding the edge of the door for support. Taking that for consent, they each removed their hats as they stepped within. The one who'd had the notebook last night stared at me for a moment. His face softened.

"How about we go to your kitchen, and my constable here can make us all a cuppa. How's that sound?"

I nodded and led the way, unable to speak. He held a chair out, inviting me to sit at my own kitchen table. The younger one, the constable, was clearly used to this duty, finding his way around my kitchen with ease. Soon we were all three seated, cups steaming in front of us.

The senior officer had passed the time until then asking me seemingly innocent questions. I'd answered automatically, one word or two at a time.

Now they shared a look before he spoke again.

"Mrs McRae. My name is Sergeant Cleaves. This is PC Evans. I'm afraid we have to tell you that your husband has been arrested."

The cup between my hands was scalding but I couldn't let go. I felt the edge of the table just below my elbows, pressing into my skin.

"Mrs McRae. Are you all right? Do you understand what I said?"

His face swam back into focus. He had brown eyes. I was surprised to see there was kindness behind them. I shook my head, trying to dispel the shock. "Yes, I am fine. Arrested? Why? What did 'e do?"

"We were called to attend an incident at the mill where he works. I believe it is run by your brother-in-law?"

I nodded.

"It seems that your husband was the cause of a very serious accident there. One of his workmates is in the hospital. He had to have emergency surgery last night.

I can't tell you much more, but he was in a very bad way when they took him in."

I felt PC Evan's eyes on me. I swallowed. "What does 'arold say 'appened?" My own eyes stayed fixed on Sergeant Cleaves.

"Unfortunately, by the time we got onsite, he had scarpered."

"I'm sorry? I don't know that word."

"I mean he'd run off. Mr Carlisle told us as much as he knew. We've yet to interview the other workers there. They were all in a bit of a state, as you can imagine. We're going back to them after we've finished here. But, as it looks at the moment, it appears your husband was operating some machinery while inebriated. Drunk, I mean."

I sunk my face into my hands, suddenly nauseous.

"This other chap may never work again. At least, not for a long time and likely never in that line of work. We finally found Mr McRae when a publican rang the station to say he had a chap who refused to leave after closing."

I didn't notice I'd sobbed aloud until I felt cloth against the back of one hand. I looked up to see PC Evans offering me his handkerchief. I nodded thank you and wiped my face.

"Mrs McRae. Is there someone we can fetch for you? This has been quite a shock. I think perhaps you shouldn't be alone for now."

I straightened my blouse, pushed my cup away and closed my eyes.

"I'm not sure. I've just put my son down for a sleep. Please" –I looked from one to the other of them– "what 'appens now?"

"We have your husband in custody, in a cell. We let him sleep the drink off before trying to get any sense out of him. Though going by the state he was in when we picked him up, I'd say he may have trouble even remembering what happened yesterday. We'll need to question him as soon as possible. Then, when the injured chap is cleared by the doctor, we'll want to ask him for his story as well. So, can we fetch anyone?"

I shook my head. "There would only be my sister, but she is pregnant, so I wouldn't want to worry her. Though of course, Rex – Mr Carlisle – will 'ave told her already I expect. Thank you for your concern." I stood. "I expect you 'ave a busy day. I am sorry my 'usband 'as been the cause of such a terrible thing. Is the one 'oo was injured able to 'ave visitors? Do you think I should?" Though it was the last thing I wanted to do, I felt I needed to do something to address Harold's actions.

The sergeant shook his head and smiled. "I don't think that would be wise, Mrs McRae. He will only be allowed family for a while anyway, apart from us."

I saw them out, shutting the front door before going back through the house and out the back door. I fell to the grass, my knees biting deep into the soft turf, as I gave into the horror of what I'd just heard. My throat burned and I lay down on my side, curled up in almost physical pain. I cried for myself, for my husband, but most of all I cried for the poor man whose life was now forever altered, perhaps even worse than my father's had been after the mine explosion. At last I pulled myself together, brushing the muddy mess from my knees and returning to the house.

Blessedly, Stephen had slept through the policemen's visit and its aftermath. I peeked into his room to see his eyes still closed, face in complete repose. I gathered up a change of clothes, went through to the bathroom and washed quickly then dressed again. I carried my muddy clothes to the wash house and dumped them there until laundry day.

* * *

Yvonne sent Rex to collect me and take me to her. The drive didn't take long and soon I was being wrapped in the sort of hug only a sister can give, pregnant tummy notwithstanding.

"Let me look at you," she said as she leaned back, holding me at arm's length. Her eyes searched my face, then she nodded. "Just as I thought. You've been worrying yourself sick, I can see!" She took the carrycot from me. "I want a cuddle with that nephew of mine. Come on through."

Rex shook his head, following us into the lounge.

I continued on through to the kitchen to make the tea for us all. Now, sitting down, watching her bounce Stephen gently on her lap, I smiled and relaxed for the first time in what felt like weeks, rather than days.

Yvonne looked up, her face sober. "So, what did the police tell you, Elise?"

I went through it all again.

Rex spoke up. "Thankfully my other chap has pulled through surgery very well. Did better than the doctors expected, but he has a long road ahead of him."

"What actually happened? The police wouldn't go into much detail."

"For starters, if I'd seen the state your man was in when he signed on for the day, I'd have sent him off with a flea in his ear. I think he must have deliberately stayed behind the others at our staff meeting. I don't even remember him being there. Apparently he had gone to start the log feeder. But, for some reason he didn't bother checking the other end of it. Brian – that's the injured fellow – had gone down there to re-grease the mechanism. That's why there were logs left over –the machine had started to jam and he was sorting it out. Now, he did everything by the book. He'd made a note in the log about what he'd found out the day before, and he'd told my foreman and hung the orange warning flag on the peg by the door. Looks like Harold either ignored the flag, or just didn't see it. He definitely didn't check in with my foreman before starting it up. I'm guessing that he was so hung over, or still drunk, that he wasn't paying attention. Brian's sleeve got caught up and tugged him in arm first." His lips were white as if he was seeing it all over again.

"I don't think you ever saw the feeder. Heavy metal ranks of plates overlap and move apart as they move the logs up to the shed. Brian's arm never stood a chance. Thank God that someone heard him scream and hit the emergency stop."

Hand to my mouth, I felt all colour leave my face and I closed my eyes in horror. I could see the vivid scene Rex painted.

"My lads acted mighty fast to get him out and stop the bleeding but it was touch and go for a while. He was unconscious by the time we got the St John's boys out to him."

When I was able to speak, I asked the only thing I could think of. "So, what did 'arold do, or say, when it all went so wrong? Did 'e at least try to 'elp?" I realised I was in tears again as I spoke, and I fumbled in my purse for my hanky.

Rex shook his head. "No, he didn't. As soon as the machine was switched off, he ran. He was gone by the time I got there from the other side of the plant. I've had to piece this altogether from what the rest of them told me. Of course, our first priority was Brian. It took a while before I even thought to ask where Harold was. I wouldn't like to say what I would have done if I had seen him."

Yvonne stood as she took over the conversation. "That's enough for us all tonight. Brian is in the best place for now, 'arold is where 'e can't cause any more trouble, and we can do nothing about any of it. So, Rex, come 'elp me get dinner on the table. Let's try to find something else to discuss for the rest of the evening."

Yvonne came with us when it was time to take Stephen and me home. As I got out of the car, she leaned around to get my attention.

"Now, you are to think about yourself and that child of yours. No moping or worrying about 'arold, you 'ear me? Like I said before, it's out of our control. The best thing you can do for 'im, your baby and you is to get good sleep and try to keep to a routine. Yes?"

"Yes, Yvie."

Back in my own home, I did my best to obey her advice. I managed well while settling Stephen down for the night, but once I'd gotten ready for bed myself, I found my thoughts returning to the horrific scene Rex had described. I bolted for the bathroom, making it just in time as a wave of nausea rose up. I clutched the porcelain, shivering in my nightdress, my head resting on the cold edge between my hands.

I finally got into bed after cleaning up my mess, turning to face the door so as not to see the empty spot on the other side of the bed. I fell quickly into an exhausted and thankfully dreamless sleep.

* * *

As I had no telephone or car, I had to go into town to talk to the police. I was desperate to know what was happening. Finding the police station was the first problem. I found a telephone box and rang the number for the directory. A friendly voice told me the address, and after asking which box I was calling from, gave me the directions as well.

I stood for a few moments on the footpath outside the station, gathering my courage.

At last I turned and walked backwards up the steps, tugging Stephen's pram. An officer held the door open for me on his way out. I smiled my thanks. My voice trembled as I told the man at the desk what I was there for. He jotted something down on a desk pad.

"Do you know the name of the officer in charge of your husband's case?" he asked.

"Yes, it was Sergeant Cleaves."

He nodded and motioned for me to take a seat. "I'll let him know you're here. Someone will come and get you when he's free." He lifted the handset of the telephone and spoke quietly into it.

I turned Stephen's pram around so he could see me, and tried to distract myself by entertaining him. About ten minutes passed before a door beside the desk opened and the young PC who'd come with Sergeant Cleaves stepped through.

"Mrs McRae? If you'd like to follow me please?"

The Sergeant's office door was ajar and the PC reached past me to hold it fully open as I manoeuvred the pram through.

Sergeant Cleaves was sitting behind a desk, reading. He looked up and smiled. "Good morning Mrs McRae. I'm sorry you've had to come all this way. I would have explained anything you wanted to know over the telephone."

"I don't 'ave one, and I didn't really want to discuss it from a public box." He waved me to a seat in front of the desk. PC Evans, I remembered his name now, sat beside me.

"So, what would you like to know?"

"I don't know 'ow this all works, and what I am allowed to know or not. But, what 'appens next? Am I going to be able to see my 'usband? And, I'm sorry but I don't know what to do about money – am I supposed to get 'im a lawyer? And pay our bills? I know that's not your area but..." My shoulders lifted in a helpless shrug as I ran out of steam.

Sergeant Cleaves smiled sympathetically. "Don't worry, I see this all the time, I'm afraid. These young chaps don't realise what they put their families through when they act so irresponsibly. I'm sorry I can only help with some of that. So, let's see if I can take those one by one. Yes, you will be able to see him, but only briefly, and not alone. It's probably best if you leave the young one in here. I'll get one of the ladies from the secretarial pool to come sit with him. As for what happens next, well, he's due to go up before the magistrate for an initial hearing as soon as there is a spot available. I'm hoping that'll happen today so we can move the case along. That's two things answered. As to representation and payment: when I saw you the other evening, I realised that you were unlikely to be in a position to go looking for a lawyer, so I started the ball rolling to have the court appoint someone to be his legal advisor in court. It's usual in cases like this."

I looked down at my son, blissfully unaware of the seriousness of our plight.

"In regards to your personal financial situation, I can't advise you at all. But it's usually best to tell your landlord as early as possible. Criminal cases end up in the local newspaper, especially when it involves serious injury, so you don't want him finding out that way. See if he's willing to give you a bit of time to work things out. Your brother-in-law is your husband's boss, so no doubt he'll see you don't go without?"

I nodded mutely, trying to think. In the end I shut the door on the rising panic over the bills and talking to a landlord I'd never met; I focussed instead on seeing Harold shortly.

"So, if you're ready, I'll get young Evans here to go get us a babysitter then he can take you through to one of our interview rooms. He'll have to stay in the room with you, and I must warn you, you won't be allowed to touch Mr McRae. Do you understand?" He motioned at the young officer, who quickly left the room on his errand. I avoided the sergeant's gaze, looking out the window, seeing nothing. The door opened after a polite knock.

"Maggie. This is Mrs McRae. She's here to see her husband for a little while. If you can sit with the lad here. Stephen, is it?"

I nodded.

"Of course sir." Maggie came over and held out a hand.

I shook it, still unused to women greeting me this way.

"Thank you Maggie," I said. I leaned over Stephen and brushed his face gently. "Maman will be back soon, ok?" I followed PC Evans out of the room and further down the hall. He opened a door and stood back.

"If you could wait here please, I'll go fetch Mr McRae." He shut the door. In the middle of the room was a simple table with a chair on either side. I took the chair closest and sat my purse on my lap.

The door opened and Harold came through in front of the officer, who gave him a nudge towards the other seat, pulled the door closed and went to stand in a corner where he could see both our faces.

I don't know quite what I was expecting, but Harold's appearance shocked me to my core. He was unshaven and his hair flopped unkempt over his face. He had clearly not bathed since I'd last seen him, days before. His clothes were visibly dirty and I noticed he had no shoes or socks on. He noticed me looking at his feet.

"Yeah, they took my laces away so I figured bare feet was easier than loose shoes. Thanks for coming." His voice was rough. He seemed to be finding it hard to look me in the face. He laid his hands on the table between us and hung his head. "So, they told you? All of it?"

I shook my head. "Not all of it. Rex had to tell me. 'arold! What were you thinking? How could you do something so..."

He looked up at last. "So what? So dreadful? So selfish? So dangerous? Obviously I wasn't thinking, was I? I am sorry about Brian. He's a mate, I wouldn't have ever done him harm on purpose! You know that's not me." He shook his head and looked away. "I was tired, and angry that I was tired. I got angry at myself after I left home that day, for blaming you. I hated that I got angry at our baby. So I went to the pub to try to stop being angry but" –he glanced over at the policeman– "I woke up the next morning in my car – late. I knew if I didn't turn up at work I'd be for the high jump with Rex, so I didn't bother trying to get back to you, just hoofed it to the mill. And I guess you know the rest. I panicked so I ran. Forgot about my car – it's probably still down there. I found a pub, figured I'd hole up there till I figured out my next move. Only this lot" –he jerked a thumb towards the PC– "well, like I said, you know the rest." He stared at me then, his expression bereft. "I don't know what to do, Elise. I don't know what's going to happen to me. They won't even tell me how Brian is."

""Brian lost 'is arm, 'arold! Just 'ow do you think 'e is?" I shook as I spoke, the scene Rex described still vivid in my mind. Seeing the look on Harold's face, I tried to regain some calm. "The sergeant told me you're going up before a magistrate, maybe today. They're going to get the court to appoint legal 'elp for you."

He nodded.

"But, 'arold. You are going to prison for this, you do know that, right?" I had worked that much out while I was waiting this morning.

He nodded again, head hanging once more.

"So, you need to tell me things. Practical things. Where do I find the landlord's telephone number and address? I'm going to 'ave to ask 'im for some grace until this is sorted."

He mumbled something.

"Pardon?"

He looked up. "Yes, I know. I'm sorry. I didn't plan any of this. You know I don't want to put you in a bind. All the paperwork is in the top drawer of the table in the lounge. I've at least got that all organised, you should find what you need easily enough."

PC Evans stepped forward. "I'm afraid that's all the time we can allow, Mrs McRae. We'll have to take him back now."

I stared at my husband. He looked empty and lost. As tragic as the whole thing was that he'd brought on himself, I found myself feeling sorry for him. "You will get through this, 'arold. Maybe they'll let me see you again soon. Goodbye."

We both stood and the PC took Harold's arm, leading him through the door ahead of me. I watched them walk away down the hall to the cells, then turned and made my way back to my son.

21

Summer 1948/1949

The next time I saw my husband, he was standing in what I was told was the dock. Yvonne was with me in the public area. I'd not been at his first hearing, only finding out afterwards that he was to remain in jail until his trial. The court had appointed someone to represent Harold, a serious young man who introduced himself to me while we waited for the judge to arrive.

"This could take a while," the lawyer said. "I've advised your husband that it would be best for everyone that he pleads guilty – judges take that into account with sentencing – but I'm not sure I got through to him. "We'd better take our seats; here's the judge."

Yvonne squeezed my hand as the court official spoke.

"All rise."

The judge took his seat. "Be seated. Bailiff, please read the charges."

The man who'd spoken before nodded and stood facing Harold. "Harold James McRae, you are charged that on Thursday the seventh of October, 1948, you acted with wilful negligence in the workplace, namely Carlisle and Sons Mill, thereby causing serious bodily harm to another. Further, you are charged with operating machinery while intoxicated, a violation of workplace regulations. How do you plead?"

Harold stared through the courtroom to me, then looked at another woman sitting nearby. "Guilty."

My head dropped. I felt Yvonne's hand rubbing my back, and heard a sigh from the other woman Harold had looked at. I realised she must be Brian's wife.

Clearly Harold's lawyer wasn't the only one surprised to hear him admit his guilt so readily. Papers rustled as the lawyers on both sides reorganised themselves. Harold's lawyer stood and spoke to the judge. I didn't really understand what was happening. Harold was led away and the lawyer came back over to me.

"The judge has set a date for sentencing. Since your husband has pleaded guilty, we don't need to proceed with the trial. It's strange though. Like I said earlier, I had advised him to do just this, but up until now he's been adamantly against the idea. This is the best decision he could have made, for him and the victim's family."

Yvonne asked the question for me. "'ow long do you think 'e'll be sentenced for?"

He shook his head. "The judge has the final say."

Yvonne hugged me to her side as the lawyer continued.

"I'm sorry, but workplace injury, especially through negligence or drunkenness, is taken very seriously. The judge will take into account how well the victim is doing, but I think you need to prepare yourself for at least two years, possibly even five." He bowed his head briefly and walked away.

Yvonne led me quickly outside. "I think you should come

back to mine, Elise. We'll collect Stephen from your neighbour and pick up a few things. You can stay with us tonight. I don't think you should be alone."

I nodded, glad to have her take charge and not having to decide anything for myself.

* * *

The following week went by without me taking much notice of the outside world. One evening Rex came home with news.

"I've had a word with that lawyer. He's sorted it for you to see Harold before they send him on to the prison. I've put my foreman in charge for tomorrow so I can drive you out there."

"Thank you Rex, that's so kind of you!" I was touched.

And so I found myself saying goodbye to my husband of less than a year, knowing he wouldn't be free for four years. Stephen would be almost school age before he saw his father again.

We met in the same room as that day after his arrest. He'd lost weight and it seemed he'd lost something else too. His eyes stared out at me, sad and lonely. "I'm sorry Elise. Will you come visit me there? But I don't think you should bring the little guy."

I swallowed, doing my best to stay calm for us both. I avoided his question, instead breaking some news of my own.

"'arold, I've 'ad to start looking for somewhere smaller, cheaper. The landlord 'as told me we 'ave to be out at the end of the month. 'e can't afford to let me stay any longer."

His face darkened. He rubbed it with both hands, shaking his head. "Why on earth did I ever go to work that day?" His voice caught and I saw his eyes fill. "If I'd just stayed away and slept it off, the worst that could have happened was Rex firing me. My mates wouldn't hate me. Brian would still be..." He swallowed. "He'd still be whole."

I looked over my shoulder at the policeman in the corner. It was a different officer this time. He stared at the wall, ignoring us both. I turned back to see Harold resting his head, face down, on the table between us. I watched helplessly, not allowed to touch him at all. Finally he sighed heavily and looked up, his face hopeless.

"It's done," I spoke with unfamiliar firmness. "You can't undo it. We just 'ave to make the best of it. I'll write you our new address as soon as I 'ave that sorted. At least Rex 'as paid me your final wages, otherwise I don't know what I'd do to cover the rent until I find work."

Harold looked shocked. "Work? But what about Stephen? You can't work!"

"Just 'ow do you expect me to support us then? I 'ave to do something. It's four years, 'arold. I can't live on fresh air and a look around!"

He almost laughed at that. It was something my maman used to say to tease us.' Her dry humour channelled through me for the first time in this surreal moment. He reached over the table, as if to grab my hands, but stopped himself.

"How many times will I have to say sorry to you, for the trouble I've caused? Of course you're right. What about our son though?"

"Yvonne 'as said 'e can stay with 'er. Apart from when she 'as 'er baby, of course. She'll need time then to adjust. She's asked one of 'er neighbours if they can 'elp for a week or so then. That's if I find something. I've never 'ad a job before."

"Time's up." The officer stepped towards me.

193

"Goodbye, 'arold. Please keep yourself safe?"

The next morning I kissed my son goodbye as he wriggled in his aunty's arms before I walked to the bus alone. Once in town, I started with the establishments I knew: the café, the library, the department and grocery stores. I'd wait quietly until someone who'd served me was free.

"Excuse me. Sorry to take up your time, but I am looking for work - anything really. Do you 'ave anything going?"

The first few shook their heads, wanting to help but unable to advise me. Now and then a question would precede the negative gesture.

"Do you have any experience working at a cash register?"

"Do you have any references? I could give them to the manager in case something comes up?"

The 'Kiwi' way of speaking often made a plain sentence sound like a question.

At one store, the lady at the counter looked me up and down with evident disdain before saying, "Oh I don't think so, dear, do you?"

I reddened and hurried out, avoiding the looks from the customers. I made my way to the library where the lady I'd met last time led me to the newspaper issues.

"Some of the businesses advertise here when they need more staff. Maybe if you start with Monday's issue and work your way through? Plenty of married women have jobs now. It's not such an unusual situation anymore. Here," she handed me a piece of paper and a pencil. "Write down anything that seems even vaguely possible, then you can either apply in person, or send them a letter. I'm sure there's something that'll suit you." She smiled encouragingly then left me to my mission.

I turned pages until I reached a section with 'situations

vacant' heading a couple of columns. I wouldn't have known what that meant before the librarian had explained. I murmured a brief 'thank God' and began to read.

There were secretarial posts, shop assistant jobs, and home delivery roles. All seemed to need either a driver's licence, or specific qualifications. I got as far as Thursday's issue before I found a possible role for me. I jotted down the details, happy that this one didn't require me to write a letter or have a work history. I returned the papers to the shelf.

"Thank you." I waved.

She waved back from the counter.

I had a few days before the factory was holding the job interviews. Yvonne and Rex walked me through the sorts of questions to expect, and helped me to put what life experiences I'd had into perspective for the work I would do should I get the job.

"I know we 'elped with family, but that still counts, Elise. You learned 'ow to follow instructions and get tasks done on time. Everything we did in the garden and with errands was training, if you think about it."

I could only hope Yvie was right about that.

"If you want to have any chance at all, don't mention that husband of yours. At the most, say he's unable to work now." Rex interrupted. He was repeating himself – we had been talking for over an hour.

Yvonne smiled, encouraging me as always. "Just be yourself, Elise. You are young and an 'ard worker. Those two things should serve you well."

When I arrived at the factory entrance early the following week, I joined a queue of perhaps twenty others all hoping for work. Right on time, the door opened and a man in a tan work coat waved us all inside.

"Just take a seat, everyone. The foreman will be through shortly to explain what's going on."

I chose a seat in the middle row. I wasn't the only woman there, but there were more men than women. The foreman came through an internal door and wasted no time.

"We're a busy place and have just landed a major new order, so we need extra bodies on the ground, if you'll excuse my turn of phrase. All I need to know is that you are willing to work hard, and listen to instructions. You'll need to be able to start tomorrow morning, is that going to be a problem for anyone? No? Ok. I have some forms here. I just need you to fill them in – that'll tell us you can read and write well enough to work here." He smiled briefly before continuing. "It's not a permanent role, it's just for the next three months. So if that's not what you are looking for, please leave now, no hard feelings."

A few chairs scraped on the floor as several of the men stood up and left, nodding to the foreman.

"Ok, that leaves about fourteen of you. We only need nine or ten. So, I'm going to have to choose. Please don't be offended if I don't choose you, it's nothing personal." He surveyed the group a moment then began to point to individuals.

As the people stood and moved to collect a form, my heart sank, fully expecting to not get chosen. Then I saw his eyes turn to me. He stared, then raised his hand to point my way. "You. Stand up please."

I obeyed, gripping my purse, my face hot.

He nodded in satisfaction. "Yep, you'll do. I need someone, shall we say, small? There's a particular machine your small hands will be just right for." He gestured with his head for me to join the other successful applicants. I smiled with relief as I walked from the chairs to the table.

*** *** ***

A month into the job, I found a room to let with a lady who took in boarders. As it was furnished, I'd only need mine and Stephen's personal things, so Yvonne helped me find a dealer who was happy to collect my bed and other furniture. He paid me a fraction of what we had paid, but it still helped to cover some of my expenses.

The work was repetitive and easy but I didn't mind. I was getting paid, my son was being cared for and I was within walking distance of my sister's home. I would get home tired and happy, knowing I was looking after myself and my son, reliant on no one else.

22

Autumn 1949

Yvonne's baby was born, a sweet little girl who reminded us both of our maman.

Stephen played at my feet one afternoon as I sat with Yvonne in the lounge while she fed the baby. I'd been watching Stephen when I heard Rex come rushing in.

"Yvonne! Are you all right? What's happened?" He shook her gently on the shoulder, panic in his voice.

"Rex? What are you doing?" Yvonne shrugged away from his hand, hugging her baby close and glaring at her husband.

He stood straight, his expression turning to surprise now. "I walked past the window and I saw…" He waved an arm vaguely before sighing. "I thought I saw you passed out." He sank down on the couch beside her.

Yvonne shook her head, laughing quietly. "Silly man, I just nodded off, that is all! I am not getting a lot of sleep, remember. 'ere, you take 'er and wind 'er while I put the kettle on." She left the room, chuckling and muttering to herself.

Rex paced up and down the room. "I hadn't realised how little sleep Yvonne is getting. It can't be good for her."

"It is normal at this stage, Rex. It will get better." I answered.

* * *

By the end of the week he had employed a woman to help with cleaning and cooking. I began to see a new side to this normally taciturn man my sister had married.

We all settled into our new routines. Of course, I didn't have a kitchen of my own anymore, so I wasn't able to invite Yvonne, Rex and their daughter home. Once a week we still had a meal with them, but now it was the midday meal rather than evening, out of respect for Yvonne's need for extra sleep.

We baptised our babies at the same service. Yvonne and Rex agreed to be Stephen's god-parents, and I was little Anastasia's god-mother.

"For Grand-mère, Elise."

"She will be so proud when you tell 'er."

My three months at work came to an end, but now that I had that experience behind me, I was able to find a replacement before my last day, ending my last week at the factory and starting the following week in the storeroom of a department store. It was even more convenient, being only a couple of minutes walk from my bus stop. Due to boarding rather than renting, I'd even begun to save a little, which gave me a feeling of security after the upheaval of the past year.

23

Winter 1949

I finally went to see Harold. I had avoided it as long as I could, delaying by writing to him regularly. Rex drove me out there after work one Saturday. We sat at a table in the visitors area, waiting for the prisoners to be shown through. Harold appeared, shuffling along in a line of other men. He broke away as he neared our table.

"Hey." He looked at me, then nodded at Rex.

"'ello 'arold." I found it hard to know where to start the conversation. The man in front of me bore little resemblance now to the one I'd married. He was unkempt and thin. I had a look at the other prisoners. It didn't seem to be a universal thing. They were all shapes and sizes. So Harold was clearly not doing well.

He cleared his throat. "So how is my son doing?"

Relieved to talk about a topic so dear to me, I told him about how well Stephen was doing with crawling and learning to stand. I told him how much he loved his baby cousin; how he would bring his toys to her when we visited, hoping to have her play with him. "And 'e can almost feed 'imself now. He is a very 'appy and settled little boy. Not really a baby anymore."

If I'd thought that would please Harold, I soon found out otherwise. His brow furrowed in a deep frown. "I hope you're being firm on him. Not letting him just do as he pleases. I don't want to come home to a mollycoddled mummy's boy!" His voice was rough and angry.

Confused, I glanced at Rex. His face was grim.

"Are you trying to pick an argument with your wife, McRae?" Rex sat forward, unfolding his arms.

Harold leaned back, a startled look on his face. "No, I'm just saying. I'm not there to discipline him, so I want to make sure she does." He jerked his head at me.

Rex leaned even closer over the table. "Let's get something straight. You're in here because you didn't discipline yourself. So why do you think you'd do a better job than Elise? Secondly, 'she' is not the way a gentleman refers to his wife. You get your head screwed on right, my man, and clean up your act. Look at the state of you!" He snorted derisively, waving a hand at Harold's general appearance.

Harold scowled. "My apologies, Elise." His apology came out forced but I nodded anyway. "You always did like to lay down the law, Mr Carlisle." The use of his last name was not lost on Rex. "As for the state of me, in case it escaped your attention, I'm in prison. Not exactly the height of sartorial elegance."

I'd not heard him talk like this.

Rex raised his eyebrows. "Sarcasm won't help you. Yes, you're in prison. That doesn't mean you just let yourself go completely. Look around. There are men here who've served more of their sentences than you, but they've made the effort to clean up for their wives or mother's visits. I'm sure they have a barber in here and they let you shower."

Harold reddened. "I don't do well washing in public." He mumbled, chin to his chest.

Rex snorted again. "You've got four years to deal with it, so you better make your mind up to that right now. You lost the right to privacy when you turned up for work in that state and ruined another man's life. If you'd served in the army, you'd have learnt that showering with other chaps isn't a big deal. You just get it over with and keep your eyes to yourself."

I stared at the floor while they spoke. The subject seemed far too personal to be discussing in such an open setting.

Rex checked his watch. "If you've nothing to say other than complaining, I'll take your wife home to your son. She's got better things to do with her time than listen to you feel sorry for yourself."

Harold reddened and scowled. "Keep your hair on. Can you wait outside for a couple of minutes then, so I can talk with my wife alone?" They glared at each other.

Rex turned to me, mutely asking my opinion.

I nodded. "I'll be fine, Rex. Really."

He stood, staring at Harold as he did so. Clearly reluctant, he turned on his heel and left the same way we'd come in.

"That's better. I might have thumped him if he'd stayed any longer. Why'd you let him come with you?" My face froze. He noticed, brows raised over a mocking smile. "What? You didn't expect me to just take that from him, did you? Who on earth does he think he is?"

I stood to my feet shakily then, finding my voice at last. "Rex was good enough to bring me to see you. Considering the damage you've done to 'is business and that poor man, I would say no one could blame 'im if 'e refused to bring me. Just 'ow do you expect me to see you? You know I can't drive! I wanted to see you. I wanted to tell you we miss you. But this" –my voice strengthened as I spoke, bolstered by my anger at this unfair attack– "this attitude of yours shames me, more than you being in 'ere. I feel like I do not even know you. I never expected to 'ave to visit such a place. I won't be back. Goodbye 'arold." Surprised at my own words and the intensity of my displeasure, I turned away without giving him a chance to respond. I clenched every muscle tight, determined to not let my nerves betray me with a stumble in my step. The door seemed so far from me but I got there without incident. I pulled it open without a backward glance and joined Rex in the corridor.

III

Part Three

24

Autumn 1950

One Friday, the day we were paid each week, the manager stopped me for a moment when he'd handed me my envelope.

"You'll find a little extra in there from now on, Mrs McRae, as well as a bit of a bonus for this week. Good work deserves a reward." He let go of the envelope, a beneficent expression lighting him up.

"Thank you, Mr Welles. I appreciate that. But why?"

"The date not mean anything to you?" He shook his head with a chuckle. "You've been with us for a year now. And you've never taken a day off for sickness or for your young lad. You've worked hard and done us proud. So, as I say, you deserve it. You'll have no trouble getting similar work in the future, should you ever need to move on. Which we hope you won't! But the war showed us nothing is set in stone."

He turned back to his office while I stood rooted to the spot. I looked down at the envelope, wondering if I should open it now. No, I thought, walking to the cloakroom to hang up my apron and get my coat and purse. I put the envelope right at the bottom, saving the amount as a surprise for later when I would be alone.

I put Stephen to bed before I took the envelope out of my purse. "Oh my!" I had expected maybe a few extra pounds, going by the way Mr Welles had spoken. But the bonus and the 'little extra' added up to an extra week's wages! My thoughts raced. I made myself a cup of tea and sat up on my bed until late into the night. My barely-formed ideas suddenly seemed within reach.

On Sundays I still had lunch with Yvie and Rex, so two days after my manager surprised me with the pay rise, I mentioned the conversation from Friday over our meal.

Yvonne put her cutlery down and clasped her hands. "Oh that's wonderful, Elise. 'e is right, you do deserve it. I 'ave watched 'ow you worked so 'ard and pushed yourself to learn. Is it very much?"

I nodded, my face glowing. "It is enough that I will soon be able to afford to look for somewhere of our own, a proper little 'ouse, rather than rooms." I kept my eyes on my plate. "You know 'ow 'ard it 'as been, working these hours and 'aving someone else look after my Stephen. And not 'aving my own space when I do get 'ome. Not that I am complaining! I know I am blessed to 'ave found work at all."

They shared a glance.

"Where is this going, Elise?" Yvonne looked concerned.

I looked up then, speaking quickly. "I was thinking, maybe it's time for us to 'ave a fresh start. In Auckland. Lucette is there, so it's not like I won't know anyone."

I pushed on, not giving either of them time to air an objection. "I 'ave been considering it on and off ever since I last saw 'arold. Now I 'ave a whole year of work experience be'ind me, I know I can find something."

Yvonne leaned forward and squeezed my hand, grinning broadly. "I am so pleased to 'ear you say that. Remember I told you that Rex used to live in Auckland? 'e knows a few people up there still. If you'd like, we could write to one or two trusted old friends to see if anyone could give you somewhere to live. I agree, there is more there for both you and Stephen, and it's not too soon to think about where you want 'im to go to school." She got up from the table and hugged me tightly.

I sighed in relief. I had been worried they would try to dissuade me. We finished our meal, dropping the subject for the time being. After clearing the dishes, I took Stephen out into the garden. While he ran off his bottled up energy, my mind conjured up Harold's face, hurt and angry as I'd seen him on my one prison visit. His letters hadn't shown any sign of forgiving me for standing up to him then.

Stephen tugged on my sleeve.

"What did you say, sweet'eart?"

"Come and see!" He led me down to the jetty, excited as only little children can be to show me some fresh new discovery in the water.

* * *

On my next visit I broached the subject of Auckland once more. "I wrote to Lucette. She was most encouraging. She says she will ask in 'er neighbour'ood about a letting possibility."

Yvonne put her cup down and got up, waving at me to stay where I was. She returned with an envelope in her hands. "I'm glad you reminded me. This came on Friday. The lady is an old friend of Rex's. She is a widow now and takes in boarders.

She taught 'im for a while and took a bit of a shine to 'im."

She held the letter out. "She does 'ave a vacancy coming up."

"Yvie, that's wonderful!" I tore the envelope open and read quickly. "Do you 'ave a map of Auckland, by any chance?"

I wrote to Lulu again as soon as I'd set the date for my move.

'Dear Lulu,

Well, it's definitely happening! Yvonne put me in touch with Rex's old school teacher, Mrs Marchand. We've exchanged letters and she is happy to have us stay as long as we need to. Isn't that wonderful? I'm not sure how far away from you she is, but at least we'll be in the same city at last. I'll put the address at the end of this. As soon as I get my head around the buses, Stephen and I will come and visit you.

Your friend,

Elise'

Though we'd corresponded over the years since we'd all arrived in New Zealand, I missed her cheerful company.

25

Winter 1950

Once again I was on my own, waiting to leave all that was familiar. Well, not quite so alone this time. I glanced down at my little boy, sitting patiently beside me. "You're not thirsty, or 'ungry at all?" I asked, as I put an arm around his shoulders and hugged him to my side.

He wriggled a little, snuggling closer. "No, Mum. All good."

There were quite a few people waiting with us. When I'd booked our tickets, the lady at the counter had been insistent.

"You need to be at the stop at least twenty minutes before the scheduled departure time," she'd said. "Otherwise we can't guarantee your seat."

We had gotten here in plenty of time, and now the bus was at least ten minutes late. Yvonne and Rex had driven us to the terminus and she had offered to wait with us.

"There's really no need, Yvie, it won't be long. And we aren't going to be alone. Look at all the other people waiting." I smiled.

"Come 'ere then, young man. Give Aunty one last 'ug before you go." Yvonne bent down and collected Stephen in a warm embrace. She lifted her chin at Rex. He sighed and got out of the car, coming around to the footpath. He looked at me awkwardly.

"Goodbye then," he said gruffly. He turned to Stephen. "Behave yourself, right, boy? Mrs Marchand runs a tight ship." He ruffled Stephen's hair. Stephen squirmed away, wrapping his arms around my leg. I lifted him onto my hip as they prepared to drive off.

"Wave to Aunty and Uncle," I said, as Rex u-turned across the road and Yvonne waved through her window. I was getting used to goodbyes, I thought. No tears this time.

The bus finally arrived twenty minutes later.

"There now. We're on our way at last. Isn't it exciting?" I said as the bus pulled into the traffic.

He bit down on the sandwich I'd given him and nodded, chewing noisily.

I pulled out a snack for myself. Now that I had nothing else to do until the other end of the trip, I gave myself over to planning our next few days. I had been in touch by telephone several times with Mrs Marchand and she seemed to be a warm and hospitable lady.

"Normally there would be another boarder above you, but now and then I cut back a bit and just have one floor let out. You and the lad have your own rooms, and there is a sitting room and your own bathroom on the same floor. You will have me all to yourselves." She was happy to collect us from the bus station, for which I was very grateful.

When we arrived, she was easy to pick out from those waiting at the terminal. Though elderly, her posture was ramrod straight, her height accentuated by her slenderness. The only signs of her advanced years was her silvery grey hair, cut to frame her face simply, and a little crepey skin at her neck. Her smile welcomed us both and I knew then that this was the right decision. While she drove home, she pointed out stores and bus stops along the way.

"Here we are then." Leading the way up the front path, she spoke over her shoulder. She smiled fondly at Stephen, holding the door open for us. "For the time being, while you get settled, I'm happy to cook dinner for us all, but when you're ready, please feel free to make use of the kitchen. Young man, what do you say to shepherd's pie for your tea after that big bus ride? Come on then, while your mum finds everything upstairs, how about you set the table for me."

I felt that she had read my mind. The day had been long and I did want just a few moments to myself. I went up the stairs. So much room! More than at my flat with Harold, even more than my room back home in New Caledonia. I sank gratefully onto the sofa in our sitting room and closed my eyes.

Dinner was almost over when Mrs Marchand turned the conversation to my future.

"My dear, I hope you don't think I've been too forward. But I have a young friend, Iris, whom I thought of when you and I were corresponding. She works at a very busy factory, and she's been able to help others who need work to get a place there. I have spoken to her, and she'd very much like to meet you. She'll pop round after work on Saturday. Do you mind?" She was earnest in her desire to help and I was grateful once more. I'd had no thought of her doing more for us than she already had, with giving us such a lovely place to live.

"Mrs Marchand, you are very kind. 'ow could I mind? I thought I was going to 'ave to spend days asking at businesses, and 'aving to learn my way around even before that. Thank you so much."

Iris arrived soon after lunch on that first Saturday and I could tell straight away that we would be friends. A little older than me, she radiated warmth and good humour. I was impressed by her friendly and respectful manner towards my landlady.

"You'll fit in fine, Elise." Iris said. "They're a good bunch in the main. It's noisy work and we're on our feet all day, but you said you've done some factory work before?"

"Yes, my first job, down in Tauranga. And you're sure they won't want me to formally apply?"

She laughed at that. "Since the war, they can't get enough staff. Most of the married women left when their men came back, and the young ones don't stay long. The boss'll just be pleased to have someone who's willing to work hard."

As she left, she pressed a piece of paper into my hand, with directions on how to find the factory.

* * *

On the bus on Monday I was determined to appear at my very best so as not to let Iris down. Soon enough we reached my stop and I joined the queue of passengers leaving through the back door of the bus. I opened my hand to read Iris's note again, checking the numbers on the buildings as I walked. It seemed I wasn't the only one heading to the factory. A few hundred metres down the road from me, a giant cooking pot protruded from the wall on an angle above the front entrance. A steady stream of workers filed in from both directions. I allowed myself to be taken along with the flow. As we neared the gates, someone tapped my arm. I saw Iris walking alongside me.

"You found us all right then."

"Yes, your note made it very simple. Thank you."

"Well done! I can take you the rest of the way in, if you like." She tucked her hand into my elbow, smiled at me and led the way to a building on our right.

We went down a narrow hallway, lined both sides with sturdy wooden doors. On the walls between the doors were photographs of solemn men, names, titles and dates in an unbroken procession going back decades. We stopped at the door marked 'Plant Manager'. Iris knocked, waited a moment then opened the door. The man behind the desk looked up inquiringly.

"Mrs McRae here for you, Mr Seddon." Iris winked at me. "See you later!"

Mr Seddon looked up. "Ah yes, of course. Come in, come in. Don't be bashful!" He laughed heartily as if he'd told a great joke, shuffled some papers about on the desk and pushed one towards me. "If you could fill this in for me, that would be great." When I'd finished, he smiled. "Excellent. You come with me, and we'll get you set up down on the factory floor." Pushing back his chair, he heaved himself upright and walked to the door. It seemed Iris hadn't exaggerated when she'd said how eager they were for workers: I had the job already!

Mr Seddon took me back down the hallway to another staircase, this one leading down inside the building. Double doors at the top and the foot of the stairs had blocked out the noise coming from the machinery. As we passed through the lower doors, it felt almost as if I was physically struck by the cacophony within.

Mr Seddon had seen my reaction, touched my elbow in

215

sympathy. Knowing I wouldn't hear him, he gestured with his head towards a small room off to one side. I nodded and followed. Once inside, the noise level from the factory floor was less overwhelming. I saw the walls were fairly thick to provide sound insulation. Another man sat behind a counter, head bent over a large book, pencil in hand.

"Mr Fredericks, this is Mrs McRae. She'll be starting on the assembly line with Iris. Can I leave her with you to get her kitted out?"

I smiled to myself when I heard I was to work with Iris, even though we had really only just met.

Mr Seddon turned back to me. "This is Mr Fredericks. He's the line foreman you'll be reporting to. I hope you'll settle in quickly." He bowed his head quickly and left.

"So, another stray Iris picked up hey?" Mr Fredericks chuckled. "Have you done any work like this before?"

"No, I am sorry. Although I worked in a factory in Tauranga, it was very different work."

"No worries. We'll get you up to speed."

Back out on the noisy factory floor, we made our way down to the back.

Through another door was a sort of anteroom, with a row of hooks from which hung a few white aprons.

"You can hang your coat on one of the empty hooks, and you'll find a locker just over there to put your bag into. Put an apron on while I find you a cap."

I did as I was told, and saw a wall of lockers off to my right. I couldn't see any actual way to lock the cubby hole, the door just closed with a latch. Mr Fredericks came over with a small padlock in his hand.

"This is your lock, and you keep one key. I keep the other

safe in my office, in case you lose yours. But if you do, and we have to make a new spare, we'll dock it from your wages." He snapped the tiny padlock in place and handed me my key.

"You can come out here to get your bag at morning or afternoon tea and lunchtime. Other than that, this area's out of bounds. Clear?"

Once I had the cap and apron on, Mr Fredericks handed me what looked like giant earmuffs.

"You'll be needing these if you value your hearing and your sanity, lass." He smiled.

He led me to my 'station'. A line of women stretched in either direction as far as I could see. Their hands continued with their work as they all snapped a quick glance up at me before turning back to the moving surface in front of them. Iris winked and grinned.

Mr Fredericks tapped my shoulder, then hers, and gestured between us, then returned to his office. Iris nodded and pulled me into line next to her. She waggled two fingers, pointing first at my eyes, at her own, and at the moving counter. I dipped my head 'yes'. Each of us stood about three feet apart. At first I couldn't make sense of what I was seeing but gradually some semblance of order began to make itself evident.

The counter flowed from left to right, and on the other side of it, about a foot higher, was a shelf filled at each station with black oblongs of some sort of wood. As the counter moved, a main section of what turned out to be metal cooking pots arrived at intervals. One woman would pick up the section, reach up to her shelf and grab a handle, push it into the housing on the side of the pot and put the pot down again. The next woman in line would be ready with a screw and tool in hand, pick up the pot and drive the screw through the base of the handle and the housing. Back on the counter, it moved to the next woman who would pick it up and check it before putting it on a second moving counter that ran behind the first.

Iris was the last in a group of three, which made me the first of the next set. The women in my group covered my station while I watched a few pots go through, then Iris gestured for me to have a go with the next pot that came down the line.

* * *

"So how did you find that, Elise?" she asked, during break time. We were in the staff canteen, sitting with about a dozen others. "Here, get this cuppa down you, you look like you need it." Iris sat down heavily in the seat next to me.

"Thank you." I picked up the cup and took a sip. It was almost scalding hot, so I blew on it as I cradled my sore hands around the cup. "I 'ope I will learn this job quickly. I was much slower than you all this morning. I 'ope I didn't hold you up."

"Don't worry love, you're not the first newbie we've trained up."

I laughed. "Yes, Mr Fredericks said I was one of your 'strays'."

At that she pretended to bristle. "Stray indeed. I'll have words with him."

She nudged me and winked. "You'll get the hang of it, don't you worry. You're not the slowest we've ever had. Ain't that right, Nancy?" She leaned around me to call down to a woman at the other end of our table.

I allowed the banter to flow around me, as the women let off steam from their morning's shift. Iris explained that with the factory being so noisy, they couldn't talk while they worked. Morning tea was a chance to catch up on each other's news.

They were clearly all good friends here.

A bell sounded, rallying the staff back out to the factory floor. Chair legs scraped on the rough concrete floor, cups and tea plates clattered on to the counter as the men and women filed out of the canteen.

The rest of the day passed more quickly than I would have expected, and by the end of it my feet were sore from standing so long. One of the other girls, Jessie, saw me holding my apron and cap and flapped a hand.

"There's the hamper, over in the corner. Just dump yours in with the rest. They get laundered tonight. We'll have a fresh set waiting for us in the morning." She took her own over and held the lid open for me. I retrieved my bag and coat and joined the throng out to the gate. Now I saw the more direct route I would take in the morning. I'd lost my sense of direction in the maze from the upstairs offices to the factory floor that morning. An elbow dug into my side, and I looked up to see Iris had caught up to me.

"So you survived your first day. Well done you!"

I laughed with her, tired as I was. "It is easy work but difficult. Do you know what I mean?"

Iris bobbed her head. "That's it exactly, Elise. Not much thinking involved, but it just keeps coming and you have to get it right every time. And it's a long day on your feet." We'd reached the gates. "My bus is this way, so I'll say good night now. See you in the morning Elise. Bye" She waved as she walked away.

The next few days passed in similar fashion, and I found the new routine becoming less of a trial. Because I was so physically tired at the end of my shift, I slept deeply, going to bed soon after Stephen. That made waking early much easier.

Though the work was demanding and I was tired by the end of the day, mentally I was able to relax.

* * *

Getting a job so quickly had at first prevented me from catching up with Lucette and her family. But one weekend, a couple of months after I had started at the factory, there was a knock on the door. Mrs Marchand was out running errands, so I knew she wasn't expecting anyone.

"Surprise!" Five voices called in unison. Lucette, Louis and the three children stood grinning on my doorstep.

"Oh my! What are you doing 'ere?" I held a hand out, grasping Lulu's and pulling her inside. "Not that I am not delighted to see you, of course!"

She laughed again as they all filed inside. She grabbed me in a quick hug. "Let me look at you. It 'as been too, too long!"

I shook my head, almost too happy to speak. I had forgotten how exuberant she could be. I turned to see Stephen coming shyly down the stairs. He'd been playing quietly in his room.

"Oh! Is this your little man?" Lucette gasped. "Don't be shy! I am your Maman's friend, Lulu, and these are my naughty children. Please, come and say 'ello."

He looked at me, eyes wide. Nodding, I gestured for him to come down. He scuttled to my side and hugged my leg.

"Stephen, these are my friends. Lulu, 'oo is not as scary as she sounds," she crossed her eyes at us while Louis stood back and the children giggled. "This is Louis."

Louis stepped forward, hand outstretched. "Pleased to meet you Stephen."

I felt Stephen let go of me with one arm. His hand came out

and Louis shook it, smiling. Without letting go, Louis stepped closer, turning, and took over the introductions.

"Stephen, this is Paul. 'e is a big boy, but 'e is not above playing with children younger than 'im."

Paul grinned and nodded.

"These are Michelle and Therese." He patted each on the head as he spoke.

Introductions over, I led us all into the kitchen and filled the kettle. As the children began talking together, Lulu and Louis helped me set out cups and glasses. I brought out a jug of milk for the children, and found Mrs Marchand's fruit cake in the pantry.

"Stephen, show your new friends where to put their plates and glasses, then you can take them upstairs and show them your room?"

"Yes mum." He scrambled down from the chair.

"Shall we go through to the living room?" I offered.

Just then Mrs Marchand arrived home and I introduced her.

"So lovely to meet Elise's friends and to put faces to names. Would you all care to stay for dinner? We have plenty." Happily they agreed. Once the meal was cooking, we gathered the children up and took them out to explore our neighbourhood.

That surprise visit cemented Lulu and her family in our lives, and many return visits were paid over the next few years.

26

Spring 1951

Life in Auckland became a happy and settled routine. Stephen's birthdays since our move seemed to have flown past with increasing rapidity. When he'd turned three, Yvonne, Rex, Anastasia and their little dog had come for a visit to help celebrate.

I had continued to write to Harold. On Stephen's last birthday Mrs Marchand had taken a photograph of Stephen and I. When I got the film developed, I paid for an extra copy to send to Harold.

Mrs Marchand and I were sitting in her living room. She was crocheting some little thing for a friend while I wrote my letter. We had been carrying on a somewhat disjointed conversation while we worked. I picked the conversation up again.

"I do think it's the least I can do to keep 'im in his son's life. But, Mrs M, the funny thing is that Stephen never asks about 'is father. Do you think that's odd?"

"Odd? No, I don't think so dear. I doubt he remembers his father very clearly, if at all. And he's not around lots of other youngsters yet, so he doesn't know anything different than having just a mum."

I glanced over my shoulder at that. She smiled and I knew she meant no offence at the 'just'. I turned back and checked over the letter once more before tucking the photograph inside it. I had taken one precaution since we had moved. At the time I felt that I was being overly cautious, but some instinct led me to not send the letters directly from here. I did not put a return address on the envelopes, and took care to give no clues as to our exact area of Auckland. I sent my letters to Yvonne and Rex's home, and they forwarded them from there.

Harold's replies were sporadic at best, and often hard to read. When I had written to tell him of our move, his response had been vicious. I'd been stung all over again by his language and had taken several days to get through it, and then only with the support of Mrs Marchand. Nothing seemed to phase the lovely elderly lady who'd taken us in.

"Don't take it to heart, Elise. He's lashing out because he's stuck. No man likes to feel helpless. He'll calm down. Keep writing to him. Then at least he'll see you haven't left him really. You'll see," she patted my hand. "And you'll know when the time is right to go see him."

I took her advice, writing as if that last one had never reached me to hurt me. Whenever Stephen did something funny, or new, or made a friend, anything really, I made a note of it so I could include it in my letters.

Having overcome so much in the short time since we were married, I believed I had grown stronger. At least I did until my next letter arrived from Harold. As I took in his opening words, I was suddenly seventeen again, my stomach clenching in shock.

'*Auckland agrees with you, it seems. You're looking good, very – fresh. I suppose I should thank you for the photograph. Still, he is my son, so it's only what I'm entitled to.*

I'm guessing you found someone to replace me up there, have you? I'm sure you've missed having someone to keep you warm after the lights were out.

You have no idea what life is like in here. All I can think of when I try to get some sleep is what you've been getting up to while I'm stuck in here. How do I know I won't be coming home to tainted goods? And I will *be coming home. You are still my wife, remember that, so don't get too used to the single life up there in the big city.*'

I stood abruptly, the injustice of his vicious barb and the thinly veiled threat shocking me physically, as if he were there in the room with me.

I went downstairs and walked in to find Mrs M wiping out some of the kitchen drawers. She took one look at me, wiped her hands dry and reached for the kettle.

"Go on through, I'll be there in a second. You can tell me all about it."

I sank to the sofa, my sobs the only sound in the room. I fumbled in my cardigan pocket for my hanky and blew my nose then wiped my face. "It's the last straw, Mrs M, 'ere, read it." I watched her face over the steam rising from my cup, my own thoughts moving slowly but surely towards a word I had never wanted to consider. She pressed her lips together, refolded the letter and looked up at me.

"He's not a very subtle man, is he?"

A moment later we were both in tears of laughter.

"Oh, Mrs M, you are so good for me!" I reached again for my hanky. "Thank you. I needed that."

Her eyes still fixed on me, she tilted her head to the side. "If I'm not mistaken, you've reached a decision, young lady."

I sent up a quiet 'thank you God' for leading me to this remarkable woman, then answered her.

"I 'ave. I think ever since 'e went to prison, a part of me knew it would come to this, but I didn't want to face it. I never believed anything would make me break my wedding vow, but this:" I gestured towards the letter. "This isn't the man I married. 'e 'as changed so much." Bringing myself back to the present, I asked, already suspecting her reply, "You wouldn't 'appen to know someone 'oo could 'elp me to get that started, would you?"

Mrs Marchand had a knack for befriending just the right person.

Within a very short time, I had an appointment with her contact, a lawyer who had the sad duty of specialising in situations like mine – family law, he called it. The receptionist showed me through after a short wait. The lawyer stood up from behind his desk, coming around as he smoothed his tie.

"Mrs McRae, I'm George Lomax. Lovely to meet you, though of course I am sorry it's under these circumstances. Mrs Marchand speaks very highly of you."

I smiled, warmed at once by his friendly manner. He held a hand out towards a pair of seats this side of his desk.

"Please sit down." He sat in the other chair once I was seated, unbuttoning the one button of his suit jacket. "Now, how about you fill me in. Mrs Marchand gave me the broad strokes, but I need the nitty gritty, if you don't mind. I'll just let you give me the whole thing, then we'll go over it again so I can step in and ask any questions that occur to me. That sound ok to you?" He smiled again.

As I felt my own mouth smile in response, I thought that his manner, though it sat naturally on him, must be a boon in his line of work. I felt that I would tell him my deepest secrets, if I had any! I did as he suggested, surprising myself with how calmly I recounted the breakdown of my marriage.

"It counts as abandonment, you see, Mrs McRae. His wilful action that day led directly to his incarceration. His treatment of you since has been witnessed by more than one independent party, escalating to that clear threat in the final letter, so we will have no trouble making the case that this is your only option."

Over the next few months I grew in admiration of Mr Lomax's professionalism. Not once did he give a private opinion as to me breaking my vows in this course of action. He went out of his way to make the process smooth and as painless as the end of a marriage could be. As he handled my 'case' we became friends, addressing each other by our first names. He was the first man in my adult life that I could say that about. Always professional, and never any suggestion of wanting more than my friendship. He was almost like another brother. I met his wife, Elizabeth, early on, as she sometimes helped when his secretary was absent and when they came for dinner, Stephen quickly became friends with their children.

27

Summer 1953-54

The bus pulled up at my stop and I hurried down the aisle to the door. I jumped down, thanking the driver with a quick wave. Straightening my dress, I hitched my purse back up over my shoulder and turned to finish my journey to Lulu's home. I walked quickly, my mind racing. Had it really been two years since I'd sat down in Mr Lomax's office? I found myself at Lulu's gate in short order. I walked down the path, forcing myself to slow down, taking deep breaths. The front door opened before I was up her steps.

"Elise! I heard the gate open but was surprised to see you. Has something happened?"

This was why I'd chosen to come to Lulu. She'd come to be like another sister. And I didn't have to think or speak in English with her, a blessing given my state of mind. I fumbled in my purse, pulling out the paper and waving it. "It's come. It's here!"

She understood immediately, her face brightening as she came down the steps. She grabbed me in a tight hug. "Oh Elise, I'm so relieved for you! Come on, let's get that kettle on.

I'm sure I can find a treat to go with our cuppa!"

She hustled me inside, her energy exactly what I needed. Drinks by our side, we each curled into one of her overstuffed armchairs, enjoying the sun streaming in through the front room window.

"Remember when we thought the two years would drag by? And yet, here we are! Really, Elise, I am so pleased for you. I know how you were so worried about what he could do. Now you can forget all about him. You are happy about it, aren't you?"

I nodded. "Yes, I am Lulu. I'm also a little sad though. You know? It really is over now. And I am sorry for my son. But, it's for the best. As you said."

"And who knows? Maybe one day you will meet someone new." She winked.

"Stop it! Once bitten, twice shy. Isn't that the saying?"

28

Autumn 1954

As I put my key in the lock I could hear Stephen holding forth in Mrs Marchand's kitchen. She was so patient with him.

"Good afternoon mon chéri."

"Mum!" He put his cup down and clambered out of his seat. I gathered him in for a hug as he nestled in close.

I held him out to look at him. "So, 'ow was your day? Did you learn something new?"

He shook his head. "Nah, just the same old stuff."

Mrs Marchand and I shared a look over his head. He'd only been at school since the start of the school year in February, yet spoke as if he'd always been there. "I won Bull Rush though. Look!" He rolled up his shorts leg to reveal a purple blotch on his thigh.

"Stephen! 'ow did that 'appen?" I glanced at Mrs Marchand again.

She shook her head, biting back a grin.

"It's ok, Mum. It doesn't hurt. I was racing away from the last tagger right at the end, and he nearly got me, but I threw myself forward, like a rugby player!" He looked very proud of himself before he checked his bruise again. " I didn't see this big branch lying on the ground. It was all twisted and I landed on it." He grimaced at the memory, then just as quickly brightened. "All the kids wanted to see my leg. The teacher made sure I was all good and someone gave me a plum from their lunchbox."

Mrs Marchand shook her head again. "He told me he'd fallen, but obviously was saving those juicy details for you. So, how about you? How was work?"

The conversation soon got boring for my boy. He wriggled down and left the room. Once he was gone, Mrs Marchand handed me an envelope.

"This arrived for you today. I thought you'd not want the boy to see it."

I stared at her as I took it from her. I looked down to see my sister's handwriting. "Thanks. I think."

"Look, you know I'm not one to pry, so I'm not going to ask. But if you want to talk after, I'm here. And whatever it is, we'll sort something out. And who knows?" She smiled. "It might be good news."

"She's not long written to me with all the usual news. And this is too soon for 'er to 'ave seen my reply. Which means this is either important or urgent. Or both." I sighed and picked the envelope up out of my lap. "Only one way to find out, I suppose." The letter knife was on the duchess. I stretched up and grabbed it. I slit the paper open and withdrew a single folded page.

'Dearest Elise,

I know it hasn't been long since my last letter, but I felt you would want to know this as soon as possible. Rex had a visit from the probation service at the mill today, looking for Harold. It appears he lied on his paperwork with his probation officer after his release, saying that he got his old job back with Rex. He hasn't been seen since his release appointment with the probation officer. There is the possibility that he is trying to find you both. I am sorry, Elise. I had hoped none of us would need to worry about him any more. Please take care, ma chérie, and let us know if there is anything we can do here.

Much love as ever, your sister'

I read it through twice before looking up at my companion. "Read it. It may end up concerning you too, if what she suspects turns out to be right." So saying, I handed the letter to her and stood up, walking over to the window. I made a small gap in the drapes, peering out into the darkness beyond.

"Elise, come and sit down." Mrs Marchand shook her head as I turned around.

"Of course he couldn't have found you. Auckland is a big city."

She was right and I felt silly for giving place to the thought. Yvonne and I had taken steps to guard my exact whereabouts. Yvonne even addressed my letters to Miss Marchand. Since Mrs Marchand had no daughters, there was no confusion. How thankful I was for that. Now I stared through the drapes, fingers gripped on the fabric.

The school holidays started soon after, and I arranged with Lulu for Stephen to stay with her for a few days. I'd spent the last week since that letter, checking over my shoulder going to and from my bus. Mrs Marchand usually walked Stephen to and from school but now she drove him. Of course he thought that was a big adventure.

On the last Friday of term, I had arranged to finish work early so I could collect him myself. I got to school a little early on purpose.

I smiled at the school secretary. "May I see the headmistress please? It won't take long."

"Of course, Mrs McRae. Take a seat." She knocked on the headmistress's door, opened it and said a few words then turned back to me.

"Go on through."

Mrs Winter looked up, a file in her hand. "Good afternoon, Mrs McRae. What can I do for you? Take a seat, please."

"Thank you, Mrs Winter. It's rather personal, but I think you need to know."

I told her briefly about Harold's imprisonment, and my subsequent divorce, subjects I'd not shared with anyone but my closest friends. "I'm only telling you now as it seems that my ex-'usband may be trying to find us. I need your assurance that none of your staff will ever let Stephen leave the school with anyone except Mrs Marchand or me. I don't think Mr McRae would 'urt Stephen, but 'e may try to take 'im." The words caught in my throat.

Mrs Winter's eyes never left mine as I spoke, her face soft with understanding. "I had suspected there was something we didn't know. But, since the war, there are so many fatherless children. I am sorry it has come to this for you." She pushed her chair back and went over to the door.

"Could I have Stephen McRae's folder please?" she called out to the secretary. "Thank you." Back at the desk, she opened the folder and made a note.

"There, it's on record, but I will also raise it in the staff room so that they are all aware of the warning. Don't worry. I will only tell them that there is a possible threat, not the details. I will respect your privacy."

29

Spring 1954

The new school term started without incident. Stephen had come back from Lulu's full of stories about his fun with her children and their pets. Life settled back into its comfortable routines. I enjoyed walking home before the sun was fully set.

At my station, partway through one morning, I got a tap on my shoulder. Mr Fredericks was behind me. He motioned for me to follow him. I glanced at Iris, who shrugged but nodded. As I left, Iris and the lady on my other side shifted to cover me.

"What is it, Mr Fredericks?" I asked, as the factory door closed behind us.

"An urgent telephone call for you, apparently." He looked at me with fatherly affection. "I hope it's not too bad. Anyway, they're holding the call for you up in the office. Best get up there."

Heart racing, I hurried up the stairs. Very few people knew where I worked, so it wasn't difficult to realise who would call me here. At the office, Mr Seddon's secretary held the telephone receiver out to me with a worried look.

"Elise McRae speaking."

"Mrs McRae, it's Mrs Winter here."

I gripped the edge of the counter. The secretary quietly left the office, shutting the door behind her.

"I'm sorry to have to telephone you at work, but I thought you should know. Stephen is fine, and safe."

My fingers loosened.

"But the teacher on playground duty has just informed me that a man was seen hanging around the fence at morning-tea time. Some of the children also told her he was asking if anyone knew Stephen McRae. Thankfully the children know not to talk to strangers so he went away without learning anything."

Grateful for the privacy, I breathed deeply, hand to my chest. How had Harold managed to find Stephen's school? I realised Mrs Winter was speaking again.

"Mrs McRae, I need to report this to the police, for the safety of the school. They will probably want to talk to you."

I shut my eyes, remembering my last interview with a police officer. I could only hope the local police would be as pleasant to deal with.

"Mrs McRae? Are you still there?"

"Yes, Mrs Winter. Sorry, I was thinking. Of course, I should 'ave realised the police would need to be told. I am sorry to 'ave brought our personal troubles to your school."

"Think nothing of it; you are not to blame. So will I give them your home address?"

Mr Seddon readily gave me the rest of the day off. "Family is important, Mrs McRae. We'll see you tomorrow. Good luck."

I'd arranged with Mrs Winter that I would come straight to the school and see the police with her. I didn't like the idea of having the police at Mrs Marchand's front door.

At the school, I told the police what I had told Mrs Winter about Harold's past and his threats.

The constable flipped his notebook shut. "That'll be all for now, Mrs McRae. We'll circulate his description and keep an eye on the school for a while. Hopefully our presence will put him off trying again. Thanks for coming in, it saves us time."

For months afterwards, I was on my guard, more aware of my surroundings than before, though I did my best to keep things normal for Stephen's sake. Mrs Marchand had gone back to walking Stephen to school, but now took the precaution of varying her route. Gradually, as the year wore on, I allowed myself to hope that Harold had given up on finding us.

30

Spring 1955

I was sitting quietly at lunch break, privately amused by some of the talk I heard flowing over me when I heard my name mentioned.

"You hoo! Elise. Over here, look over here."

I looked around to see a hand waving further down the table.

When Nancy saw she had my attention, she continued:"You doing anything Friday night?"

Unsure where the conversation was going, I shook my head. "No, I don't tend to go out in the evening. Why?"

Her grin widened. "There's a dance on at the community hall. A new band is playing and we need more girls to make up numbers. You got a nice dress?"

I lowered my eyes to the table as Iris nudged my side.

"Go on, Elise. About time you started acting your age. Time enough for you to be a grumpy old lady like me when you start getting grey hairs." She laughed as I stared at her through narrowed eyes.

"I've never gone to a dance, Iris. I wouldn't 'ave a clue what to wear, or if I even can dance."

She considered me, leaning back to get a better look. She nodded once, then turned to Nancy. "She's in Nanse. I'll get her tarted up, don't you worry," she shouted, her words starting a round of clapping and whistles from our workmates. I buried my hot face in my hands, wishing they'd find something else to talk about.

On the factory floor, I was for once grateful for the usual din from the machinery. No one bothered to try to make themselves heard. We had to keep our eyes firmly on our station and the conveyor belts that carried the goods along our production line, which meant the younger girls couldn't attempt to catch my eye to tease me that way.

As we walked out through the gate that evening, I found one person hadn't forgotten completely. Iris appeared beside me, touching my arm to get my attention.

"Now, we have a few days to get you sorted. How about I come to yours tomorrow after work, and we can figure out your glad rags?" She laughed as she saw my face. "Oh don't be like that. A young girl like you deserves to let her hair down now and then. It'll only be for a few hours, it won't kill you."

I realised I didn't actually have a choice. She'd made up her mind: I was going and that was that. I gave in with ill grace. "All right, I'll go. But I know I'll just end up sitting looking after the coats all evening."

On the bus home, guilt gnawed at me as I acknowledged I owed her thanks for putting her own needs aside to do what she felt would help me. I made a mental note to improve my behaviour the following day. Which I promptly forgot when we inspected my wardrobe.

"See what I mean?" I sighed as I threw my best dress on my

bed, on top of all the clothes I owned. It didn't make for a large pile. "I just 'ave what I need for normal everyday things – work, groceries, taking Stephen to school or 'is friends, and this," I waved a derisive hand at the dress Yvonne had given me. Up until now I'd always thought it the prettiest dress I could ever want. But now it seemed old fashioned and too young. It certainly didn't seem to be something to wear to a dance.

Iris snorted. She stood on the other side of my bed, hands planted on her hips and a smile on her face. "Are you done feeling sorry for yourself? I know it's not your usual idea of fun, but seriously, Elise, when was the last time you did something that was just for you? Oh, I know you enjoy taking that darling boy of yours to the playground or the zoo, but that's different. A dance is exactly what you need. A chance to be surrounded by people your own age, enjoying some cheerful music and having an evening that is just for fun!"

I laughed then. "My own age? Iris, you're not exactly elderly you know. There's not that many years between us. But I am sorry, it's not very grateful of me, when you've taken time away from Jim to sort me out."

She nodded, a satisfied smile on her face. "That's better, though I don't think you quite got my point. This is supposed to be all about you, you silly goose! Now, give me that." She waved an imperious hand at my spotted dress. I handed it over, curious now. She held it up by the shoulders, shaking the full skirt out and turning it to the light. "Hmm, yes, I think we can do something with this. Like you, it just needs a bit of updating." She winked.

* * *

Friday arrived and I fairly ran out of the gates to catch the first bus. At home I washed up and ate an early dinner. Mrs Marchand had been only too pleased to sit with Stephen for the evening when I told her where I'd been invited.

"Just what the doctor ordered!" She beamed. "I think I'll get us some fish and chips, how does that sound, Stephen?"

"Yay!" he shouted, running around us in circles. We laughed at his enthusiasm for such a simple meal. He ground to a halt by her and threw his arms around her. "Thank you, thank you!" He grinned.

I left the two of them to plan their evening while getting ready to buy their dinner. I dampened my hair then brushed it into place. Mrs Marchand had let me use some of her hairspray. I patted my head as the spray dried, wincing at the odd texture. I put on the dress, adding the belt and blouse over the top. Iris had worked her magic with what I already had, showing me how to mix things up to modernise my appearance. At work the day after her visit, she'd handed me a little makeup, quickly showing me how to apply it in the ladies room over lunchtime. I'd gasped at the change I saw in the mirror. "I have cheekbones!" I'd said, turning from side to side as Iris laughed at me.

"Well, wash it off now, or we won't have time to eat. Come on."

I did my best to apply it again as she had shown me, checking both sides of my face for any lines or unevenness.

"Shoes, there. Necklace." I muttered the list to myself as I completed my wardrobe. I gave myself a last appraisal in my bedroom mirror, nodding to myself. "That will do, Mrs McRae." I had kept my married name even after the divorce. I'd not wanted to give any reason for gossip or scandal, especially since everyone knew I had a child. But saying that surname still made me sad at times. It was a constant reminder that I had somehow failed. I'd taken several weeks to come to terms with my new status, before I'd felt able to go to Mass. I thought everyone who saw me could see the shame of 'divorced woman' written on me. Lulu had been stern with me when she discovered why I wasn't going.

"Elise! That is quite enough of that thinking. Do you think our God doesn't know, just by you staying away from church? Do you think He only sees you when you walk through those doors?"

I'd sat back in my seat, her words hitting me like a punch. I felt my breath escape in response and sat speechless for a moment. "I …" I stopped, blinking rapidly. I swallowed. "I never saw it that way." A short, almost bitter, laugh burst from me. "Of course, you are right. I have been stupid."

She'd reached over, patting my hand as it lay on the arm of my chair.

"You aren't alone in that, my friend. We all act stupidly sometime or other. The real question is, what are you going to do to fix it?"

Of course my answer had been to go back to church the very next weekend, and to go to confession. Even so, now and then the sadness over what might have been crept to the front of my thoughts.

As I shut my wardrobe door with the mirror on its inside, I rolled my shoulders back and mentally tucked the sadness away in a drawer, determined to at least try to enjoy the evening. I made my way downstairs, to find my son and landlady donning their coats in the hallway.

Stephen looked over. "Mummy! You look lovely!"

I could feel a blush behind the makeup as I smiled. I hugged him. "Thank you, Stephen. Do I still look like me though?"

He laughed, shaking his head. "Of course you do. Funny Mummy!"

Mrs Marchand caught my arm. "Your ride will be here soon then? You have your key? We're off now to get the fish and chips, or this one won't get to bed on time! You have a wonderful time, Elise! That's an order!" She wagged a finger at me, a grin on her face as she spoke.

"Yes, ma'am. I promise." I waved them off and shut the door. Five minutes later I heard a car horn toot. I took a deep breath. "'ere I go then." I opened the door, locked it behind me, and walked quickly down the path to the car before I could change my mind.

Nancy turned around in the front seat as I settled behind her. "You came then. I thought you might chicken out once Iris wasn't there to twist your arm." She laughed to take the sting out of her words. "Elise, sorry, Mrs McRae" –she winked at me before gesturing to the man behind the wheel– "This is my beau, Mr Jones."

The community hall wasn't too far away, and we pulled up alongside the curb after about a quarter of an hour's drive. I heard music pouring out from the partly opened doors even before I'd opened the car door. Nancy hopped out quickly, holding my door as I climbed out from the back seat. She was wiggling, moving her feet already in excitement. She laughed as she slammed my door behind me.

"I've been so looking forward to this. I love a good dance. Best exercise you can have. Especially with a handsome man like mine to look at while you do it." She grabbed my arm and that of Mr Jones, pulling us with her to the hall doors. He grinned at me. "Looks like we have to do as we're told."

Inside, Nancy released my arm and took off her coat, handing it to the hat check girl by a counter on our left. She grabbed her beau's arm again and dragged him to the dance floor, dropping her purse on a table as they passed it. Despite my own nervousness, I had to laugh as she took the lead on the dance floor, gyrating to the upbeat tune.

I turned away at last, handing my own coat over at the counter and looking around to see who else I knew there. The sea of faces was daunting: I was worried about anyone catching my eye if they were strangers. I slowly walked to an empty table and sat down. A body detached itself from the dancing throng and came my way. She grinned and flopped into a chair next to me, breathing hard and staring at the dancers.

I looked her up and down. "Jessie! I didn't see you there. You look lovely in that dress."

"It's my absolute favourite. That's why I love coming to things like this – and it's a great excuse to show off my legs!" She threw her head back and laughed. It was infectious. "So, I came over to drag you up there. You won't draw a chap to you while you sit there looking like someone's chaperone! Come on, it's easy enough, I'll show you what to do."

I shook my head, my fear flooding back. "No, not yet, please Jessie. Let me get used to the music for a while. Please?" I begged.

"Not a bit of it." She stuck out her hand and grabbed mine, dragging me from my seat. "The only way is to dive straight in." And with that she suited action to words, pulling me into the middle of the crowd, spinning me around and grabbing my other hand as well.

Soon I had no room left to think of anything but keeping up with her, my eyes fixed solidly on her feet, straining to hear her shout the steps over the band. At one point I lost grip on her and bumped into someone behind me. I muttered an apology but daren't turn away from my excitable and talented partner. The song ended and in the brief pause before the next started, I threw a plea-filled look at Jessie and hurried back to my table. She laughed again, giving in with good grace. I found my hanky in my purse and pulled it out, patting my steaming face as the music began again.

"Excuse me. Would you like a cool drink?"

I came out from behind my hanky and glanced up. A young man stood before me, a hopeful expression in his eyes and a glass in each hand. As I looked, he held one of the cups out to me. "I figured you could use it after that exertion out there." He jerked his head towards the dance floor.

I smiled. "Thank you, that is very thoughtful." I took the glass and sipped. The cool sweet liquid was just what I needed. A slight lemony freshness lightened the sweetness.

"May I sit down?"

I nodded so he drew out the seat opposite me, turning it slightly so that he could see the dancers and me with just a slight turn of his head.

"I don't know how they keep it up, one song after another." He grinned at me, a lopsided widening of his generous mouth. He was slender and angular. I suspected he wasn't quite as lacking in stamina as he was pretending. He had the look of someone who worked hard physically for a living, nothing spare on him at all. I took another sip so he wouldn't catch me staring. "I'm Rob, by the way. Rob Swinlea."

"Elise McRae. Pleased to meet you. And thank you again

243

for the drink."

Mr Swinlea bobbed his head. "You're welcome. I have a confession to make."

I smiled nervously.

"I do have ulterior motives for bringing you a drink. I thought if I got you some refreshment first, you may consider saying yes when I ask you to dance with me." Now he was back to grinning broadly, a boyish expectancy on his face.

I couldn't help but return the look. I had come here thinking only about keeping my work friends happy so I could say no another time. Though I had worked out it was considered the way to meet boys — men — I'd not allowed myself to think in that direction. And here I was, without doing anything to attract attention, being asked to dance already, a couple of songs into the evening. "You must not 'ave seen 'ow terrible I was then. You will put your toes in danger. I've never danced before, you see."

He looked surprised. "Really? I thought you did pretty well, considering how your friend was pulling you all over the place. Are you French, by the way? I couldn't help but notice a bit of an accent there."

I blushed, and hoped the low lighting wouldn't give me away. "Yes, though actually from New Caledonia."

"Well, Miss McRae from New Caledonia, would you do me the honour of dancing with me to the next song?"

That startled me. He'd naturally assumed the 'Miss'. I didn't want to lie, but then I wasn't actually married anymore, was I? Would I be misleading him if I didn't correct him? The song began, and taking my silence for consent, he stood and held out his hand. And so I left the subject of my name at the table.

He was definitely a better dance partner than Jessie. He took each of my hands gently, placing one on his own shoulder, and putting his own free hand carefully on my waist. Our other hands were clasped together just below his shoulder and slightly outstretched. Holding me closer than I'd been to anyone since before Harold's imprisonment, he used his own steps to guide me in the movement of the dance. We sidestepped and moved around in a small circle, facing first one way then the other. As the song progressed, he nodded and used our joined hands to twirl me away and back, stopping me with the hand back on my waist. To my surprise I forgot to be nervous, and found myself having fun. He kept it to a few simple movements and repeated them, so gradually I was able to anticipate and relax into the music.

We broke apart as the song came to an end, the dancers all stopping to catch their breath as they applauded the band. The singer appeared to be their leader, and spoke a few words into the microphone, thanking us all and introducing the next song. It was slower than the last few songs. I heard sighs of relief around me as couples and groups of girls dancing together decided to stay or take a break.

"Shall we?" Mr Swinlea asked.

"Yes," I surprised myself with the ready answer. He took my hand again, drawing me close with the hand that had been on my waist, now at the small of my back. Unsure where to look, I stared at his shoulder.

"This is called a waltz. It's even easier than that other one." He murmured close to my ear. "One, two, three," he counted quietly, helping me hear the beat and move in time with it.

By the time the song ended I was ready to sit down. He seemed to sense that, and holding onto my hand still, led me back to my table.

Jessie and some man were sitting there. She grinned broadly as we approached. "Look at you go, Mrs M! I didn't think you had it in you."

I felt a sinking inside as Mr Swinlea's hand froze in mine. He looked down at me, confusion on his face. I swallowed hard.

"I — I should 'ave said before. Could we move over there please? I will explain." I stared back, putting every ounce of sincerity I could into my gaze.

At last he nodded. We threaded our way through the tables to a quiet spot near the far wall.

He leaned against the wall, hands thrust into his pockets. "So, you're Mrs McRae? Is there a Mr McRae?" His voice sounded hard now.

Slowly I nodded. "There is, but 'e is not 'ere. I, that is, we are divorced. I am sorry I didn't tell you before, but it is not something I talk about. Jessie" —I pointed back over my shoulder— "and my other work friends only know that I was married. They don't know the details, or why 'e is not with me. I 'ave let them come to their own conclusions. I am not proud of it."

He considered me carefully, eyes searching mine. "I guess I don't need to know more than that. I'm sorry I jumped to conclusions."

"Thank you, and there is no need to apologise."

He smiled then and I sighed with relief. He pushed away from the wall, grabbed my hand and led me back the way we'd come. He pulled out my chair and pushed it back in once I was seated.

"Jessie, is it? Elise here — "

I bit my lip at his boldness in using my Christian name so

casually.

"— tells me I have you to thank for persuading her to come tonight." He sketched a short bow in her direction.

The band was taking a short break as well, the room instead now filled with the hubbub of multiple conversations at each table. Smoke rose from several of them as men and women lit up cigarettes and leant back in their chairs, as relaxed there as they'd been active before. When the band started up again, Jessie took no time to grab her partner and drag him as she'd dragged me earlier.

Rob and I laughed as we saw the poor chap struggle to keep up with her.

"So much for the man being the lead." He chuckled in my ear.

While the dancing continued, we sat and talked. He told me that he lived on a farm, but had come home to visit his friends. "I didn't know anything about tonight until I arrived at Terry's." He grinned ruefully. "But they wouldn't take no for an answer, so here I am. They even had these fancy rags for me so I wouldn't embarrass them." He waved a hand at his suit. "I'll have to remember to thank them as well."

If this was the start of anything serious, I thought it best to get that something out in the open. "Rob? I need to tell you – I 'ave a son. 'is name is Stephen and 'e is six, almost seven."

"He is a lucky little boy to have you as his mum. I'd love to meet him."

This man continued to surprise me. Not that I had any experience, but I had been given to understand, from listening to the chatter in the break room, that single young men weren't at all interested in children or other people's domestic situations. From what I'd heard, they thought of themselves as free from what they called 'complications'. His face fell at my silence.

"Sorry, maybe that was a bit forward of me. I would understand if you aren't ready for him to meet me. It's only our first date after all."

My face burned at that word. Date? "No. You caught me by surprise, that's all." I thought quickly, then smiled. "Maybe it is better sooner than later."

He grinned, relief written all over him. Leaning forward, elbows on the table, he looked at me seriously. "I'm not normally this forward, so please don't think badly of me. Would you mind giving me your address? So I can come meet him, and maybe we can go for a walk together?"

As much as I liked him, I wasn't sure I was quite ready to tell him where we lived. "Would you mind if we meet somewhere instead? Maybe the zoo? Stephen loves it there. It may be easier that way, don't you think?"

He nodded. "Whatever you're ok with. I just really want to see you again. Soon." He blushed. Part of me considered it critically. So that's what I look like when it happens to me. Another part of me felt for him, touched that he would be so open with me.

"I'd like that too. What about tomorrow afternoon? Or is that too soon?"

"No, that's perfect! Shall I meet you both at the main entrance, say one o'clock?"

We sat there, grinning at each other, until Jessie and her friend came back, flopping into seats, panting from the dancing.

By the time the evening was over, we'd got in a couple more dances and learned more about each other. He waved to me as Nancy's chap drove us off.

Going to work the next day I suspected break times would be trying, knowing Jessie as well as I did by now. Sure enough, as I sat down at the table for morning tea, she pounced.

"Here she is, the dark horse. How's the dancing feet this morning?" She cast a leering glance along the table. Nancy and a few others laughed as I reddened and drank my tea. Iris arrived just then, tapping the woman next to me on the shoulder.

"Oy, you're in my seat. Up you get." The woman grabbed her drink, apologised and hurried off to another table. Iris sat down heavily, now between me and the teasing further along. She smiled at me and leaned forward. "Ignore them, Elise. Get on with your tea, and let me handle this." She spoke so only I could hear. Then she turned to the others. "So Jessie, who's this new fella Nancy told me about? From all accounts he didn't stand a chance once you clapped eyes on him."

Around the table a shout of laughter arose. Those who had been following Jessie's lead in teasing me now turned on her with glee, begging for more gossip.

I whispered a thank you to Iris's back.

* * *

Mrs Marchand had been delighted when I'd told her of my plans to take Stephen to the zoo. "Wonderful! It's about time you two had a proper outing." She promised to have him 'ship shape and Bristol fashion' by the time I got home, so I'd only need to sort myself out.

"I'm back! 'ello?" I called, as I came in and shut the door behind me. I looked up as I heard footsteps coming down the stairs.

"Mum, Mum! Are we really going to the zoo? Right now?" He jumped the last couple of stairs and ran into me for a cuddle.

Laughing, I assured him we were. "But just let me freshen up. We 'ave time before the bus." I extricated myself and climbed the stairs to our rooms. He followed behind, chattering excitedly about the animals he wanted to see first.

Mrs Marchand waved us off. I'd told her about meeting Rob, but asked her to leave it to me to tell Stephen.

"Now, 'e's not quite a friend yet, you understand." I explained as we walked to the bus stop. "I only met 'im last night. But I told 'im all about you and 'e wanted to meet you. I 'ope you will like 'im too."

"Is he old like you, Mum?" He was holding my hand, so now I jiggled his arm through our joined hands.

"Cheeky! Your maman is not old. Rob is a grown up though. I didn't ask 'is age. Grown ups don't tend to do that. So don't you either, all right?" I gave him a stern look, but he just grinned as he skipped beside me to keep up.

Being a Saturday afternoon, many of the passengers on the bus were families as well, and got off at the same stop as us. I smiled at the excited chatter coming from all the children, and once or twice caught the eye of an already tired-looking parent. As we approached the main entrance, I slowed to separate us from the others, checking to see if Rob was here yet.

"Is that him, Mum?" Stephen pointed off to one side.

I looked. "Yes, it is. Thank you. Come on."

We changed direction. As soon as he saw us, he pushed off from the wall and met us partway. We shared a smile, then I did the introductions.

"Stephen, this is Mr Swinlea. Mr Swinlea, this is my son, Stephen. Say 'ello, Stephen."

Rob stuck his hand out to shake Stephen's. Stephen looked up at me and I nodded. He stood up straighter, squaring his shoulders and took Rob's hand.

"Pleased to meet you, Master McRae." Rob said, striking just the right note with Stephen. "Shall we go in then? What are we seeing first?"

Stephen's face glowed and he jumped with excitement. "The lions! They are the king of the jungle, so we have to see them first!"

Rob and I shared a smile as he answered. "Lions it is then."

We joined the queue to the admission counter, moving slowly and steadily forward. When it was our turn, Rob stepped in front of us.

"Two adults, one child please." He turned and smiled, handing Stephen his own ticket to hold.

"Thanks Mr Swinlea!" He grinned.

"Yes, thank you Rob. You didn't 'ave to do that."

He sketched a short bow of his head. "My pleasure. Now, shall we see if they have any of those bags of peanuts for when we get to the elephants?"

"Yes please!" Stephen dropped my hand and grabbed Rob's. I laughed at the look of shocked delight on Rob's face.

For the rest of the visit, Stephen hardly left Rob's side. I trailed along sometimes beside them, often just behind, quietly thrilled at their instant bond. I saw how starved my son was for male company. Now and then Rob would grin back at me, eyes crinkled.

While we were waiting for our bus home, Rob turned to me.

"I know this is early days. But I reckon we hit it off pretty well, don't you?" Taking my smile for agreement, he continued: "So, could I take you out to dinner? I'll be back in town in a couple of weeks. Maybe just us? I'm happy to meet you somewhere, if that makes you more comfortable."

"Yes, I'd like that. Very much."

He waited till our bus arrived, then waved goodbye.

31

Summer 1955/1956

By the following week I was old news, thanks to Iris's ready intervention the day after the dance. Break time went back to safe and familiar routines, other subjects dominating the attention of my colleagues.

Iris and I had lunch out on Tuesday, the better to talk without prying ears. We found a bench near a grassed area just down from the factory and laid out our lunches on a tea towel she'd brought from home.

"Now, start at the beginning and leave nothing out." She picked up a sandwich expectantly.

I laughed, took a bite of my apple, and filled her in.

"Is there anything more I should know, Miss?" Iris grinned at last.

"Well, I'm meeting 'im next Friday for dinner. 'e is taking me there." I pointed down the road towards the restaurant which was just out of sight. I knew she'd know where I meant.

"And you kept that till last?" She threw her hands in the air in mock exasperation. "It's like blood from a stone with you, Elise!"

We gathered up our things as she continued to tease. We got back to the locker room just in time to put it all away and get our work coats back on.

*　*　*

Our dinner date resolved any doubts I may have had, and I was happy to have him drive me home. My respect for him grew with every conversation, as we learned more about each other. At the same time, I could see how he was filling a void in Stephen's life I hadn't realised was there until that visit to the zoo.

One Sunday, a few weeks later, Rob arrived to take Stephen and me out for the afternoon. Once in the car, Stephen wriggled to the middle of the seat so he could see out the front. After a while his attention turned to Rob and he began to ask about the parts of the car. I sat quietly listening, marvelling at Rob's patience with the stream of questions. He explained about the gears and the pedals, and let Stephen lean closer to watch the sequence of movements as we pulled away from a stop sign.

We reached the point beyond which Stephen and I had never been. Rob adroitly turned the conversation to our surroundings, pointing out landmarks and a few famous buildings. As we got closer into the city, the streets became steeper and narrower. I told Stephen to sit back in his seat behind me, my nerves at the tightness of the roads making me firm with him. Rob threw an amused look my way.

"There's nothing to worry about. I've driven here heaps of times. I grew up here, remember? Relax!"

I did my best to follow his advice, but though he knew the

roads and what to expect at the top of a slope or around a bend, I didn't. So I really only relaxed once we stopped and got out of the car. I stretched to ease out the knots in my arms and legs where I'd braced myself in my seat. Stephen was turning slow circles, taking in the tall buildings surrounding us. Rob locked the car, came to the footpath and took my arm.

"Come on lad, how about you grab your mum's other hand? We'll keep her safe on both sides, hey?"

We walked three abreast along the almost deserted street. I saw why Rob had suggested a Sunday afternoon: though no shops were open, it meant we didn't have to wait for cars to pass, or manoeuvre past other walkers. Rob proved to be a fount of knowledge of the city, satisfying even my child's usually insatiable appetite for information. He showed us the Town Hall, the Court Theatre and the Chief Post Office building as we walked. Like Stephen, I craned my neck to better see the magnificent and ornate structures, feeling dwarfed by them.

"They can't really build like this anymore. Brick and labour is so much more expensive. Hard to believe it's only about forty years ago that they opened this, isn't it? You'd think it was over a hundred years old." Rob's voice was infused with awe as he spoke.

I glanced over briefly. I think perhaps it was at that moment that I knew for certain I was in love with him. Not for him a small or self centred existence. The thought shocked me even as it happened. I stared back up at the building to hide my own expression while I compared him to Harold consciously for the first time. Harold's behaviour now took on a more general significance. Up until now, I'd only seen it in terms of how much it had hurt me and Stephen, and the damage to his colleague's life. In that moment, though, I saw it as part of a whole way of looking at the world. I gave myself a mental shake, shutting down that meditation for now. Time enough to examine it more deeply when I was alone. I smiled down at my son to anchor myself firmly in the fun of the day.

"What do you think, Stephen? Would it be 'ard work, building those walls with all those 'eavy bricks?"

He nodded vigorously. "It must have taken hundreds of years!" He stretched his arms wide in emphasis, with a child's typical exaggeration.

We walked a circuit encompassing several large city blocks, ending back at the car.

"This next place won't look like much at the moment, but I thought you'd like to one day be able to tell your mates that you saw it like it is right now." With that cryptic comment to Stephen, Rob went silent, smiling away to himself as he drove us through the city towards the harbour. The water shimmered in the afternoon sun, the road at times appearing to head straight towards it, at others twisting away around stores and offices.

At last we pulled off the road, parking in an empty, unsealed space between the road and the sea.

"Come on." Rob got out and led the way over the rough ground. Just as we caught up to him, a movement caught my peripheral vision. I turned to see a man walking quickly towards us from the other side of the parking space. Rob was still talking to Stephen; neither of them had noticed the stranger.

"On the other side you can just see the northern part of Auckland," Rob said. "They've just signed off on putting a bridge across here."

I moved closer to Rob, something in the way the man was walking made me nervous. I reached for Stephen's hand.

Stephen stared. "What, all the way to those?" He pointed to a cluster of buildings, made small by the distance. "It's miles away!" He looked up at Rob, a look of disbelief.

"Rob." I whispered. He didn't hear me, instead shaking his head at Stephen's question.

"It's true. The government has made a whole new department to get it done. There'll be heaps of workers wanted – engineers, builders, all sorts. They want it to be like a highway over the water. It's going to take a few years I reckon. What do you say to going over there? We can buy tickets to catch the ferry at the office over there." He pointed to a building nearer the sea.

The man was getting closer. I moved between him and my son. Rob looked at me at last, a question on his face. I flicked my eyes towards the stranger.

Stephen was still staring up at Rob. "Will you work on it?"

"Rob! I think we need to go."

"No, not in my line. But —" Rob spoke to Stephen, and didn't hear me.

"What're you doin' with my wife?"

My stomach knotted as the voice whipped out. Harold had found me.

Rob stared, first at Harold, then at me.

I gulped and turned to face Harold, keeping Stephen between Rob and me. Harold was just a few feet away now. I heard Rob take a step, realising he meant to move in front of me. I reached back for his hand and squeezed, then gently pushed him back.

Stephen spoke. "Mum, that's the man from school. Do you

know him?"

I was grateful once more to the discipline his school had instilled: he had seen the 'stranger' but not identified himself.

"It's all right, Stephen. Yes, I know 'im. Stay with Rob, please." I spoke without taking my eyes off the figure in front of me. "So it was you. I don't know 'ow you found 'is school, but it doesn't matter. They reported you to the police, you know."

Harold made a sound somewhere between a laugh and a grunt. "I'm his father, and your husband. I have rights."

"We aren't married anymore, 'arold, you know that. I am not your wife. And you 'ave no rights to Stephen. You gave up your rights with your threats and behaviour. "

His lip lifted in a sneer. "Your church doesn't let you divorce. And what about your vows?" He put on a sing-song voice as he quoted: "'till death do us part'. Did you forget that, Elise? Anyway, you do what you want, but a man is entitled to see his son." He took a step closer, leaning to see Stephen behind me. Stephen whimpered.

"No!" I surprised myself, my own voice strong despite the churning in my stomach.

Harold straightened and for a moment I got a good look at him. He had shaved and cut his hair, but his face had new lines in it. His hair was greying and receding, and the sour smell of old beer wafted from him.

I stood even straighter and surprised myself again by taking a step toward him. "No, I am not your wife, and 'e is no longer your son. You only 'ave yourself to blame, 'arold. You abandoned us that day you left 'ome and chose the bottle over me." I realised the truth as I spoke it.

Harold's shoulders sagged but his face stayed hard.

"I don't know what you thought you'd achieve by this – ambush. But you need to go and not come near us again. I will report you to the police if you do."

Rob cleared his throat and came up beside me. "Look mate, you best be on your way. You heard the lady, no need to make this a big scene."

Harold lifted his gaze, glaring at Rob. "And who the hell do you think you are? This is between me and her, so back off!"

Rob stiffened.

I put a hand in front of him. "It's ok, Rob, I can manage. Why don't you and Stephen go get those tickets? I'll be right there." I glanced at him quickly, reluctant to take my eyes off Harold until Stephen was out of reach.

Rob nodded. "Come on, little guy, we'll wait for your mum over there."

I heard Stephen's footsteps move away and I let go of the breath I didn't know I was holding. I turned back to my ex-husband. Now we had no audience, his face softened and he tried to grab my hand.

"Elise. Please. Can't we try again? I can change. I got another job. I got a place to live. Please?" His tone wheedled, grating after the viciousness of minutes before.

I snatched my hand away. "I said no, 'arold. That's final. Go back to Tauranga, it's for the best, really. You need to put us be'ind you. After all, we were only married a few short months. We don't even know each other now." I stared, hoping against hope that he would finally see sense.

At last he shuffled backwards, hands stuffed in his trouser pockets. "I didn't mean any of it you know," he said as he moved away. "What I said in those letters. I was just so ... alone. And I guess I lashed out."

I almost felt sorry for him. "Goodbye 'arold." I turned at last and began walking towards Rob and Stephen. Though I knew I had done the right thing, I couldn't help feeling saddened at the state Harold was in, to have tried something so desperate. The next moment, something hit me from behind and arms wrapped around me, dragging me to the ground. I bit back a scream, even now not wanting to scare my son.

"You think I'd just let you walk off?" Sour breath washed over my face as the words were growled at me.

I struggled as one arm tightened around me and the other hand moved up to grab my hair. Some instinct kicked in before he could get a good grip. I twisted my head to the side and bit into his arm.

"You little …" he snarled. But before he could finish I felt his weight being pulled off me. I rolled over in time to see Rob launch a fist into Harold's face, knocking him to the ground. Harold groaned, curling up on his side but made no attempt to get back up.

"Mummy, Mummy!" Stephen was crying as he tried to hug my head, on his knees behind me.

"I'm ok, my darling, I'm ok. Let me sit up." I let him climb on my lap and check for himself. He looked at me, a hand on each side of my head.

"You were so brave, Mum! You bit him good!"

I laughed then, wrapping my arms around him until he begged for air.

Over his head I watched as Rob marched a defeated Harold away to the ferry office. By the time he came out again, we were on our feet, Stephen brushing the gravel and dust from my skirt. I held both hands out as Rob drew close but he evaded my hands, instead pulling me in close, hugging me as tightly as I had hugged my son moments before.

"It's all over now." He pulled back, frowning at me. "Remind me never to get on your bad side, Elise!"

* * *

As the ferry left the terminal with us onboard, a police car drove up to the ferry office. I shared a look with Rob. Stephen was so excited to be on the ferry; for the time being he was distracted from the drama in the car park.

Rob spoke again. "Are you sure you're ok?"

I nodded. "Yes, I'm fine Rob. I may be a little sore tomorrow though."

He put an arm over my shoulders, pressing me to his side. "I know we've not known each other very long. But I think you know how I feel about you, don't you?"

I stared out across the water. I could almost feel him studying my face. I wanted to give him a simple answer, knowing all the while that it wasn't a simple situation. I had been married, divorced, and had a child. His was a more straight forward past. I knew how the church viewed marriage after a divorce. If I loved him, as I was more and more sure of each day, could I put him through all the trouble involved?

"I do, Rob. And I feel the same. But it's not just about that is it? It's not just us. What will your family say when they know I'm divorced, not a widow? That I 'ave a child already? That my ex-'usband is a criminal? They'd never accept me." To my chagrin I felt tears burn and I blinked rapidly to clear them.

"They will have to accept you because I love you. Do you hear me? I am of age and I can make my own choices. Elise," He turned me to face him, his expression serious. "I won't say anymore today, but please, think about it. I think you know what I want." He leaned in and kissed the top of my head.

I thought about little else over the next week. Rob had dropped us home, chatting normally and keeping Stephen engaged. I put my son to bed after an early supper, before settling in the lounge with Mrs Marchand over a cup of tea.

My normally unflappable landlady let out a gasp when I explained what had occurred on our outing.

"Oh, my Elise! I wonder how he found you?"

I shrugged. "I don't think he left Auckland after that scare at the school, so maybe he moved up here. I think he just got lucky today. Who knows?"

She snorted. "Not so lucky for him in the end though, was it? And you are sure you're all right? Nothing broken?"

Laughing, I assured her as I'd done Rob earlier. "I'm absolutely fine, Mrs M, I promise. I may 'ave a bruise or two in the morning, but at least now we know 'e is be'ind us once and for all. I was more scared for Stephen than myself. I couldn't let 'arold take 'im. Any bumps or bruises I 'ave are nothing compared to that." I stood up and went through to the kitchen to rinse with our cups. On my way to the stairs, I popped my head through the living room door. "I'm off to bed. Good—"

"Not so fast, young lady." She gestured sternly for me to come back in. "I'm pretty sure you have something else to tell me."

Sighing, I sat down. "I don't know 'ow you do this." I shook my head at her seeming prescience. "I think Rob is going to – propose." There. I had said it aloud.

She studied me carefully. "And?"

"And, I'm divorced, I 'ave another man's child – a man 'oo

262

just attacked us this afternoon. Not exactly a straightforward situation!"

"He knows all that, Elise, and it's plain to anyone who sees him that the man is crazy about you. Don't give me that look! If he has already begun talking along those lines, he's considered it all and is ready to face it with you. So, any other excuses?" She laughed, waving a hand as if swatting my worries away. "Elise, I know you've been badly let down and hurt by Harold. But you're young, too young to give up on being loved properly. Think about it. Pray of course. You know I am here, whatever you decide."

* * *

On Saturday evening, Rob arrived to take me out to dinner. Throughout the meal, the conversation was light. Mrs Marchand's advice hadn't left my thoughts in the days since.

"Shall we?" he said as he bundled the serviette on the table and stood. We walked back to the car, arm in arm. The next moment, he reached into a pocket and sank to one knee beside me, the streetlight sparkling on the little jewelled ring in his hand. His grin up at me seemed blurry. I didn't notice that it was my own tears that were causing the blur.

"Elise McRae, will you do me the honour of becoming my wife?" His grin looked nervous now.

Now the moment had arrived. I gave a silent prayer of thanks, a flood of peace washing away all my concerns. "I will, Rob. Yes! I will," I gulped back my tears, trying to steady my voice.

He removed the ring from the little box, took my hand and slipped it onto my finger. Then he stood to hold me, kissing my ear. "Thank God for that! And I promise never to get drunk and end up in jail!"

I smacked him on the back in mock disapproval. "Rob!"

He looked at me, laughing."What? Is it a taboo subject now? Do I need to start a list of what I can't talk about?"

I hugged him again, arms around his waist as he stood tall and strong in front of me. "Why am I only now seeing 'ow silly you can be?"

He threw his head back, his laugh reverberating down the empty street. "Come on, let's go tell that son of yours."

Mrs Marchand had gone to see some friends, so Stephen was staying at Lulu's for the evening. All the way there, Rob drove with one hand, the other holding mine.

We pushed through the gate. Louis opened the door, smiling when he saw Rob standing close to me.

"Come in, come in," he whispered. "They crashed out only an hour or so ago. Lulu's just putting Stephen's things back in 'is bag."

We followed him silently through to the lounge.

"Do you want a cup of tea before you go? I was about to make our supper drink?" As he spoke, his eye fell to my hand. He looked at our faces, a smile spreading over his own face. "Really? I knew it!" He shook Rob's hand, congratulating him before giving me a hug. "I insist you stay for a celebratory drink. Sit, sit!" He ushered us to the sofa and left the room.

Lulu rushed in moments later. She stared at my hand as she entered. She leaned over me and squeezed me in her arms. Then she hugged Rob as well.

He laughed. "I've never been hugged by two women on the same day before! Unless you count my sisters."

Lulu stood smiling from me to Rob until Louis returned

with a tray of drinks.

"Come and sit down, Lulu." I said with a laugh.

"I managed to find something a little stronger than tea." Louis placed the tray down carefully, the glass bottle rattling against the cups. "Who's for a little brandy in their tea?" He held the bottle expectantly.

Rob eyed me, brows raised.

"Go on, one drink won't undo that promise!" I grinned.

Lulu and Louis looked confused.

"A private joke, don't worry. Yes please," Rob said.

"Not for me, though, thank you. Just a little milk."

So Lulu and I stuck to tea, the men lacing theirs with a splash of the golden brandy.

"A toast to the 'appy couple." We raised our cups together.

* * *

Iris, Lulu and I were out to do some last minute shopping. As one decision after another was checked off, I compared this experience with that other time, when I was a mere sixteen-year-old, frightened by the state I'd found myself in, and pulled along by circumstances over which I felt little control.

"Elise! Did you hear me?" Lulu had shaken my arm to get my attention.

"What? Sorry, I was away with the fairies."

"That much was clear. So, what were you thinking to make you forget your friends?"

I swatted her in mock annoyance. "If you must know, I was thinking back to the last time I was shopping for a wedding. It was very – different."

Iris took charge then, leading us to a bench seat nearby. "So tell us then. I mean, we know your ex wasn't a patch on your Rob, but apart from that?"

I tried to pick just the right words. "I think last time, I was so young, for a start. And I made a mistake. I just didn't know 'ow much that would take over my life. I love my son, you both know that! But everything after that just 'appened to me. I thought it was what I wanted, but it all went wrong so fast."

I reached into my bag for a hanky. My friends sat in silence, but I could sense their sympathy as I continued: "And now, it's like night and day really." I smiled. "Rob is so respectful of me, he talks to me – treats me – as an equal. You know what I mean?"

Though I now knew my future husband was my junior by more than three years, I saw a maturity in him I'd never seen in my ex-husband. Already I went to him whenever I had a problem, trusting in his wisdom and strength.

There had been just one fly in the ointment. We had known we would have to face it, but the church's stance against remarriage after divorce saddened me. Since moving to this city, I'd come to see the local church as my home, as it was Mrs Marchand's. Rob was, I think, somewhat relieved that it was not to be an option. And I understood. His experiences at the hands of the Catholic school staff were enough to explain that reaction. But that's his story, not mine, to tell.

"I'll ask my mates. Someone's bound to have an idea where we can try."

Which is why, soon after he'd told his family of our en-gagement, we had an appointment with various ministers. Anglican, Methodist, and Baptist churches either said no once they heard my full story, or they had no space available to fit us in. The last one we approached was a Presbyterian church.

Pastor Michael welcomed us to his office with a smile. "Please, take a seat. Can I offer you a cup of tea?"

We accepted, feeling a warmth we'd not experienced with any of his contemporaries of the other denominations. Growing up Catholic, I had no idea of what to expect from any of them, and was rather taken aback by the modern buildings. If I'd not known it was a church, I could have been forgiven for thinking this one was a community centre or something similar.

Once we had our drinks, he sat down at a third chair in front of his desk, putting me even more at ease. "Now, I understand you have a bit of a complication with your upcoming nuptials? Fill me in, and I'll butt in if I think of anything."

Rob did just that, taking charge in a way I appreciated.

Pastor Michael turned his attention to me. "Mrs McRae. My sincere commiserations for the troubles you have had to face. It's not something anyone can be prepared for, but at the tender age you were, I'm not surprised that it's had such a lasting impact on you. And I commend you for doing all you could to make the best of things at the time. It must have been very difficult." He paused.

I nodded, eyes stinging at the depth of his understanding.

"Now, I must also apologise for the treatment you have had from the Christian community. Sometimes we are so much harder on our own members than the outside world! That said, I understand that principles are only of any use when they are maintained. I do know the basis for the stance of churches in situations such as yours."

I swallowed. I was suddenly unsure where this oration was heading. I saw that priests weren't alone in their skill at using a lot of words to say simple things.

267

He smiled again. "Doesn't mean I agree with them. In fact, we Presbyterians believe that divorce can be forgiven like any other 'sin.'" He held up a finger on each hand, hooking them in the air. "So, yes, we would be happy to marry you here in our humble church." He stood and walked around his desk. He picked up a book, clearly his diary, and flicked through a few pages. "How does Saturday, six weeks from now, work for you? Will that give you enough time to get things organised, invitations and the like?"

Rob grabbed my hand, sighing in relief. "That is perfect, ta Pastor. Do you do that reading of the banns thing? Do we need to turn up on Sunday?"

Pastor Michael flapped a hand. "No, we don't worry about that. You're not considering making us your permanent church are you?"

We shook our heads.

He laughed now. "If I restricted who I'd marry based on their decision of joining us, I'd not get a lot of practice marrying folk! No, we just need to catch up closer to the time, to nail down the details for the day, but other than that, I need some contact information for my diary here, then you can get on with the other hundred things on your plate before the big day."

After that, my wedding planning came together quickly: Iris offered to fix my hair on the day, and Mrs Marchand took charge of the flowers for my bouquet and the church. Her garden was well admired by the ladies of the parish.

* * *

Stephen and I were going to live on the farm where Rob

worked. A rural town called Morrinsville, almost two hours south of Auckland. It meant I would have to finish at the factory of course. And Stephen would have to change schools.

"Mum, will I be in the big kids' class at the new school?" It was the latest in a long line of questions Stephen had for me since I had told him about Morrinsville.

"Yes, my love. Rob 'as spoken with the 'eadmaster already. Now, do you 'ave your present for your teacher?" We had gone shopping to choose a 'goodbye' gift.

My last Friday as Mrs McRae dawned bright, clear, and for once in this sub-tropical city, dry. I rode the bus to work for the last time. My work friends took the opportunity to tease me every break time that day, some like Jessie, giving way to their ribald tendencies, while others pretended to commiserate with my loss of freedom. I'd had to give a little more detail about my past when they found out I was to be married, and not at my own church. Many assured me they would be there tomorrow to see me walk down the aisle.

Stephen had raced home from school to finish packing his things. We were to move into our own home right after the ceremony and wedding breakfast the next day. When I got back from work, he was waiting impatiently in the hallway for me.

"Mum! My suitcase, my bag and the toy box are all full. And I'm not done." Mrs Marchand appeared in the hall from the kitchen, wiping her hands on her apron. "I've told him not to panic. Anything that doesn't fit in the car, I can box up and mail to you. But I don't think I've convinced him."

I pulled my son into a hug. He wriggled, putting up his new big-boy resistance before giving in. "Do you 'ear that? So you can look forward to boxes arriving, or we can come back for the rest when we come to visit. Come on, time for dinner. You need a good sleep tonight so you can be fresh for walking your maman down the aisle."

This was something Rob and I had talked through. We both felt it important that Stephen be involved in the ceremony, rather than a spectator. I'd written to Papa, telling him the date once it was set, and assuring him I understood if he wasn't able to afford the trip. I'd suggested the idea about Stephen and Papa had written back, enthusiastically supporting the suggestion.

"I will come over as soon as possible after your wedding, but knowing young Stephen can fill my shoes makes it easier. Tell him I am counting on him to do me proud! I am looking forward to meeting this Rob who seems to have made you so happy again. Leon sends his love, as do Odette and Edmond. Did I tell you Odette has had another child? They are both doing well, though your brother-in-law sounds as though it is all rather overwhelming, being surrounded by girls! More next time, but know your Papa is there with you in spirit if not in body. Give my regards to your fiancé."

* * *

One o'clock the next day, I stood at the front of the Presbyterian church, my son on one side, my soon-to-be husband on the other. The minister spoke the well known words, while Rob and I faced each other, repeating our parts in turn. At the appointed moment, Stephen reached around to hand our rings to Pastor Michael. We slipped the gold circles onto each other's fingers. When we kissed as husband and wife for the first time, a cheer went up from my friends. Stephen's arms came around me from behind, squeezing me tightly.

We turned to face the crowd. My eyes stung as I realised how many people had come to share our day. I looked at Rob's family, now my family too, his sisters dabbing at their eyes with dainty handkerchiefs while they smiled fondly at their 'little' brother.

Later that day, the three of us arrived at the farm cottage as a real family. Rob opened the door and then looked back at me. He grinned down at Stephen, came over and swept an arm behind my back, the other scooping my knees up. Stephen whooped and ducked around to go inside ahead of us. I grabbed Rob's neck as he carried me over the doorstep, my head tucked into his shoulder.

List of Main Characters

Family

   Elise - youngest of five children

   Yvonne (Yvie) - Elise's older sister

   Leon - Elise's older brother

   Maman (Leontine) - Elise's mother

   Papa (Edmund) - Elise's father

   Grand-mère (Anasthasie) - Elise's grandmother, Maman's mother

   Edmond - Elise's oldest brother, the firstborn in the family

   Odette - Elise's oldest sister

Other

Rex - Yvonne's husband

   Lulu - Elise's friend from the ship

   Harold - Elise's first husband

   Stephen - Elise's son

   Mrs Marchand - Elise's landlady

   Iris - Elise's work friend

   Rob - Elise's second husband

Glossary - French terms & Phrases

The meanings and usage of some words have changed over time. These are as Elise would have used them.

Collège	Middle school between eleven and fifteen years of age
Lycée	High school between fifteen and seventeen years of age
Université	University
Ma chérie/Mon chéri	Feminine/Masculine terms of endearment
Madame/Mme	Equivalent to Mrs
Mademoiselle/Mlle	Equivalent to Miss
Père	Father (as title of a priest)
Oncle	Uncle
Gagnon	Technically - a farmer or peasant, deriving from an old word meaning to till the ground etc. It sounds similar to the Old French word for 'guard dog' - hence the giggle in class.
Cimetière	Cemetery
Merci	Thanks
Bataillon du Pacifique	Pacific Battalion (during WWII)
Bonjour	Hello/good morning
Salut	Hello
Bonjour tout le monde	Good morning everyone
Asseyez-vous	Sit down
Je vous bénis ma chère	Bless you my dear
Bisque	Smooth, creamy soup
Cepes a la savoyarde	French starter dish of wild mushrooms with ham and Vegetables
Bouillabaisse	Traditional Provençal fish soup

Acknowledgements

This book has been decades in the making. Without my biggest cheerleader and prayer warrior, Jeffrey, I don't think I would have ever got it started, let alone finished. You are the best husband, friend and listener in the world, I love you and I thank you. You corrected me when my plot went wayward, pulled me back on track every time I allowed things to distract me and believed in me when I doubted. You always value the time I spend writing and creating. Praise God for you. Thank you for allowing me to share your late mum with the world – at least, one possible version of her story.

Aimée, thank you for the hours spent in archives, sorting through all the information we compiled from the family and online records, and for trying to put some kind of logic to my thoughts. To the rest of our children, thank you for putting up with the late dinners, the help-yourself nights and the weird answers to your questions when my brain was still inside this book or any of the online learning I took on to figure out this author-life.

Marianne and Gary, and Graham, thank you all for the research, and the personal anecdotes and memories of the real Elise and her ancestors that helped shape the heroine of this story. Each of you gave me clues to the story behind the lady we loved.

Lauren, my sister in Christ, the staunchest of friends, always ready to fellowship over coffee to talk about our favourite subject, the Lord and His Word. Our conversations have been a welcome refreshment. Thank you for being you.

Rachel, my editor. You are a God-send! You haven't just edited, you've educated me in so many ways. You pushed me to write better, to think past the obvious and to at least try to grasp some understanding of better grammar and format! Thank you for your generous nature, and your willingness to find a way to get things done.

Julia, thank you for being the connector God's called you to be. You put me in touch with Rachel, you went ahead of me in this writing and publishing lark and set the pace – which I've yet to meet! Thank you.

All the movers and shakers at The Self Publishing Formula, especially James and Mark for leading from the front, and sharing all they have learned freely with us through You Tube. You inspired me to get on to your How to Write a Bestseller course, marking a turning point in my writing. Thank you for reaching back and helping the rest of us follow your lead.

Suzy K Quinn. Thank you for that Bestseller course you did with SPF. You made sense of the scary world of writing and editing. I so appreciated your no-nonsense approach and your ongoing encouragement since.

The 'librarians' at One Stop For Writers - thank you! Your tools and layout were integral to turning my ideas into a sensible plot and turning my names on a page into real characters with emotional depth. I came back to your site time and again over the last several years and I'll be back for the next book.

Without you all, there would be no book. Thank you and bless you.

Author's Note

This story is loosely based on the early life of my late mother-in-law. She passed away before we knew much of the facts about her, as she was of a generation and disposition that didn't talk about these things. I have done my best, with the help of research by various family members and my husband's memory of her, to flesh out the few facts we have to build a feasible story of her childhood and those early days in New Zealand. As one cousin put it, they were an ordinary family just trying to get by.

I have aimed for accuracy with historical events and places mentioned, but if there are any errors, I apologise and ask for your forbearance.

You can keep in touch by email: marikaywriter@gmail.com

The Flower Grower's Daughter is my first book and will be the first in a three-part serial.

About the Author

Mari Kay is a Christian wife and mother with the desire to write good stories with a touch of romance.

Mixing her interest in genealogy and language, she has completed her debut work, The Flower Grower's Daughter.

As well as writing, she bakes, dabbles in mixed-media art, and hangs out with her now-retired husband.

You can connect with me on:
- https://www.discipleyourself.com
- https://www.facebook.com/MariKayCreations
- https://ko-fi.com/marikaycreations
- https://www.kobo.com/nz/en/ebook/the-flower-grower-s-daughter?sId=afb0f781-4975-4f80-a8ba-d3c449382f69